MW01119906

CARRYING
CAPACITY

SYLVAIN P. CODERRE

Tellwell Talent
www.tellwell.ca

ISBN
978-0-2288-3319-2 (Paperback)
978-0-2288-3320-8 (eBook)

TABLE OF CONTENTS

PREFACE

I am not a writer. I am a simple city Gastroenterologist. Clinical medicine is fascinating, rewarding in countless ways, but does not fully satisfy my passion for creativity. It is with this spirit of creation that I have assembled, in this novel, a whole host of ideas that have been percolating in my head for years. I tried to write it as a whimsical reflection on some interesting issues of the human condition. While some of these ideas are random, there is a plot to this book! There is a point, a message (or at least food for some serious thought at some point!)

Disclaimer:

The following is a work of fiction. Names, characters, businesses, places, events and incidents are either the products of the author's imagination or used in a fictitious manner.

Any resemblance to actual persons, living or dead, or actual events, is purely coincidental.

For the most part.

There may be a teenie weenie bit of resemblance that is not coincidental. Or in some cases a lot.

But otherwise purely coincidental.

Sylvain Coderre, Calgary, Canada, ©

CHAPTER I

THE CURLING RINK

"**G**ood evening to you Lynne, how are you tonight?"
Lynne Nanton knew what joke was coming.
"I am doing great Paul, how are you doing?"
"Fine Lynne, fine. Like a bag of salt!"

Paul Riverside was a regular curler in Calgary's South Mountain Sunday night curling league. The league was a typical curling league as far as age distribution: old and older. The league was made up mostly of aging doctors and their spouses. Most of the doctors were males, perhaps reflective of medical school admission numbers from that era. About half of the male doctors brought their wives to curling. Curiously, since a doctor specializing in cosmetic surgery had joined the league, the male doctors seemed to be aging faster than their spouses!

Since Paul had retired three years ago, he had more time on his hands and was the league organizer. For that reason, Lynne had significantly more interaction with Paul than any other curler in the league. Paul was predictable with his comedic opener, but remained a charming, sweet man. It was not clear to Lynne why Paul seemed to be stuck with this one joke: had he sheltered himself in his books and then his medical practice? Was it due to his obvious social awkwardness? Either way, despite being a Doctor, who are notoriously cheap, Paul was a good tipper, so Lynne put up a smile to his weekly introduction.

The secret to getting a good tip from Paul was laughing at his joke. The secret to the rest of Lynne's tips was very clear: a V-neck shirt that exposed a good portion of her very generous bosom, a neckline that complimented her otherwise stunning good looks. This method of generating tips had worked for most curling leagues, and the doctors' league was certainly no exception.

The atmosphere on this night was particularly jovial. One of the regulars, Dr. Warren Mcallum, had enjoyed a big win over his archrival tonight. Lynne liked to call him Dr. Warren. Dr. Warren was unaccustomed to winning. When he won, everybody knew it.

"Good evening Lynne," Mcallum said. "Did you watch my big win tonight on sheet four?"

"No, I didn't unfortunately, it's been quite busy here tonight."

"I finally beat that Dennis Parkwood tonight. Parkwood is the fissure in my anus. For once, I won't need to hear him babble on about his great shots. I was going to have 'He died with Dennis Parkwood's broom up his butt' engraved on my tombstone. I can now change that!"

"That's great news, Doctor Warren. Happy to hear it."

"I am celebrating tonight, Lynne," Mcallum said. "Two Coronas and this little box of peanuts, please. Hey Parkwood, look what I bought, would you be interested in taste of my salty nuts!"

Warren Mcallum exploded in his usual high-pitched, roaring laughter, which was somehow both headache-inducing and endearing. Lynne could not help but to genuinely laugh out loud.

Mcallum's wife, Jeanne de Lavérendrye, was quick to intercede. Jeanne, an absolute dove, followed behind him and said, "Ignore him, Lynne, he is a child. Speaking of children, when is the big day for you?"

"March ninth. Can't wait, three more months!"

2

Lynne was anxiously awaiting the big day. She was thirty-two years old, and she and her husband Don had been trying to have kids for seven years now. Seven long years! Seven years of regularly timed, clockwork sex, with very careful attention to abstinence the days leading up to her mid-cycle to avoid wasting any of Don's precious few gametes.

"No Don, no. You have to load up for next Friday." Those words all too commonly came out of Lynne's mouth as Don was getting riled up for some conjugal action. This was followed by years of testing, injection drugs, clinic visits, that eventually led to the famous Dr. Julian Northgate.

Julian Northgate was not a curler. If he were though, he would clearly have fallen into Warren Mcallum's FIGJAM category. Dr. Northgate was a world-renowned fertility specialist. Initially trained at the University of Alberta medical school, Dr. Northgate had completed his Reproductive Endocrinology Fellowship Training

Program in San Diego. Somewhat surprisingly to everyone, he chose to return to a relatively small fertility center in Calgary. "Better to be a big fish in a small pond then small fish in a big pond," Northgate had repeatedly said.

It was clear when you first met Julian Northgate that he had no issues whatsoever with self-confidence. Julian Northgate loved himself. As Lynne and Don had repeatedly interacted and gotten comfortable with many people at the clinic, several of the staff had commented that there was no room in Northgate's heart for him to love someone else. That might explain why this handsome thirty-four-year-old doctor had never married, and by all reports had no significant other in his life at all currently.

To say that Julian Northgate was handsome was a gross understatement. He quite simply was sculpted from the Rock of Gibraltar. Six foot two, blond, blue eyes, strong cheek bones, perfect facial symmetry, and teeth that made fresh snow look relatively dull. He obviously was very fit, with carefully chiseled muscles, which he liked to show off with an unusually tight set of hospital greens.

Despite his obvious arrogant personality flaw, Northgate was able to exhibit a kind, caring side, often marked by hand holding and welling of tears from his piercing blue eyes. This side of his personality, and of course the amazing results his clinic had published, was undoubtedly what made him the most sought-after specialist in not only southern Alberta, but western Canada.

Lynne Nanton had seen a different side of Julian Northgate's personality that was not pleasant. To Lynne, it was a side that was creepy and scary. This side of Northgate's personality only came out when he and Lynne were alone together.

On their very first visit to the clinic, Northgate had sent Don away to the lab to, as he put it, "Bang the specimen container". Both Don and Lynne had found this quite amusing at the time, as Northgate was a very charming person, who was very likely their last ticket to having children of their own.

After Don had left for the laboratory, Northgate and Lynne were alone in the last clinic room down the very long hallway of the clinic area. It was then that Lynne saw a very different person. Northgate got extremely close to her, and spoke in a low, chilling voice, that almost extruded visible slime out of his mouth.

"You realize your husband is why you can't have kids," Northgate said.

"Pardon, Doctor?" Lynne replied.

"There is nothing wrong with you," as he inspected her carefully with his steely blue eyes, repeatedly, up and down.

"You mean that all my tests are normal?"

"Yes. Your tests are normal," answered Northgate, getting progressively closer to her. "You are perfect. In every way."

"It's very warm in here," Lynne said, as visible sweat oozed from her perfectly bronzed forehead and neck area.

"It is very hot in here," Northgate said. He carefully eyed the bead of sweat now dripping down her cleavage, waiting awkwardly until it came to a rest in the hollow between her well-rounded breasts. "Let me get you a towel."

As he got up to go to the sink for a towel, Northgate grabbed Lynne's chart in an apparent attempt to cover the embarrassing physiology that was difficult to hide in tight greens.

A knock on the door, which sounded to Lynne like canons on Remembrance Day, interrupted this horrific encounter. Lynne bounced to her feet to open the door.

"Doctor Northgate, a Doctor from Cochrane is on the phone, asking to speak to you right away," said the clinic nurse, Sandy Bridgeport, who had become Lynne's favorite person in the world.

"That's fine, we were done here for now. I was just telling missus Nanton that her laboratory tests are all normal. She is perfect! See you in two weeks for results of your husband's tests, missus Nanton."

3

The drive home from that first clinic visit had been a quiet one. Don Nanton was replaying his lovemaking episode with the laboratory jar. His chubby cheeks seemed even chubbier today, as they were beet red from the events of the morning. Don had not been as faithful to gym visits as Lynne had in recent years, to the point where the extra forty pounds he was carrying made him feel extremely insecure about his marriage and life in general. "What does she see in him?", "How did a hot woman like her end up with a guy like him?" were questions that he assumed others were asking. The additional burden of being told he is "responsible for their fertility problems", by many doctors including Julian Northgate, further compounded his profound anxiety.

Don thought of breaking the ice by providing Lynne with a detailed account of his sexual encounter with the specimen container, but decided not to. Some day, it would be a funny topic of discussion, in the right moment with the right crowd. Don could not help at least sneaking a peek into the humor of the moment. Don had always felt an attraction for shorter women, like Lynne, but his companion in the very public clinic bathroom was much shorter. In fact, she was three inches tall. Rather than dinner and candlelight, the romantic atmosphere was created by the constant hissing of the toilet's faulty flush valve assembly. The container had a well-manufactured firm and tight body, with a mouth that was both perfectly round and dangerously sharp. The firmness and symmetry of her mouth and body were matched by the circular, equally firm, pink lid. Don recalled thinking, as he got close to the pivotal moment, of the geometric challenge placed by depositing the specimen from a horizontal structure to a tiny vertical one. He had regretted not planning and practicing this unique technique ahead of time, but did manage, possibly due to his Engineering background, to find the correct angle and get the job done. He certainly did not want a re-do experience!

"What are you smiling about?" Lynne said.

"Oh, nothing important, ignore me."

Lynne found it easy to ignore Don in this situation. She was rattled, and constantly replaying the events of that first clinic visit in her mind. *Did I read too much into this?* she wondered. *Maybe beneath that fine exterior lives a socially uneasy person, who is well meaning but has words that don't quite come out right. Doesn't explain the situation in his greens though, but did I imagine that as well?*

As usual, Lynne had done her research on Julian Northgate prior to that first visit. No complaints whatsoever to the CPSA (College of Physicians and Surgeons of Alberta). Incredibly high rating of 4.8 out of five from hundreds of patients in RateMD.

After replaying the clinic visit in her mind several times, that day, Lynne concluded that she misinterpreted the situation. *I need to put this behind me. After all, he is the best, and we are desperate for his help.*

4

"Here I am, flying on Canadian Airlines from Quebec to Toronto, and suddenly the oxygen masks fall from the compartment above. I am thinking, Warren, maybe you should have listened to the pre-flight instructions from the stewardess!" Another high-pitched laughing outburst from Mcallum ensued. Nobody could make Warren Mcallum laugh as loud as Warren Mcallum. His infectious laugh did bring a smile to all those still present in the bar: Jeanne de Lavérendrye, Paul Riverside and his wife Audrey, and one of the few female physicians in the league, Dr. Patricia Richmond.

"Honey," Jeanne said, "you need to get into the twenty-first century and call them flight attendants."

"Sorry dear, I keep forgetting that name change. Too many changes in society: soon women will be wanting to vote!"

"Warren, are you sure that this plane story happened to you?" Riverside asked, laughing. "Seems to me that Dennis Parkwood told me the same story."

"Parkwood has told me this story, and so many of his other stories, so many times, that I can't tell if they happened to me or not anymore. As I was about to tell you, the plane then dives twenty-thousand feet in about five seconds, to regain proper pressure in the cabin. I'm shitting bricks at this point, as are the frantic stewardesses. Oops, sorry dear, flight attendants. Riverside, when they tell you that you might not feel the flow from the oxygen masks, you don't. I am sitting next to this older lady, and we have three masks for the two of us. She is looking totally calm, while I am sucking as hard as I can on that yellow plastic, trying to grab any molecule of oxygen I can! I grab the second mask. Same. At this point, I think I am a goner, and the only thing I remember is having Céline Dion's Titanic song in my head as the plane is diving!"

"At any rate, you, or should I say, Parkwood survived. What was wrong with the plane?" Riverside said, after all the laughs had died down.

"According to the pilot, there was no real depressurization. Just a computer malfunction. At this point, the pilot tells us that "We are over Ottawa, but I think we will soldier on to Toronto". I think? I think? Can I get a second opinion? Take this plane down!"

This was followed by Mcallum's high-pitched laugh, and a huge round of laughter from everyone, including Lynne, who could not help but be listening in on the conversation.

"Could you make your stories any longer?" Patricia Richmond said. "I think I might use them to put my patients to sleep in the Operating Room tomorrow! Who needs anesthetics?"

"Honey, we should go and let mama here get some rest," said Jeanne.

"You are right dear, let's go. Good night everyone, see you next week for more of Parkwood's, I mean my, stories. Good night, Lynne."

"Good night Doctor Warren. See you next week."

5

"Mister Barren, there is a visitor for you at the desk."

The unit clerk at the Privatklinik Hohenegg in Zürich was aware of the clinic's rigid privacy policy. Patient confidentiality was of paramount importance to the success and reputation of this highly respected mental health institution. Admissions could not be confirmed or denied. Visitors not specifically listed in the patient's chart were to be turned away without discussion or explanation. But this visitor somehow carried a very different feeling with him.

"I haven't had a visitor in the four weeks I have been here," Ruprecht Barren said. "Do I know him?"

"Just give me a moment, sir." The unit clerk interrupted the intercom discussion briefly, then returned. "He says that you have never met, but feels that you are deeply kindred spirits. He believes that he can help you with your condition in ways that traditional medicine cannot."

"Is it my birthday, today?" Ruprecht said.

"No, sir. Today is June 26, 2016. Your birthday is in four days."

Ruprecht Barren felt no better since his admission almost a month ago. His instincts were leading him to meet with this mysterious visitor. Even false hope seemed better to Ruprecht than no hope at all.

"Does he look dangerous?" Ruprecht said.

"Not at all, sir. My feeling, which is shared by our charge Nurse tonight, is that his intentions are pure and genuine. Unfortunately, your Doctor has left for the day, and we can't receive her blessing for the visit."

"I will see him. Can you give me five minutes to clean up?"

Ruprecht Barren was a proud man. Born and raised in the small East German town of Wurzen, Ruprecht proved to be goal-oriented from a very young age. His father was a mechanical engineer, who amongst many other inventions had created the Lifket electric chain hoist. The success of the company and the hoist had put this little town of less than twenty-thousand inhabitants on the map. At the tender age of seventeen, Ruprecht moved away from home to follow in his father's Engineering footsteps, at Leipzig University. Ruprecht was an only child, and quite attached to his parents, particularly his father, who he idolized. He was pleased to move out, but especially pleased to live only thirty-minutes from Wurzen on the Autobahn.

Ruprecht's skill and determination made him a natural leader with his University peers. During his busy second year of Mechanical Engineering, Ruprecht led the Leipzig youth in the 1989 Monday Demonstrations against the communist German Democratic Republic. His left shoulder is tattooed with 'Heldenstadt, 31090', a personal tribute to the title of 'Hero City' that was attributed to Leipzig after the October 03, 1990 unification of Germany. Ruprecht was scooped up by BMW headquarters in Munich, and after a series of steady promotions, became the Chairman of the Management board in 2015.

Ruprecht's heart always remained in Leipzig and Wurzen. His attachment to his father never wavered, and when his father passed away at the beginning of 2016, the emotional trapdoor that had been kept closed by the weight of a chaotic lifestyle opened, spiralling Ruprecht into a cycle of burnout, depression, and suicidal thoughts. Not knowing where to turn, but knowing he needed help in the most confidential manner possible, Ruprecht turned to this famous Psychiatric center well removed from his home.

Ruprecht's room was as dingy as the rest of the unit. As his visitor slowly opened the door, rays from a beautiful Zürich sunset behind him seemed to deflect of the man's shoulders, filling Ruprecht's being with a sense of serenity that he had not experienced in months.

"Good evening, mister Barren. My apologies for the unannounced visit. My name is Soul Fernandez. Doctor

Soul Fernandez. I am a Professor of Ecology at Florida State University, and truly honored to meet you."

Ruprecht extended his hand to greet his visitor.

"Doctor Fernandez, please call me Ruprecht. What can I help you with?"

"Please call me Soul, Ruprecht. I will get right to the point of my visit, Ruprecht, and leave you to your well-deserved privacy. I am here because I believe we can help each other. I would like to introduce you to a cause that you can help me achieve. In turn, this cause will fill you with a sense of achievement that in addition to your medical care, will help you out of your current state. I have followed your career from afar, and have seen you at your best when you are fully engaged in improving the world and the plight of your fellow human."

"You're referring to Hero City, no doubt. Those were great times. I fear that the chaos and pace of my life and my years of placing importance to false idols have made me unable to cope with my father's passing. I am no longer able to interact with the world in a way that my potential allows. I am in a desperate state of waking death."

"I would like to replace the emptiness of greed and guilt by a sense of altruism and achievement, Ruprecht. My cause will take you to unimaginable heights. Work with me and we will reprogram your neurons and brain transmitters to the point where you can return to your previous existence with an invigorating outlook and sense of fulfillment."

Ruprecht reflected. He was not certain whether it was his piercing look, or the way Soul made the rays of sunlight dance off him, but Ruprecht was having difficulty making visual connection with his visitor. While his eyes were muddy, the emotional connection with Soul was clear and certain. It was a connection Ruprecht desperately needed. He was left with no doubt that further discussion with Dr. Soul Fernandez was key to his recovery.

"Carry on, Soul. I want to hear more."

6

It got very quiet when Warren Mcallum left a room, but particularly that night, as Lynne was now alone in the curling rink with the ice maker, Yves Lavallée. Yves had just moved to Calgary from Quebec City, at the encouragement of his cousin, Jeanne de Lavérendrye. Yves had never curled or seen a curling rink before, but South Mountain had abruptly lost their ice maker, and Yves had learned the art from the city's best ice maker.

As Lynne picked up the last empty glasses and beer bottles, she could not help but reach down to her now six-month pregnant belly and wish her due date could arrive sooner. She had been constantly in a state of worry that something would go wrong given the tense circumstances surrounding the conception. She again thought of Dr. Northgate, and the second visit with him.

With Don and the nurse present, he was sweet as her mother's sugar pie. Patient, caring, empathetic: everything you would want in a doctor dealing with vulnerable couples.

"If you don't mind, I would like to examine Lynne alone now," Northgate had said to Don and the nurse. While this had seemed normal at the time, it was later strange to Lynne that a Doctor would not keep a nursing chaperone with him during such sensitive examinations.

After they had left the room, Northgate wasted no time in adopting his creepy disposition with Lynne.

"Your husband's tests confirm that the issue is with him. There is a zero chance that the two of you can conceive a child with Don's almost complete inability to make useful sperm."

"You mean conceive in the natural way," Lynne said, "but with the technology of the clinic anything is possible, right?"

"I am not sure Lynne. Even I can't turn a pile of turd into a diamond." Northgate obviously felt that was quite funny. Lynne was not amused. Northgate got closer to Lynne, and repeated, "The bottom line is this, Lynne: it is becoming very clear to me that only I can make you pregnant."

"You mean you and the clinic can make me pregnant."

Another saving knock on the door, another quick exit, and another quiet ride home wondering what she had just been offered as a treatment for her fertility issues. No matter what was meant by this discussion, Lynne was clearly going to initiate a complaint with the CPSA this time.

7

"Lynne, h-i h-am edding ome." shouted Yves Lavallée, who was standing at the bottom of the stairs leading from the curling ice to the bar area. "De h-ice is clean h-and ready for tomorrow. I will leave h-unless you want to throw a few rucks!" Yves laughed hard at his joke. Lynne could not see him, but she could imagine his big toothless grin, surrounded by his unshaven face and possibly the world's worse skullet.

Lynne smiled and replied, "I am fine Yves, go ahead. Just wrapping up and will be done in fifteen minutes."

"Do you need a ride ome?"

"Thanks Yves, all good. I will call Don when I am close to finished, we live very close."

"Sounds good Lynne. I will close the lights in the rink and downstairs. Bye."

"Thanks Yves, I will lock up. Bye."

And with that the curling ice went dark, and the faint glimmer of light emanating up the stairs from the lobby area disappeared.

8

A few minutes later, Lynne heard the unmistakable rumble of Yves' 2005 Ford-150 engine starting, driving out of the parking lot loudly, then fading away into the night. It was a sound she had heard many times growing up on her Saskatchewan family farm. A few loose ends to wrap-up and she would be on her way. Lynne jumped as she heard a second booming sound from the back of the curling rink.

What was that? she thought. *Settle down Lynne. You are a bit on edge. That is Yves' storage job on the curling brooms.*

Yves did have a bat habit of placing all the brooms on one side of the broom storage box, only to have it topple over within minutes.

Turning her back to the curling rink, which was now dark other than the illuminated Coca-Cola advertisement on the far west wall, Lynne opened the fridge behind the bar and started the process of stocking the fridge for the next day.

Good night for Alexander Keith's brewery, Lynne thought, as she placed the final bottles into the fridge and closed the glass doors. Closing the doors always came with gush of fresh, cold air, which was most welcomed at any time but particularly for a woman just starting her third trimester.

Tonight, the gush of cold air felt particularly good, and particularly long. Lynne was still feeling a definite hint of a cold breeze hit her back.

That's weird, thought Lynne. *Did I not shut these doors correctly?*

As she walked towards the fridge doors, Lynne realized that something was different. The soothing reflection in the fridge's glass doors from the Coca-Cola sign had vanished. Turning around abruptly, Lynne stared into a now completely pitch-black rink.

"Where is the Coca-Cola sign?" Lynne said, out loud this time, with a rising level of anxiety brought on by the two distinct changes to her end-of-shift routine.

The cold breeze was still there. Realizing that the fridge doors were indeed correctly shut, Lynne's feeling of relief from this cold air turned to a smothering feeling of fear. She felt the freezing cold air hitting her skin, starting a chain reaction of goosebumps from head to toe. These quickly turned into numbing sensations rising from her feet to the base of her neck with alarming speed.

Something is very wrong, she thought.

"Don, is that you?"

No response.

"Yves, is this your idea of a joke?"

No response.

Then lights out everywhere. Upstairs, fridge light, curling rink, Coca-Cola sign. All gone.

"What the hell?" Lynne scrambled behind the bar, tripping over her bar stool, reaching out for the light switch that she knew too well was just to the right of the hard liquor cabinet. With an outstretched hand, she moved her left index finger up from the base of the switch. Only the switch did not feel like hard plastic.

It felt like a warm finger.

Stumbling backwards, Lynne's flight or fight response kicked in. Her pupils were now as dilated as arteries pulsing through warm cheeks on a hot summer day. A feeling she feared she would never again experience.

Lynne could now see the faint outline of her attacker. Very tall. Very broad shoulders.

I can't fight this guy. Run Lynne, run! Get to the back stairway and rear exit!

Lynne got up and started running. She had the advantage of knowing exactly where all the tables and chairs were. Somehow, she managed to get to the back door without stumbling into any of the multiple obstacles in her way. As she reached for the door, and tried turning the handle, she realized that the intruder had barricaded it from the outside.

The sound from a few minutes ago was not Yves' sloppy broom storage job.

Lynne now realized that her attacker had not followed her to the door. He was still near the bar. There was only one way out: the main entrance down the stairs at the other end of the bar.

"Lynne, there is no way out of this one. This is it for you," said the chilling voice.

"Do I know you?" Lynne had tears streaming down her face. "Why are you here?"

"The why is not important. The how is. I don't want to make this any more painful for you than it has to be Lynne."

Lynne could feel and sense the intruder was getting closer to her. Strangely, there was a hint of compassion and empathy in his last statement.

"I'm pregnant. I am due in three months. Please, you can't do this."

"I know Lynne, I know. And that is exactly why I have to do this."

She now felt her attacker very close. Lynne shoved her intruder and started running to the door across the bar. Only this time the intruder had moved the chairs, and she tripped over the very chair Warren Mcallum had been sitting in. Lynne fell hard to the ground.

Her assailant moved in swiftly. Wrapping his legs around her pelvis, one arm around her chest, one arm around her mouth. Lynne was completely frozen against her attacker.

"Shhh Lynne, it's going to be OK."

Lynne felt a damp cloth across her mouth. She slowly began feeling as though she was drifting away. Her resistance disappeared, as did the grip of the intruder on her body.

She thought of her parents, who never approved of her choice of husbands. She thought of Don, who would see his world fall apart. She thought of her unborn child. She thought of her unborn children. Lynne wondered what they would look like. Would she see them where she was now going?

As Lynne fell into a complete sleep, her assailant took out a surgical scalpel. With a precise right-handed movement, the blade plunged into Lynne's neck. Blood was now pouring out of her left carotid artery. As promised by her murderer, Lynne's life drifted out of her body in painless fashion.

And with that, three souls left our planet Earth.

9

Bzzz-Bzzz.

Bzzz-Bzzz.

Soul Fernandez could hear the vibration of his cell phone. In the darkness of his Tallahassee condominium, he could not find it. After several attempts at reaching out for it, he inadvertently knocked it from his bedside table to the ground.

Bzzz-Bzzz.

Shoot, I hope I didn't crack it, it costs a ridiculous fortune to replace the darn screens! Picking the phone up off the ground, he brushed a finger over the screen and realized it was intact. *Phew, I don't have time for that.*

There would not be a lot of places for the phone to hide anyways. His condominium was not much bigger than a standard hotel room. One open room with a kitchen on the left, a family room on the right, which led to a small bedroom and ensuite. For a man with such an impressive resumé and international clout, Soul Fernandez lived in a very simple residence.

"Hello?" Soul said, in an excessively forceful tone. It was the tone people use to try to betray the fact that they are sleeping, as though sleep was somehow something they should be hiding.

"Soul, it's me."

"Sorry, I am not sure who 'me' is?"

"Primera."

"Primera. Sorry, I didn't recognize your voice. I was half asleep. What time is it?"

"One AM your time, Soul. Eleven PM over here."

"Are you alone, Primera?"

"Yes I am. I just got back home."

Soul waited. Dead silence from his caller.

"Primera, are you still there?"

"Yes I wanted to tell you that it's done."

This time it was Soul's turn to sit in dead silence.

"That is good news, Primera. Everything went as planned?"

"Better than I expected."

"The shipment came in on time?"

"Yes."

"Excellent. La Fuente will be happy. And the incision?"

"Perfect."

"Excellent again. La Fuente will be doubly happy."

Another pause. This time Soul interrupted.

"Are you OK, Primera?"

"I am fine."

"You stand steadfast in the glory of our plan?" Soul said.

"Machiavelli would espouse that glory is a worthy goal. The end justifies the means to achieve that glory."

Soul paused before answering.

"That is excellent."

"14U14US, right Soul?"

"14U14US. Correct, Primera. Call me in two days for an update."

"Will do. Good night, Soul."

"Good night, Primera."

So, it begins, thought Soul. Though he was exhausted, and had a very busy week starting, he would not fall asleep for several hours.

CHAPTER 2

CHANDLER ON
THE JOB

1

"Detective, we just got a call. They found a dead body at the South Mountain Curling Club."

Jayne Chandler had just arrived at the police station when she heard the news from the young Constable. She had not yet had time to remove her coat or get her coffee. Everyone in the department knew that you could get away with talking to Chandler in the morning before her coat was off, or before she had her first coffee, but not both.

She looked up at the young corporal with her steely glare, which was familiar to everyone. No words were uttered, or needed to be said.

"S-s-s-sorry to barge in on you like this D-d-detective, but Police Chief Hunter wanted me to let you know ASAP."

Another steely glare, with just as many words in her reply, was followed by a quick departure by the Constable.

Detective Sargeant Jayne Chandler had become a legend in the Calgary Police Department. Born and raised in Calgary, she was an only child of two parents who were both high school teachers. Her parents would have loved for Jayne to follow in their footsteps. Jayne realized early that she had important personality flaws that limited her potential as a teacher. Firstly, she did not like to talk. Secondly, and perhaps most importantly, she did not like people, although she could tolerate people when they were dead. With that realization, Jayne enrolled in the local Bachelor of Arts/Criminal Justice program. At the age of twenty-two, after receiving the Gold Medal from her University program, she completed police academy with flying colors, and was promptly hired by the Calgary department. Her love for reading, and the absence of anybody else in her life or hobbies other than work, made Jayne's general world knowledge vast and eclectic. Jayne Chandler was an avid reader in her personal life, and immensely by the book in her professional life.

Despite her small five-foot stature and slim build, Jayne had a toughness that far outmatched most of her larger-sized, often male, colleagues. Her resting face was severe and intimidating. She liked her hair cut very short, one inch below ear level, and straight. This had earned her, amongst her more literary-inclined colleagues, the tag of Detective Jayne Austere. Her sharp awareness of the world around her probably meant that Jayne knew of the nickname, but if she did, she had not let on. This resting face was not easily approachable, which had dramatically limited any form of a social life. This did not bother Jayne, given her overall impression of people. On rare occasions, when someone was able to burst through her stern look, Jayne's smile would radiate like the crack of dawn on a beautiful spring day. Her smile turned this plain, dark, stony-faced woman into a soft, gorgeous, radiating beauty. It was something to behold, but usually only very brief. Few people could say they had ever seen that side of the Detective.

It did not take long for Police Chief James Hunter to realize he had hired a gem. During her first few months on regular patrol duties, Jayne showed a penchant for taking even mundane cases deeper than anyone would have thought to, occasionally solving crimes well beyond her pay grade. Most notoriously was the case of judge Mikka Heikinen. Chandler had stopped the judge for speeding, going 130 kilometers per hour in an 100km/hr zone.

"Where are you driving at such a fast speed this morning, sir?"

"Just heading to IKEA for furniture officer, trying to beat the morning rush."

"Morning rush? It's eight AM on Saturday sir, I think you will be alright."

"Maybe, but that store is crazy, and my item is at the end of the store. Damn place makes you walk a full circle before you can get to what you want!"

Chandler had detected a clear nervousness in the perpetrator's laugh.

"I understand, sir. Can I see your license and registration?"

"Sure, Officer. Here they are."

"You seem awfully nervous and sweaty over a speeding ticket, mister... Heikinen? Did I pronounce that right?"

"Yes, Officer. JUDGE Heikinen," perhaps trying to gain favor and trust from the young officer. Detective Chandler stared back at him, expressionless. Judge Heikinen had picked the wrong police officer to try to impress.

"Is that a Finnish name sir?"

"Yes."

"Mister Heikinen, it's July, why the winter gloves in your passenger seat?"

"Bad arthritis, Officer. Cold mornings make my fingers very bad." Heikinen tried to push them away from her view, subtly. Not too subtle to get it past Chandler.

"Your wife doesn't come with you to shop for furniture, sir?"

A silent response was accompanied by a worried look. This was all the response Chandler needed. Sensing something was up, Chandler asked, "Can I see those gloves, sir?"

Not waiting for a reply, Chandler walked over to the passenger side, where she saw the blood covering Heikinen's suspicious gloves.

"Sir, I am going to need you to get out of the car."

"What? I…"

"Sir, put your hands behind your head, and stay leaning against your driver door please!"

Speaking into her radio, Chandler called for help. "Dispatch, I am going to need some back-up here. Deerfoot and Glenmore heading south on Deerfoot."

Chandler reached down and popped the trunk, where she made the grotesque discovery.

"Dispatch, we have a suspected murder scene here, I am going to need that back-up, and fast!"

Looking back at the judge, with that cold look. "Judge unless IKEA is accepting returns on body parts, I don't think you are really heading there, are you? I see why your wife isn't helping you to shop!"

Moving his head to look at her, Heikinen said, "How the hell did you know?"

"Finland hates Sweden. No self-respecting Finnish man would shop at IKEA!"

Chandler almost made herself laugh. But it took much more than a joke of that calibre to get even a snicker out of her.

This arrest, and many others that followed, did not go unnoticed by the administrators in the police department, particularly Police Chief Hunter. At twenty-three years of age, Chandler was a Detective Corporal. At twenty-four, a Detective Sargeant. Record advancement, unseen in this, or any, police force.

2

"Can you take him with you?" said the Police Chief, sheepishly poking his head into Jayne's office.

"You serious, Jim?" asked Jayne. "Can this day get any worse?" Normally a young Detective would not be in a position for such honesty with her boss, but Jayne was different. Being direct with people was both her strength and possibly her worst weakness. The Police Chief recognized this strength and did not bat an eye at the obvious criticism of his son.

"I figured you might need the help."

"Help? Are you fucking kidding me, Jim? Help? From what I hear, on his best day, he will triple my workload! I know he isn't a shining light, but isn't there a faulty streetlight you can send him too? Please Jim!"

"I would, Jayne, but he is wallowing away as a fourth-class Constable and I need to try something to kick-start his career. At some point I must provide evidence to justify a promotion. Responding to false house alarms and monitoring crosswalks is not the type of stuff that gets you Police Captain. I would like him to get used to working with a partner on more challenging assignments. So, I will periodically assign him to shadow Detectives during their investigation. You, Detective Sargeant Jayne Chandler, will be my guinea pig in this project."

Before Jayne could response, the Police Chief exited her office, smiling ear to ear. The same could not be said of Jayne.

3

"Good morning, John. The Police Chief wants you to catch up with Detective Chandler," said the young Constable who had started Jayne's day off on the wrong foot. Little did he know, or maybe he did, that sending John Hunter to her now was going to exponentially add to her miserable start.

"Chandler?" said John. "Moving up with the big boys, or big girls, or actually she is a small girl. Whatever, you know what I mean."

The same meteoric career rise that followed twenty-five-year-old Detective Sargeant Jayne Chandler could not be said about John Hunter's flat school and career trajectory. To say that high school was difficult for John would be a massive understatement. His high school mates nicknamed him "Goal post Huntee", for his many "off the post and in" exam marks, which barely reached minimum performance. The nickname could also have applied to his hockey prowess, which was significant. He was captain of his high school hockey team, for a record four years, and led the River Crest High School to three straight city titles. Physically, John had a clear presence. Six foot three, square shoulders, firmly muscular everywhere, with large brown eyes that women would disappear in: and many women did. His cognitive skills were much less accomplished. Following his less than stellar high school academic performance, John took a gap year to 'find himself'. One gap year became two gap years. The size of that post high school gap matched his own gap teeth, which made John look even less smart, but was also curiously cute and endearing. Word around the department was that if John's IQ was one point lower, he would be a tree!

After two years of odd jobs, somehow, mysteriously (or perhaps not so mysterious with a sprinkle of nepotism), John was allowed into the police academy. With a few more lucky bounces off goal posts, John managed to complete the twenty-four-week course in proper time. He was hired (another 'mystery') on the Calgary force, as a fourth-class Constable. Two years into the force, he continued to be assigned to mundane, simple tasks, and his rank had not changed.

Today, two twenty-five-year-olds on radically different career trajectories were going to be paired up.

This was not a match made in heaven.

4

"La Fuente, it's Soul."

"Doctor Fernandez. Guten morgen, or it is guten tag for you in the sunny Florida Panhandle?"

"It's the morning, sir."

"Soul, I do appreciate the dramatic flair of my nickname. "La Fuente". I love it!"

"You are my source. La Fuente."

"I get it, but when it's just you and I, call me by my first name."

Ruprecht Barren was a no-nonsense, direct person. There was no room in his life for histrionics.

"Understood, Ruprecht. I just wanted to tell you that it has started."

"When?"

"Late last night, or early morning for you. Primera pulled it off."

"Primera. La Fuente. I sure do love you, Soul Fernandez!"

"We will need more shipments. Very soon," Soul said.

"Consider them on their way."

"Our cause is pure, and the correct one. We MUST succeed."

"Let's succeed. But let's also remember one thing, Soul. It's just life and death after all."

Ruprecht Barren was a changed man. That phrase was his motto since 2016, when the radiant Soul Fernandez entered his gloomy hospital room. Ruprecht had always been about diligence, effort, organization, all leading to a self-imposed obligation for success. Now, he considers success a by-product, and sometimes not, of those key traits.

"Yes, you have told me that before, Ruprecht. Not sure I agree with or follow your new mantra. But I am pleased that we are in this battle together."

"The shipment will be sent by tomorrow, Soul. Keep me posted."

"I will. Thank you Ruprecht."

5

"We found the body right here, Detective Chandler. We haven't moved it."

Jayne acknowledged lead Investigator Isabella Lake with a brief nod of the head. Isabella was also considered to be a smart cookie in the Department, and was one of few who had garnered Jayne's genuine admiration and respect.

"Thanks, Inspector Lake." Jayne reached out to her in her usual cold handshake. A moment of relaxation in her stone face showed that she was relieved to see Isabella on the job. This relaxation disappeared when Jayne looked back at her partner for the day. Her partner looked at them with a gap-toothed smile that was not great for Jayne's blood pressure.

"Give me what you got so far, Inspector," Jayne said.

Without the need for any notes, Inspector Lake started.

"This morning at nine AM, the South Mountain curling club ice maker, a mister Yves Lavallée, arrived for the usual start to his Monday morning." Isabella had gone to a French-immersion school since Grade one and had a full proper pronunciation of the difficult French name. "Mister Lavallée comes in an hour early, to get the ice ready for the ten AM stick league."

"Sorry to interrupt, Inspector. Stick league?" Jayne said.

"Yes, Detective, stick league. Some curlers, usually more senior, have trouble bending down to throw their rocks. They use a long stick to push the rock down the ice."

"Seriously?" replied Jayne. "Why bother. Give it up. Sorry, carry on, Inspector."

"As is his usual routine, mister Lavallée went to the ice first. He turned on the lights of the curling rink, but this time the lights did not come on. That led him down to his workshop at the end of the rink, where the main breakers are. Mister Lavallée noticed that the main breaker had been turned off, which of course he thought was very strange. He turned his thoughts to the last person who left the rink, missus Lynne Nanton, and whether she might have for some reason wanted to completely shut off all power.

Mister Lavallée raced upstairs to the bar area, to see if perhaps missus Nanton had experienced an electrical issue requiring her to kill the electricity to the whole place. As he climbed up the stairs, he noticed a smell that was not familiar to him, but that resonated in him as something worrisome. After taking a few steps into the bar area, mister Lavallée found the body in its current position. He knew she was gone. He did not touch anything. The landlines were down also. He used his cell phone to call 9-1-1 and I was dispatched with Captain Lahr here. Since then, the rink manager has come in and is in his office downstairs."

Jayne briefly glanced at Captain Michael Lahr, an officer with over twenty years of experience in the force. This was certainly not Lahr's first rodeo.

"Upon discovering the body, Captain Lahr and I immediately cleared the rink of the curlers that were arriving. The front doors were closed and locked. We came back upstairs and did a preliminary search of the area. Nothing out of ordinary, other than the body and this chair that was knocked over. We did leave mister Lavallée and the rink manager downstairs, where they currently remain. Both are very shaken obviously."

Detective Chandler ignored that last comment, and knelt to visually inspect the body. Lynne Nanton's remains were surrounded by a pool of blood the size of a small wading pool. She was on her left side, with her left arm bent under her thorax, and her right arm hanging over her abdomen. Her blood-drenched sweater had lifted as she had fallen to her final resting place, exposing her protuberant abdomen. Her right leg lay very straight, covered by her slightly bent left leg.

Inspector Lake continued. "As you can see, Detective, the victim has a ten-centimeter cut over her left carotid artery area. What is unusual is that the cut is very clean. Like a surgical incision. The assailant didn't make a straight cut. It is curved at both ends. Almost looks like the sick bastard made it look like a smile!"

"You can't make a perfect incision like that unless…"

"Your victim is sedated, correct Detective," intervened Lake. People don't usually cut off Jayne Chandler, but Isabella could. Jayne would see it as sign of her enthusiasm and competence. "Which is why I looked hard for puncture marks anywhere in her body and found none."

"A sedated patient, but no injection sites?" Jayne said.

"Correct again, Detective. But look closer at her mouth. There is a faint, red, dry area all the way around it. I think our killer went old school. Inhaled anesthetic agent in a rag. Only missus Nanton must have had a local allergic reaction to it."

"All of this would explain the lack of any other bruises, scratches. No sign of a fight whatsoever?" asked Jayne.

"None. Only a small bruise on her left knee, which I think happened when she tripped on this chair, in the dark."

"Is that it, Inspector? Jayne asked.

"One last note," Lake said. "I noticed two very small letters that were written on both sides of her belly button. CC."

"CC?" Jayne said.

"Yes, Detective. Sorry, I have no idea what it means."

"Excuse me, Inspector Lake and Detective Chandler," interjected John, "but you didn't mention that the victim might have been pregnant."

"Nice work, Hunter!" Jayne said. "Inspector Lake, please record fourth-class Constable John Hunter's brilliant conclusion that this woman, who is obviously in child-bearing years, who also has a massive abdomen, might, and he did say might, be pregnant!"

"I will make sure to put that in my report," Isabella said, smiling. "Thank you, Constable."

John turned away from Jayne and smiled at the sympathetic young Inspector.

6

"CC?" Jayne muttered. "CC?"

Jayne was completely enthralled by this case. Not only was there a dead body, which she loved, but a brain-teasing puzzle was clearly huge value-add.

"Curling Club?" Jayne said out loud.

"Calling Card?" Captain Lahr said.

"Maybe it has no meaning other than a reminder for her to do something," John said. "I do that sometimes when I need to pick something up at the grocery store."

"Let me be clear on this one, Hunter," Jayne said. "You mean to tell us that you would use a sharpie, on your abdomen, to write out your grocery list? CC then might refer to 'cold-cuts' or 'Coca-Cola'? Inspector Lake, let's look closer at her belly. Are you sure you don't see any other written letters anywhere else? Like MC for Mac and

Cheese? Or better yet, please check on both sides of her anus for DH: Donut Hole!"

"Nothing of the sort, Detective," Isabella said, trying to control her laughter for the sake of the Detective in training. "But all the theories at this stage have been noted."

"Alright, back to work," Jayne said. "Inspector Lake, is this ice maker still here?"

"You mean Yves Lavallée?"

"Yes, him," Jayne said. "But there is no way in hell I can pronounce that name. We will need to simplify that for me please."

Jayne Chandler had always lived in Calgary. She had zero interest in travelling. She had zero interest in any other language. She was as anglo as anglo could get.

"Hunter, can you go get him? He is downstairs. That means down those stairs."

"Yes, boss." Hunter hurried out of the room. Despite the instruction to go down the front stairs, Hunter dashed to the back stairs. He tried to open the far door, but like Lynne, could not get it open.

"I forgot to mention that, my apologies," said Isabella, "that door was barricaded. I presume by the intruder but will check with the staff."

"Thanks Inspector," said Jayne. "No worries about the omission in the report. Hunter, I think you have tried the door long enough. Again, the OTHER stairs!"

As Hunter finally headed downstairs, Jayne turned to Isabella.

"Holy crap. That boy is good-looking, but how many lobotomies has he had?"

"He's sweet," Isabella said. "Maybe he is just trying too hard."

Jayne Chandler stared back at the Inspector, with a distinct look of doubt in her eyes.

7

Inspector Isabella Lake and Captain Michael Lahr were dispatched to interview the rink manager and to search for more evidence. Detective Chandler had ordered them to "Fingerprint the dickens out of everything, and don't forget that main breaker!"

"That poor guy," Isabella said. "He is so scared that he can't think straight."

"Not convinced that fear has anything to do with it," said Michael. "You know what they say at the station: what's long and hard on John Hunter?"

"What?"

"Grade three!"

"That's bad, Lahr!" Isabella said. "I noticed you were refraining from your usual corny jokes around Chandler."

"For sure, she definitely scares me! When she was talking about the stick curlers, I wanted to chime in that it's a way for aging curlers to "stick it out anyways", but thought best not to!"

"Probably good that you didn't. You drive me to drink, Lahr. Sure could use a cider right now!"

"Cider? I love cider,". "That reminds me of a joke. What is a murderer's favorite drink?"

"I don't want to know."

"Homicider!"

"Stop, please, just stop!" Isabella said, as Michael fist pumped her with pride. "Let's go back upstairs and join the others. Enough from you."

8

John Hunter brought Yves Lavallée up to the bar area. The body was now resting in the customary black bag.

Detective Chandler launched into her questions for the ice maker, ignoring his visible discomfort with the presence of the body and blood in the room. She was not impressed with the stench of tobacco in the room, and the bald head with the few remaining strands flowing halfway down his back.

"Mister..."

"Yves Lavallée, miss."

"Detective will do, sir. Can I call you Eaves?"

"Like de gutter h-around my ouse?"

"Yes, like that."

"If you must." (under his breath, "*C*alisse *d'anglo. Eaves?*")

"Apparently you have just started working here. How many weeks have you known the victim, sir?" started Jayne.

"H-eight," replied Yves. Yves had not warmed to Jayne, and was glaring at her.

"What do you hate?"

"Nothing. I ate nothing."

"I'm not interested in what you had for breakfast today, Eaves. It's a pretty straightforward question: how many weeks have you known her?"

"H-eight Osti de Tabarnac! One, two, tree, four, five, six, seven, h-eight!" (*Calisse de tête carrée!*)

"Got it! Thank your sir. When did you last see the victim, Eaves?"

"H-I was finishing my shift h-around ten PM last night. Before h-I leave on Sundays, Lynne h-always secretly makes me my special drink. Some vodka, mixed h-in with an orange glass of juice."

For the next thirty minutes, Yves recounted the details of how he left Lynne around ten PM last night. He went through his routine of leaving the rink last night, and how he came to discover the body this morning. He confirmed that the back door was not barricaded by the curling staff. Yves repeatedly emphasized how much he liked Lynne, and how tragic this would be for her husband Don, who he had met on a few occasions when Don picked Lynne up from work. Yves had noticed there was a table of four left at the bar near the time he left. He didn't know the curlers very well, except for his cousin Jeanne de Lavérendrye, who Yves noted was still there near closing time.

Jayne was softening up to Yves. Yves was clearly a warm, caring person. Jayne could see that there was not an ounce of malice in him. In her mind, she was placing him at the bottom of her suspect list. She was even getting used to his accent, though there were many points that needed clarification along the way. "Lynne was a oot and an oller!" took an especially long period of time to sort out.

"One more question, sir," Jayne said. "First, let me try this. One more question, Yves."

Wow, she did it. She sounded almost not like a complete western anglo!

"Not perfect, Detective, but close. Tanks for the h-effort!"

Even Yves was starting to like Jayne. They say Calgary and Quebec City are sister cities. This was being re-enacted right before John Hunter's eyes.

"Beautiful moment, both," John said. "Let's hug it out!"

Jayne glared at him, again. But perhaps with fewer daggers this time.

"Ok, maybe let's not," John said. "But beautiful moment nonetheless."

Yves' warmth seemed to have rubbed off on Jayne. Her body language and facial expression towards her new-found, imposed partner was ever so slightly softening.

"OK, one last question, Yves." (even better said this time) "Lynne had two small letters etched in her abdominal area. CC. One on either side of her belly button. Do you have any idea what that might mean?"

"CC. CC. H-I ave no h-idea, Detective. Let me tink for a minute." Yves was deep in thought. "You mean there was a C, then the ole of er belly button, then h-anoder C?"

"That's right."

Yves' faced lit up. "h-I got it! Lynne really liked her abs, maybe that was it."

"Abs?" Jayne said. "You mean she liked her abdominal muscles? I don't understand, Yves."

John Hunter clued in.

"He means Habs, Detective Chandler. Lynne liked the Montreal Canadiens."

Jayne was about to dismiss John's intervention again, with the same viper's tongue as she used previously, when Yves saved John.

"Dat's right h-officer Unter. C, then the ole, which h-is like h-an o, then anoder C. Club de Ockey Canadien. Way to go Lynne!"

"A true fan," John said.

Jayne looked perplexed. Firstly, John had said something quite smart. Second, could the combination of skullet Yves and lobotomy John crack this code?

Move out Robert Langdon, we have two new faces to crack the Da Vinci code. Jayne thought.

"Well, not sure gentlemen, but I will take your hypotheses into consideration," Jayne said. A faint smile formed at her mouth. John and Yves could not help but see it, and notice how significantly prettier it made the Detective.

"I have finished our preliminary search of the building and fingerprinting, Detective." Isabella Lake had returned with Michael Lahr. "Captain Lahr got a list of the curlers in the last Sunday league. Apparently, a bunch of old Doctors. I have to say, to this point, there is not much in the way of useful clues."

"Thanks, Inspector, let's divide the list and conquer, shall we?" replied Jayne.

"You don't need me h-any more, Detective?" asked Yves.

"No, Yves. "(impressing Isabella Lake with her new-found accent). "Thank you for your help. We will let you know if we need you again." Jayne extended her hand in what was an unusually warm handshake.

"Last ting. Captain Lahr, I notice that you smoke. Can I bum you for a cigarette?"

Captain Lahr could not resist. "You can have a cigarette, but the sodomy is not necessary!"

This time, Isabella laughed genuinely, and to everyone's surprise, so did Detective Chandler. Our two Da Vinci code crackers smiled, in a manner unconvincing that they got the joke.

CHAPTER 3

CURLERS'
INTERROGATION

1

"How did it go this morning?" said Police Chief Hunter. Once again, Jayne had not settled into her office yet, but she would show proper deference to the man who had hired and promoted her to what Jayne considered her dream job.

"It's a troubling one, sir. We believe the murderer used a rag with anesthetic to put the victim, Lynne Nanton, to sleep, then slashed her carotid with surgical precision. The victim was a young woman, who appeared to be in late stages of pregnancy." Jayne omitted the observation raised by the chief's son.

"Any leads?"

"None at this stage, sir. I have only interviewed the curling rink ice maker who discovered the body. He seems clean. Inspector Lake talked to the rink manager this morning. He wasn't there all-day Sunday. He did provide us with a long list of curlers from the Sunday night league.

Inspector Lake went through the rink for fingerprints. An autopsy is pending."

"Any family?"

"Just a husband, sir. His name is Don Nanton. He doesn't know yet. We tracked him down at his work. I sent Inspector Lake and Captain Lahr to find him and break the news. They have more skill and experience at breaking bad news."

While Detective Chandler certainly did not lack self confidence, she was insightful enough to appreciate her strengths and limitations. Difficult emotional conversations would not be on her list of strengths. Her colleagues had joked, of course without Jayne's knowledge, that receiving bad news by way of a text would be warmer than receiving it verbally from Jayne.

The Police Chief nodded. While his preference would be for his lead Detective to break the difficult news to family, he realized that this sort of empathetic discussion was not Jayne's strength. Her avoidance of such discussions early in her promising career was less than ideal. Like anything else, these skills need to be practiced and honed, which would not happen if Jayne kept sending others to do the difficult deed. He would broach this with her at some point, but not now. In some way Police Chief Hunter was happy to discover this flaw in his star Detective, as it gave him something to constructively criticize during their annual report meetings.

"Was there anything stolen from the rink, Jayne? Was this part of a burglary?"

"The manager told Inspector Lake that nothing appeared to be taken from his office, or at first glance from anywhere in the rink. His office door was locked when he arrived this morning, just as he had left it Saturday."

"What's next?" asked the Chief.

"Once Inspector Lake and Captain Lahr return, I will send them out to the victim's house to look for any clues. In the meantime, I am rounding up the curling Doctors and will interview them back at the rink."

"You will bring my son again?"

Jayne did her best not to hesitate. "For sure. Just for you, Jim."

"Thanks. How did he do this morning? Was he helpful to you?"

"He is showing signs of improvement, Jim. Though as you know, the bar was set low. He was able to understand and interpret the ice maker's thick French accent at one point, which proved very helpful."

"Then there is hope? Fantastic!"

"I wouldn't get excited, Jim. It's one bright moment surrounded by a lot of days of mental darkness. It's like the sun poking through thick, dark clouds for that one second on a cloudy day."

"Harsh."

"I know, Jim. But I know you as a straight shooter, who is aware of your kid's limitations. That's one of the things I appreciate most about you, Jim. Your ability to see through the crap in this world and get to the point."

"Thanks for the compliment. To me and my son."

"Don't get too excited too quickly, Jim. As they say, even a stopped clock is correct twice a day."

Jim laughed. There are not many people that can speak to him this way. If breaking bad news would be a criticism during Jayne's annual evaluation, her honesty would clearly be a strength. Police Chief James Hunter spent his days with administrators and local politicians who made him feel like his job was to be placed every morning in a giant vat of bullshit, and his task was to try to escape from this vat alive. This was bad enough during the days, but was even worse during the many rubber-chicken dinners with sides of cauliflower and broccoli that he had to endure with this group. These painful social events made his interactions with Jayne, which were doused in honesty rather than hypocrisy and lies, particularly refreshing. Even if it was at the expense of his only son.

"I will leave and let you crack another case, Detective. Thanks for the update."

As he turned and left, Jayne had a fleeting thought of whether she should have toned down her criticism for John. This was rapidly dismissed in her mind. Honesty came first and foremost.

Sometimes the truth hurts, and if you don't want to hear it, then don't ask, Jayne thought.

2

"Let's go, fourth-class Constable. Back to the curling rink. We need to interview some potential witnesses at one PM." Jayne turned around and started walking. She was a woman on a mission. "We will take my car. I need to stop for a coffee, or I am going to die."

"Excellent, right behind you, Detective." John was starting to see the excitement in his new-found duties.

Spending entire days with a radar gun in hand was clearly not as thrilling as a murder investigation.

As they sat down in her car, John asked. "Do you like Tim Horton's, Detective?"

"I do. Why?"

"Do you know that the one at Glover and 150th avenue near here gives cops free coffee?"

"You kidding me? That would have been useful information two years ago. I can't even think of how much money that would have saved me!"

Jayne could not help but think that this might be the second moment for John in her "Even a stopped clock is right twice a day" statement from a few minutes ago.

"Thanks again, John. That was very helpful."

"Glad to be of service, Detective Chandler."

3

"Alright class, we will get started, please be seated."

Professor and Doctor Soul Fernandez loved his job. He loved lecturing about his favorite topic and passion: the environment. He loved his research and the eventual impact he could have on our planet. This part though, he did not enjoy: trying to get three hundred first-year University students to get quiet and settle into their seats.

"This morning, we will cover a topic that is near and dear to my heart: the concept of carrying capacity"

The most spacious auditorium in the Department of Biological Sciences was majestic in appearance. As you looked up from the podium, the lecturer could see three columns of seats, with four intervening sets of stairs. The seats on the two outer thirds were garnet in color, with the middle section gold. Garnet and gold. The traditional Florida State University (FSU) colors. Straight ahead at the top of the auditorium were the large windows of the state-of-the-art audio-visual control center. Right above the windows was a huge replica of the University's logo: the stately figure of a member from the Indigenous Seminole band. Having the ability to stand at the front of this auditorium, and lecture to this enthusiastic group of young people was something that Soul never took for granted. Even today, after a sleepless night, the room and his bright audience energized him. Every time he stepped up to this microphone, Dr. Soul Fernandez thought of his family and their humble beginnings.

"Everything has a limit. This auditorium has a limit. There may be room for a few more people today, but that is it. Not much more than a few. Similarly, every natural ecosystem has a limit, and a finite limit of resources that can support a finite number of living beings in its populations. As you sit in this lecture today, your working memory has a limit: two or three new pieces of information that you pay attention to will get through your working memory into long-term memory. While I think I have your attention, let me make my three main points today very clear.

One: our planet can be viewed as a single ecosystem. Two: our planet has a limit, quantitatively expressed as carrying capacity. Three: our world is fast approaching, if not already approached, its carrying capacity. Stated otherwise: WE HAVE ENOUGH HUMANS ON THIS PLANET!"

Soul Fernandez was the last of eight kids, who grew up in the La Perla area, in San Juan Puerto Rico. San Juan is reputed to be a very dangerous city. La Perla is the very dangerous part of this very dangerous city. La Perla's claim to fame is its consistent appearance in the 'ten most dangerous neighborhoods in the world' list. A pearl has been described as a hard, glistening jewel. La Perla was not glistening. It was not a jewel. But it was certainly hard.

Soul was somehow shielded from the harshness of his home area. Being the last of eight kids, his five brothers and two sisters fiercely protected and defended him. Soul knew that the world around him was replete with drugs, narcotics and gangs, but he did not live that world. His father Toto was not educated beyond high school, and began his career working as a labourer in the harbor. However, Toto became noticed by all his co-workers because of his exuberant, charismatic personality. Toto was hired by a local tourism company, which managed to organize weekly festivals that attracted a growing number of tourists during Soul's childhood. Toto knew that protection of these tourists was paramount, and he enlisted the help of Soul's brothers in the growing business. By the time Soul had reached high school, Toto was owner of the tourism company and had enough money to send Soul to a private boarding school in San Juan. If his siblings resented Soul, they never let on. When Soul asked Toto why he chose him to send to private school, his father answered, "I have worked all my life to remove the hard cover and show the world two pearls in my life: my neighborhood and my youngest son." The business is now with Soul's brothers. His father passed from liver disease in 2015. Toto never saw the crowning moment for his tourism company when in 2017, they managed to attract Luis Fonsi and Daddy Yankee to La Perla to film their monster hit video, Despacito.

"The concept of carrying capacity is tied to the concept of environmental resistance. When a population first starts growing, it can grow quite fast, as it has all the resources it can want and need available to it. However, the more it grows, the more the environment creates a resistance to that population's growth. The environmental factors that resist growth include living organisms, such as infections, plants and predators, or non-living things, such as oxygen, minerals and space. When the population growth meets the realities of environmental resistance, the growth flattens out. The point where growth flattens out is called the carrying capacity. This concept can apply to a small area, an entire ecosystem, or the Earth as a whole.

Stated otherwise, you just cannot keep piling in population numbers to a system, such as the planet Earth. The environmental factors have limits and will resist. Again, WE HAVE ENOUGH HUMANS ON THIS PLANET!"

How did this little boy from La Perla Puerto Rico become such an important world-wide figure? First, he knew he would have to leave his beloved island. The saying amongst his baseball team was that "You can't walk off the island." You had to swing the bat. Soul was excellent at the swinging part. Only problem was that he was not particularly good at actually hitting the baseball. With the realisation that sport was not going to be his way off the island to bigger and better prospects, Soul turned to schoolwork. With his first-class education in San Juan, and the family's growing success in tourism, Soul applied and was accepted to many universities and programs. He settled onto the Ecology, Evolution and Organismal Biology program at the University of Kansas. He excelled there. Soul's combination of acute global conscience and inherited charisma made him a prime catch for a PhD program with the Ecology and Evolution group at Florida State University. After sailing through his PhD in less than three years, Soul was hired as an Assistant Professor in 2009. 145 publications later, he was promoted to be a full Professor in 2017. Eight years to this title is a feat that has never been seen at FSU, in any faculty across campus.

"Our time is almost up. I realize I presented a lot in the past two hours. You will need to take your time to digest all of this. Work through some examples of the logistic population growth model, particularly calculating the population size (N) for each example ecosystem's carrying capacity, or K. But I want to bring you back to my original statement about the number of humans on our planet. Estimating the earth's K is not an easy feat. Over ten years of research have led me to these numbers. Our current earth population is 7.7 billion people. Most scientists estimate the Earth's carrying capacity at nine to ten billion people. Let me tell you class, they are wrong. Their estimates are based on flawed data about forests, which are shrinking, projected reductions in emissions, which are not happening, and ignore the presence of CO_2 producers such as Betsy the cow and Scruffy the cat.

My data is clear: Earth's carrying capacity is AT MOST eight billion. We are there folks. Have I mentioned this to you? WE HAVE ENOUGH HUMANS ON THIS PLANET."

Silence in the room. Soul stared out at the audience, which was now dead silent.

"You have two jobs to work on for next class. First, you can look at my numbers in example 4c in your workbook, and you can verify my eight billion calculation for K. Secondly, we can discuss solutions to this problem. I have a few myself, some of which you might find distasteful and controversial. Thank you for your attention."

A round of applause followed. Such a response is not common in a University, but had become commonplace for Dr. Soul Fernandez. Soul found himself surrounded by many students who flocked to meet and question him.

Now I know how Jesus felt, he thought, as he gladly and patiently answered their questions.

4

It was helpful that a good portion of the Sunday night medical curling league were retired, or semi-retired doctors. This was particularly true of those who stay late for drinks. As Jayne and John arrived upstairs, they could see a table with five gloomy faces: Dr. Warren Mcallum, Jeanne de Lavérendrye, Dr. Paul Riverside and Audrey Riverside. Dr. Patricia Richmond was just racing in from her morning Operating Room slate, and had just finished getting a round of hugs from her friends.

"Hello folks. I am Detective Sargeant Jayne Chandler, and this is Constable John Hunter. I am sorry we are meeting under these circumstances. Lynne Nanton, the bartender, is dead. An apparent murder. The ice maker identified one of you as being amongst the last to leave. We will now proceed to interviewing each of you individually. For your information, the body is no longer here and has been moved to our morgue. I thank you all in advance for your cooperation."

John's mind had drifted since Jayne's opening line. *She didn't say fourth-class Constable this time. She must be warming up to me.*

"Constable Hunter?" Jayne seemed to have noticed Hunter's daydream, and wanted to jar him back to the earth.

"Yes, Detective?" His heart was pounding, like a little kid caught sneaking into the Halloween candy stash before October 31st.

"Let's go downstairs to the curling office. Folks, you can come down one by one, the order doesn't matter."

5

The first to speak to the two police officers was Dr. Warren Mcallum. He was the most visibly shaken of the group. While gregarious and loud at times, Warren Mcallum was a very kind man, deeply empathetic to all those around him. His patients loved him and were crushed when he announced his retirement two years ago.

"Hello, sir, please have a seat," said Detective Chandler, in her more common serious tone.

"Thanks, Detective. This is incredibly difficult for all of us. Lynne was a big part of our curling fraternity."

Warren's voice quivered, his eyes leaking tears down his cheeks.

Misreading his body language, Jayne began hammering away with her questions.

"Your full name, sir?"

"Doctor Warren Mcallum."

"How long did you know the victim, Doctor?"

"I have been curling in the Sunday league for as long as I can remember. Probably twenty years or so. Lynne was the regular Sunday bartender for the last five years, I would say. She was our favorite bartender we have ever had. Engaging, bright, and best of all she always laughed hard at my jokes."

"What is your specialty, Doctor?"

"Hepatology. It's the field of medicine that deals with..."

"Liver disease, I know."

"Sorry, Detective, most people don't know what I do, or did."

"I am not most people. What do you mean, "did"?"

"I retired two years ago. Best decision I ever made. Spending more time curling and golfing. Curling better now, but it hasn't helped my golf game at all."

"I hear ya," said John. "My usual shot shape has earned me the nicknamed Dole with my golf buddies. I slice like a surgeon's blade."

"Probably not the best analogy in this context, Constable Hunter," snapped Detective Chandler. John immediately wiped off the grin he had displayed.

Warren Mcallum wasn't certain what to make of Constable John Hunter. *Maybe I like this guy, but how the hell is he involved in such an important investigation?* he thought.

Jayne picked up on Mcallum's puzzled look. "He is just in training, Doctor. He should only be observing, correct fourth-class Constable Hunter?" said Jayne, with a glare that Hunter now recognized.

Jayne continued for fifteen minutes, uninterrupted by her imposed colleague, clarifying with Mcallum the events of the evening, the time he left the rink, Lynne's condition when he left, and any other details that he may find useful to share."

"That is all I can think of, Detective," Mcallum concluded.

"Thank you, Doctor. I have no more questions," Jayne said.

"Thanks, Detective. So very sad to lose Lynne, and the twins. Her husband must be devastated."

"Twins?" said Jayne. "How do you know that, Doctor?"

"I may be a Hepatologist, but Lynne was huge from the time she started showing! Plus, she told my wife Jeanne. That cinched the diagnosis!"

"Astute indeed. Thank you, Doctor," concluded Jayne. That will be all. The Constable will escort you upstairs. Constable Hunter, can you bring up someone else when you come back?" As opposed to their introduction, this time Jayne got up, and warmly shook the affable Doctor's hand.

"Can do, Detective." John replied to the command.

6

Next came Jeanne de Lavérendrye and Audrey Riverside, both of whom presented sympathetic and heartfelt statements. They answered similar questions to Warren Mcallum. Unfortunately, as in the case of Warren, when they left around ten PM Lynne was in good spirits and appeared safe within the confines of the curling rink. Jeanne and Audrey could not imagine anyone having ill feelings or wanting to hurt Lynne, who they considered a model citizen.

"Did they steal or vandalize anything?" asked Audrey.

"No, ma'am. According to the rink manager, everything was in its place this morning," Jayne said.

"Impossible to believe this happened, right here in this building," Jeanne said.

With no new information emerging that would help move the investigation closer to finding the perpetrator, Jayne dismissed Jeanne and Audrey.

Dr. Paul Riverside followed, who was able to provide more details about Lynne's character, given his direct interaction with her as league president. But nothing helpful to produce a suspect. The highlight was Paul managing to get a smile out of Detective Chandler with his famous "Fine, fine like a bag of salt" line.

7

The final person questioned was Patricia Richmond. Jayne was getting tired. Her face was quite red, in part from blushing, in part from her classic tell that she was tired: vigorously rubbing her eyes and cheeks with her left hand. The desire to complete this part of the investigation trumped her fatigue, and her hunger pains.

Dr. Richmond was an imposing woman physically. She appeared to be close to six feet tall, with a substantial amount of wavy, red hair. Her hair contrasted sharply with her fair skin and blue eyes.

The line of questioning was like the previous four.

"Hello madam, please have a seat. What is your full name?"

"Doctor Patricia Richmond."

"How long did you know the victim, Doctor?"

"Not long. I moved from Edinburgh Scotland six months ago. This is my first year of curling in Calgary. I have only met her once or twice, as I don't always stay for drinks. Nice lassie though. Shame what happened."

"Why did you move from Scotland?" asked Jayne. Patricia Richmond seemed to be at too senior a stage in her career to contemplate such a big move to Canada.

"Personal reasons. Wasn't professional. It certainly wasn't because I did not love my country. I am a proud Scot you know. We invented pretty much everything: steam engine, television, penicillin, and the phone! Alexander Graham Bell was a Scotsman you know. Just like curling, we invented it, but Canadians take credit for it!"

"I didn't know that, Doctor," Jayne said. She thought of pursuing the ambiguous "personal reasons" statement, but decided to shelve it for another time. Her stomach was starting to do the call of the lion. "What is your specialty, Doctor?"

"Anesthesia. That is why I arrived here late. My apologies for that, but I was in the Operating Room this morning."

"You put people to sleep all day?" asked John. "My grade nine Social Studies teacher would have been great at that. What a bore!"

Richmond smiled as she answered. "No, not just that. Anesthesiologists have many other roles. Some of us run Intensive Care Units. Some are involved in chronic pain clinics. Some of us give epidurals to women in labour."

Jayne intervened. "Before you ask, Constable, epidurals are a needle that goes into women's spine when they are in labour, to help with the pain of contractions." Richmond nodded, smiling again.

"Do you use inhaled anesthetics in your practice, Doctor?"

"Less and less. I haven't used any since being in Canada."

"Why is that?"

"Do you know what a systematic review of the literature is, Detective?"

"I do. But you might have to explain for my colleague here."

Richmond now turned to John Hunter." It is when you take all the studies that have been done on a subject, analyze them together, do a fancy statistical test called a meta-analysis, then come up with conclusions. It's a way to increase your patient population, especially for topics where large studies are not easy or feasible."

"Thank you, Doctor," John said.

"At any rate, a systematic review published by one of my Scottish colleagues, concluded that using an intravenous anesthetic, Propofol, was better that inhaled anesthetics on a number of points, including post-operative nausea and vomiting, pain control, and overall patient satisfaction with their operation."

"If you were going to use one, which one would you use?" asked Jayne.

"There are a number out there. Some called the volatile halogenic anesthetics: halothane, isoflurane, desflurane, sevoflurane. Then there are oldies like ether and nitrous oxide."

"Laughing gas," Jayne said. "What you would undoubtedly call a fart, Hunter."

"Have to say," John said, grinning. "My friend Pete's can make you pass out!"

"Doctor Richmond. Could those be put in a rag and put someone to sleep?" Jayne said. She couldn't help but smile at the thought of how this process would work.

Richmond was amused at the dynamics between her interrogators. She found Detective Chandler's exasperation at her colleague quite entertaining.

"I guess so, I have never tried! We usually use a mask. Can I ask why you are interested in these agents, Detective?"

"Confidentially, our preliminary investigation suggests that the victim may have been put to sleep with an anesthetic administered by a rag, before having her carotid artery severed."

"Awful. Absolutely awful. For her and her twins."

"How did you know she was having twins?" interrupted John. This time Jayne was quite interested in the answer. "Did Lynne tell you this?"

"No. I guess I just assumed she was based on how big her belly was. It was practically touching us when she was using the cash register!"

Jayne decided to let this one go as well.

"Can you measure these anesthetic agents in the blood?" This was less of a question to Richmond than Jayne making a note for herself to ask the Pathologist doing the autopsy today.

"Again, I have never had to," Richmond said, "but I would guess that most if not all of them would be possible to measure by a blood test. Or even perhaps measure them in the patient's breath."

"Thank you. It's been a long day for everyone. A few last questions. When did you leave the rink last night?"

"I said bye to the young hen at ten o'clock."

Jayne caught a puzzled look from John.

"Hen is Scottish for a woman, Constable," Jayne said. "You can stop looking around for the farm animals now. Read a book occasionally, will you? What did you do then, Doctor?"

"I stopped at the cludgie downstairs for a minute. Then I jumped into my brief."

"Constable, this is not her underwear, this is her car," pre-empted Jayne. By now, Patricia had buried her face in her both her hands, laughing. "And the cludgie is a toilet."

"And then I drove right home and went to bed. Six AM wake-up for a seven AM Operating Room start."

"Thank you, Doctor. That will be all. Appreciate your time. The Constable will escort you upstairs, then all of you can leave. Have a good evening."

8

Five minutes later, the curlers had left. Jayne had tracked down the curling manager, thanked him, and both she and John jumped into her car.

"What now, Detective?" John asked.

"It's four o'clock. I will drive you back to the station, then I need some time to make notes and put some of this information together."

"Would you like my help in putting the case together?"

"No, thanks."

"Would you like my impression of the folks we met today?"

"No."

"Any preliminary thoughts you want to share with me?"

Jayne did have some. But she did not feel up to any further conversation with John Hunter right now.

"I think I am too tired right now, Constable. Let's meet in my office at eight AM tomorrow morning. Inspector Lake just texted me and will have a report on her interview with the victim's husband and what she found in their house."

"Sounds good, Detective."

The rest of the drive was quiet. This day had proven to be very motivating for John Hunter. Eight AM Tuesday morning could not come fast enough.

Chapter 4

Morocco, 2016

1

"Good morning ladies and gentlemen. I would like to thank the organizers of the 2016 Climate Change Conference for inviting me to give the opening address. It is great to be here in the beautiful city of Marrakech. My name is Doctor Soul Fernandez, and I am a Professor in the Ecology and Evolution group at Florida State University."

A warm round of applause followed Soul's introduction. To this group of political leaders and environmental activists, he needed no introduction. Dr. Soul Fernandez was a world authority in climate change, and had been a central figure in the birth and redaction of the Paris Agreement signed a few months earlier that year. It was a natural fit for the chair of the conference to invite Soul to kick off the first major event since the signing of the historical agreement.

"I am not here to present you with slide after slide of data supporting the worrisome, and in fact fatal changes, which are occurring in our climate. I do want to present an overview of the key areas on our planet that are in jeopardy, for two reasons. First, this will frame the seriousness of what we will be undertaking in the next nine days. Second, these are areas that the scientific community will need to monitor closely as we implement the changes needed to reach the Paris agreement targets. But before I start, I do want to emphasize one point. One key point that I want you to hold in your hearts and minds as we move forward in the following week."

Soul paused and looked around the room. Soul had a penchant to drama, and enjoyed the opportunity to create some amongst this group of leaders. He also recognized that on a practical level, many of his audience members were listening to him through live translators and were a few seconds behind him. The packed boardroom was deathly silent waiting for him to continue.

"The Paris Agreement is a bare minimum. If we fail to implement it, and I would strongly argue that we cannot fail, we are not reaching bare minimum targets. If, or should I say, WHEN we succeed in implementing it, we cannot rest on those laurels. We have to strive further."

Dramatic pause again.

"The Paris Agreement is a bare minimum, ladies and gentlemen."

2

"I have been given ten minutes to speak to you today. In that time, I want to recap where we are in the world of Ecological and climate change science. The world that we know in 2016 has changed. That is not the problem. The fundamental problem is the RATE at which it is changing.

Those who choose to turn a blind eye to the science of climate change will constantly argue that "The Earth is changing, because it always has, and always will". They are partly correct. The Earth has been known to change its temperature over its existence. It is not uncommon for the Earth to see a four-degree Celsius temperature rise. But over five thousand years! We are currently seeing that four-degree rise over one hundred years! That is not "normal progression of nature" as the nay-sayers state. This is one hundred percent created by humans: and we must stop it!"

Soul proceeded to show four slides of NASA Earth temperature maps starting in 1890, then 1935, 1980 and 2015, to emphasize the recorded dramatic shift in our planet's temperature ratings.

"We are heating up. What does that affect? Let's start with water. Many of the negative impacts of this temperature rise affect water. Glaciers are melting. We are seeing that. This causes the oceans to rise, creating havoc for the majority of the world's population that lives within one hundred kilometers of a coastline. This is not a scare tactic created by climate scientists. As you will see in the next few slides, there are concrete changes to rising ocean levels impacting many people in a very real way, most notably the inhabitants of the South-Pacific island of Tuvalu."

"By the year 2100, scientific data shown in this slide predicts a sixty-centimeter rise in ocean levels. Yes, sixty. SIX-ZERO. More water in some areas leads to major floods. Paradoxically, smaller glaciers in some areas causes deadly drought. Our planet is seventy percent water, our bodies are seventy percent water. If you remember only one deleterious effect of climate change, remember its life-threatening impact on water. People who ignore climate change are a threat to our existence. With the effects of climate change on water, those people may have a harder, or easier time, burying their heads in the sand, depending where they live!"

A much-needed laughter break ensued. Those in attendance want to hear about this topic, but it does not make it any easier to hear and digest.

"Not done with water yet. People automatically equate rising CO_2 levels, which by the way, as you see in this slide, is an undisputable fact, simply with rising Earth temperature levels. Rising CO_2 levels is killing our oceans and its ecosystems directly. It is basic Biochemistry, as shown on this slide. Add CO_2 to H_2O and you get H_2CO_3. Carbonic acid. Acid. Ocean acidification is rapidly killing our coral reefs, and in turn killing the species in those ecosystems. And I forgot to add this point. As you see on this slide, more CO_2 leads to rising ocean temperatures, which leads to more water vapour, more heat from yet another important greenhouse gas, and the potential for torrential rains with flooding."

Dr. Soul Fernandez started this talk with a captive audience: now you would describe the crowd as in a trance.

"Two last points, as I do want to stay on time. Thus far, I have focused on water, and I think appropriately. But there are key land areas that we need to consider when protecting our world and measuring the impacts of our changes. The first is the Arctic permafrost, which is thawing at an accelerated pace. The permafrost is a hidden, but major, source of CO_2. More thawing, more CO_2, and the vicious cycle shown on this slide spins and whirls. The last key ecosystems, and certainly not the least, are the rain forests. A changing environment in the world affects these forests and their rich animal and plant life, while reductions in these key consumers of CO_2 affects the rest of the world. And to those who don't feel that humans are causing climate change, I ask this question: who is then deforesting these areas? Is it the guy on this next slide? E.T.? Maybe E.T. didn't go home after all, did he? Did his spaceship land in the Amazon and good old E.T. started hacking away at the trees?"

Another welcomed reprieve from the difficult topic declared itself as a raucous laugh and a prolonged round of applause.

"There it is folks. This is serious. I will stop talking now, as it is time we move onto concrete action. And please remember: the Paris Agreement is a bare minimum! Thank you."

A standing ovation at these types of conferences is not a common occurrence. When Soul Fernandez finished speaking, standing ovations were the norm.

3

"Inspiring speech, Doctor Fernandez. You have moved nations to their feet."

"Thank you, Miss Marie Meadows."

"That is correct. How did you know that?"

"I have studied your career and actions for some time now, Marie. Can I call you Marie?"

"Certainly, Doctor. Then you must know that I am the Secretary of the United Nations Affairs Division. The Division has been heavily involved in the creation of the climate change reports."

"Please call me Soul. What can I help you with, Marie?"

"Don't take this wrong, Soul, but I feel that your words, our words, are falling onto deaf ears. I am starting to disbelieve that we can actually stop the Earth from falling apart."

"You must believe, Marie. A little faith makes the impossible happen. Faith can move mountains, after all."

"It seems like the world would like to place more faith on the anti-climate change scientists. People like Doctor Patrick Moore, the so-called 'Sensible Environmentalist'. His arguments of the natural flux in Earth's temperature, and that we are currently in one of the coldest periods in our planet's history, are gaining traction in the media. Doctor Moore also talks about how CO_2 fluctuations have always come AFTER temperature changes. I must admit that hurts the cause and effect argument."

"There will always be ways to present data in a light that supports an argument," Soul said, "even the frivolous argument of those ignoring climate change."

"He isn't the only one, though. Doctor Tony Heller points out that our current temperatures are lower than in the 1930s. That from 1910 to 1940 the Earth warmed as fast as between 1970 to 2000. That after our ancestors walked across from Siberia to North America ten-thousand years ago, ocean levels rose quickly but that rise has now tapered. These are problematic arguments for us."

"Surely an organization like the United Nations can have a say in the messaging," Soul said.

"We can, but it makes our lives difficult when independent agencies like NASA talk about the Greenland ice mass growing again, and that we are heading to Earth cooling for the next ten years due to a weak solar cycle. We can control the message, but we don't control what the average person decides to place their faith in. It feels like we need more than faith, Soul."

"On that point, I cannot disagree. Sometimes faith needs a little nudge from people in the right places. Are you in the right place, Marie?"

"What do you mean?"

"Can we move into a private area? This backstage area can get loud and busy with such a large conference."

"Certainly. I just left a meeting room down the hall, which is now empty."

"Show me the way, Marie."

4

Marie Meadows lead Soul Fernandez one hundred meters down the conference corridor. The corridor was lined with identical twenty-people meeting rooms, all named after African countries.

"Let's go in here," Marie said. "The Namibia room should be empty for the next hour."

After they sat down at the front of the room, Soul started.

"Do you have close interactions with the United Nations Security Council, Marie?"

"Of course, I do. The Security Council doesn't wipe its ass without first checking with the Affairs Division. My longstanding presence there gives me a unique position of influence at the United Nations."

"That is excellent."

"Why do you ask? What do you have in mind?"

"What would you say if I told you I had a plan that I believe would have even more meaningful effect on saving our planet than the Paris Agreement?"

"I would say I would be very interested."

"You talked about the scientist nay-sayers. While I disagree with most of them, I believe Bjorn Lomborg, the 'Skeptical Environmentalist', can help our cause. He projects that the trillions of dollars spent on reaching the Paris agreement will only lead to microscopic benefits."

"How does that help us?" Marie said.

"It means we need to consider some back-up plans. Plans that will be distasteful to some. Still interested?"

"Yes."

"What would you say if that plan involved some casualties?"

"I would still say that I am very interested. As would many members of the United Nations and the Security Council."

"What if those casualties involved family and friends of key members of the United Nations and the country leaders it represents?"

Marie hesitated for a moment.

"I would want to know more. But still interested."

"And you feel that a critical moment in this process, you, Marie Meadows, Secretary of the United Nations

Affairs Division, could exert a deciding influence on your Council?"

"I could. I need more details, Soul. Your plan seems dark. But somehow, you strike me as the light that can turn blind humans into see-ers of the truthful and correct path."

"Excellent. Then I will continue, Marie."

CHAPTER 5

CHANDLER VS NORTHGATE

1

Detective Chandler had a restless night. It felt as though she woke up on the hour every hour, then spent thirty minutes trying to get back to sleep. Visions of the dead body were troubling her. The lack of leads to this point was concerning. Babysitting a twenty-five-year-old was irritating. In the middle of the night, every point of frustration seems to get amplified. Even the interruption of her morning before she could sit down and have a coffee was annoying her at four AM. At six AM, having woken for the fifth time, Jayne hopped out of bed and got ready. She was even annoyed at all the money she could have saved if she knew the Tim Horton's on Glover gave out coffee to police officers!

Not today, she thought. *Today I am going to get a free one.*

She arrived at her office an hour later, and prepared for her meeting with Inspector Lake. Jayne felt in a better mood. The smell of coffee permeated the office air. Her bagel was half eaten. She was about to meet the most competent person in the Department for some news. Jayne felt ready to crack this case today.

"Good morning, Detective," Police Chief James Hunter said, "I just brought you over your new apprentice. He seems good and ready for another day in paradise."

John Hunter walked into Jayne's office, smiling.

What a buzz kill, lamented Jayne.

"You look a little sleepy, Detective," continued James. "Bad night sleep? Here's a little pick-me-up for you. When I was John's boy-scout counsellor back in the day, I would get the troops going at six AM with the following saying:

"Awake awake 'tis morning,
The bird is on the wing.
Wait, wait, it's absurd,
The wing is on the bird!"

"Sounds really inspirational, Chief," Jayne said. "Yes, we are ready for you, Inspector." Jayne waved Isabella Lake into her office. Great timing. Captain Lahr once again was at her side.

"I will leave you all," James said, "Good luck with the case."

"Good morning, all," Isabella said. "I will get right to it if that's OK."

"That sounds perfect," replied Jayne.

"After we left you at the curling rink, Michael and I went to meet Don Nanton at his work. Not going to lie, that was the toughest discussion I have ever had with someone."

"I'll bet," said Jayne. The sympathy she expressed was more directed to the Inspector than the husband.

"Obviously, the poor man's world was shattered. Lynne was his entire family in Calgary. They were desperately looking forward to starting this family in three months. They were living in an apartment right now but had made plans with a builder to start a house next summer. Don has no idea whatsoever as to who would have a beef with Lynne. Her family and friends adored her. She was very popular at work. The clinic staff had taken quite a shine to them and Don felt that they were rooting for them."

"Clinic staff?" said Jayne.

"Lynne and Don had been trying to conceive for seven years. For five of those years they had assumed it was her endometriosis." Isabella turned to John. "It's a problem where the lining of the woman's uterus, or should I say womb, grows outside of the womb into her other female parts."

"Thank you, Inspector," John said. "I have heard of the condition. It's apparently quite common. And painful. In a way, it's like the woman is having periods inside her own body."

"That's a very good analogy, Constable," said Isabella. "You are correct in saying that the disease causes intense pelvic pain. It can also lead to infertility. Lynne's pain was so debilitating that she could only stand to work part time. That's what led her to taking the job at the curling rink. Four hours an evening, five evenings a week. At any rate, they recently changed fertility clinics and got re-tested. Turns out Don was the main problem. With special fertility techniques they were able to get Lynne pregnant."

"What's the name of this clinic?" Jayne asked.

"Conception Opportunities Calgary. It's run by a Doctor Julian Northgate, who Don speaks very highly of."

"Isabella," said John. "You did say Conception Opportunities Calgary, correct? COC? Is it possible that the belly button letters were not 'club de 'ockey canadien' as per Yves Lavallée, but represent this clinic?"

"Very impressive, John," said Isabella.

Jayne was speechless from John's verbal upper cut to her chin. The Detective prided herself in her ability to read people, and John Hunter was now clearly confusing her.

"Impressive that I figured it out before you did?" John said.

"Yes. But mostly that you were able to say COC without Captain Lahr here chiming in with a bad joke!" Isabella said.

"I was trying to be serious," Michael said. "This is a serious investigation, Inspector. Laughing at banal jokes about the male genitalia during a murder investigation is inappropriate. It clearly would have been a...dick move!"

Isabella and Jayne could not help but smile.

"You're hopeless," Isabella said. "Can I carry on? There's more."

"Yes, please carry on, Inspector," Jayne said.

"When Captain Lahr and I took Don back to his home, I asked him to enter his computer passwords so we could access Lynne's files. Lynne had a fertility clinic folder. Most of it was just general information about the clinic. One document was entitled 'issue'. When I opened that up, I found the following notes:

December 13, 2018 visit:

- *Northgate gets too close to me*
- *He stares at me a long time*
- *He can't stop looking at my cleavage*
- *Blames Don*

? is he just awkward? am I imagining this
No complaints from Alberta College. Good RateMD ratings.
March 07, 2019 visit:

- *Creepy again*
- *Says that only HE can get me pregnant*
- *I must do something this time. But I need him!*

June 20, 2019 visit:

- *No problems on this one*
- *Spent most of the visit with Nurse Sandy Bridgeport*
- *In Vitro Fertilization treatment scheduled in two weeks*

"Were there any notes after that?" Jayne asked. "She must have attended the clinic for the In Vitro Fertilization and then follow-ups after she got pregnant?"

"For sure she would have," Isabella said. "But maybe everything else went well?"

"Did she file a complaint with the medical College?" Jayne said.

"I checked on-line. I don't see anything for Doctor Julian Northgate. Not one complaint."

"Does Don know about this?"

"I don't think so, and under the circumstances, we didn't think we could tell him."

"Good idea. Can we go visit this clinic and Doctor Northgate today?"

"Booked. I spoke to the Head Nurse, Harriet Stubley. They are expecting us at noon. They don't know yet about the murder."

"OK. I will make an announcement to the entire staff. Then I will start with the Head Nurse, Doctor Northgate, and Nurse Bridgeport. Inspector Lake, once you go through Lynne's file, let me know if there are any other clinic players I should interview."

Isabella left the office. John Hunter did not.

"That will be all Constable. See you at 11:30 AM."

"OK, boss."

"And by the way, great work with the COC idea. I guess you aren't fully retarded."

"Thanks, boss. I think."

John smiled widely at Jayne, a smile that for the first time in their relationship, was returned.

2

Detective Sargeant Jayne Chandler walked into the room full of worried and upset clinic staff. She approached the discussion much in the same way as her curling rink introduction: direct and to the point.

"Hello, folks. I am Detective Sargeant Jayne Chandler. This is Constable John Hunter, Inspector Isabella Lake, and Captain Michael Lahr. I am sorry we are meeting under these circumstances. Lynne Nanton, one of your patients, is dead. An apparent murder. Our team will be interviewing some of you, and going through the clinic and the victim's files for any possible clues. Please try to continue your usual daily activities, we don't want to hamper your patient care. I thank you all in advance for your cooperation."

Jayne started leaving the room. She felt the shock in her audience. She could see the dismay in the staff's eyes. She stopped, and added, in a much warmer tone, "I realize that you are all caring people by the nature of what you do for a living. This will be difficult for you and I am sorry for that. Our Department does have counsellors available on stand-by. Let me or anyone from the team know if you would like to avail yourself of that service. Thank you."

The police team left the room.

John had noticed the change in the Detective's speech, but was not comfortable bringing it up to her as they walked into the main clinic office.

3

"Hello. Is it OK if I am first to be interviewed? I am expected in the procedure room as soon as possible. Sorry if I am messing up your schedule."

Nurse Sandy Bridgeport had walked into the office. Her pants were typical purple nursing scrubs that nicely contrasted a lighter-colored top studded with a multicolor arrangement of hearts. Nurse Sandy was petite, five-foot tall at most, with long blond hair and radiant blue eyes. Nurse Sandy exuded a great deal of warmth and compassion. She was clearly in the right profession. When sick or distressed, Sandy would be exactly the type of person you would want to see walk in the room.

"No problem at all," Jayne said. "You are…"

"Sandy Bridgeport. I am a Nurse in the clinic."

"Yes missus Bridgeport, welcome. Please have a seat. This is Constable John Hunter. Is it OK if I call you Sandy?"

"For sure, Detective. I feel terrible about what happened to Lynne. She was a real gem. We all loved her and Don here. They were so close to their dreams coming true."

"Yes. Awful situation. Tragic. She seemed well-loved by all. How long have you worked in the clinic, Sandy?" asked Jayne.

"Three years. After I graduated from Nursing I worked in Labour and Delivery for two years, then I moved to the clinic essentially at the time it opened. There is a whole group of us who moved to the clinic at the same time and are still here. That's what makes it a fun place to work. And of course, we get to bring babies into the world."

"Babies are delivered here?" asked John.

"No, sorry about that Constable! We don't bring them into the world. That usually happens in the hospital Labor and Delivery wards. We sort of make them here."

"You are like the Japanese car factory, and the hospital is the dealership." John said.

"That's right, I never thought of it that way," Sandy said. "Very clever, Constable!"

John was falling in love.

"Interesting analogy, Constable Hunter," Jayne said. "If we can move back from cars to babies, Sandy what do you do in the clinic?"

"Doctor Northgate likes the nurses to be involved in every aspect of the clinic. And we do. That means anything from triaging referrals, taking patients' histories, moving patients and their partners through the clinic, and of course the procedure areas."

"Do you like doing all of that?" Jayne asked.

"Yes. I have always felt that variety is the key ingredient to a happy career. We get that here."

Not much variety in my usual traffic duty, thought John.

"You said a group of you moved over here three years ago," said Jayne. "That means most of the staff here, including you, have known Doctor Northgate for three years?"

"That's right. He is a great person to work with. He is kind to his patients, pays well, and as you will see not hard to look at!"

Darn, I hate him already, thought John.

"Everyone at the clinic likes Doctor Northgate?" said Jayne.

"Yes, for sure. Though if you interview everyone here, they will probably all tell you that while we do love him, there is no greater love in the world than Doctor Northgate for himself."

"That kind of guy hey," smiled Jayne.

"Speaking of loving yourself," John said, "I have to ask Nurse, are you involved in the collection of the male specimens?"

"I hand them the container and direct them to the bathroom. But I, nor does anyone else, get "involved" with the actual process!" Sandy and John laughed. Jayne smiled. "That's not how Nurse Stubley got the title of 'Head' nurse!"

That one caught Jayne, who was now joining the group laughter.

"You obviously have a great sense of humor," John said. He was now fully in love with Nurse Sandy.

"You have to in this place, sometimes," Sandy said.

"Sorry to get back to business, Sandy," Jayne said. "Can you think of anyone, clinic staff or otherwise, who would have an issue with Lynne Nanton?"

"I can't, no."

"Were there any difficult interactions in the clinic that you witnessed?" Jayne said.

"Absolutely not."

"Specifically, with Doctor Northgate?"

"Not that I saw, Detective. The interactions between Lynne and him were especially positive, I thought."

"Thank you, Sandy. We will let you go to your procedures. Appreciate your time, and your sense of humor!" Jayne said, shaking her hand, as did John.

"My pleasure. Sorry I could not have been of more help. Have a great day."

And with that, John watched the new love of his life leave. Jayne could not help but to smile, both from the jokes and Constable Hunter's puppy-dog eyes as Nurse Sandy left the room.

4

As much as Nurse Sandy brought warmth to the office, clinic Head Nurse Harriet Stubley brought with her an Arctic cold front that very rapidly changed the room's atmosphere. She was the antithesis of Nurse Sandy. Nurse Stubley looked to be in her late fifties. She wore black nursing scrubs that would best have been a full-size bigger, as they excessively hugged the many rolls of fat that she displayed throughout her body. Nurse Stubley had curly, salt and pepper hair, which was too long for a woman of that vintage. As she sat down, John and Jayne's eyes could not help but to migrate to the situation on Nurse Stubley's chin. It was obvious that she either developed serious eyesight issues, or that she lost her facial hair tweezers several years back.

If Nurse Sandy was the clinic's rose bush, Nurse Stubley was its Saguaro cactus.

"Welcome, Nurse." Jayne said. "How do you say your last name. Is it Stooblee or Stubbly?"

"It is said Stubbly but spelled S-T-U-B-L-E-Y," Nurse Stubley said.

"That's an interesting name," John said. "What nationality is it?"

"My father was German."

"Stubley is your maiden name, then?" Jayne said.

"Yes, it is. I have always been Stubley. Born Stubley. Remain Stubley. Will always be Stubley."

Please don't laugh, John thought. *Please don't laugh. Quick think of something sad. Lost puppies, lost puppies, lost puppies.*

It was Jayne who broke first. When the huge smile spread across her lips, John could not hold it in anymore. He tried to make it seem like a cough, but did not hide his laugh very well.

Nurse Stubley looked puzzled.

"I am sorry, Nurse," John said. "Detective Chandler and I just shared some jokes with Nurse Sandy. Still lingering. Nothing to do with you!"

"I see. That Sandy can be quite funny if you are into that crass kind of humor."

Quick thinking, John, thought Jayne. *You saved our ass!*

"My apologies, Nurse Stubley," Jayne said. "Let's get going with questions, shall we?"

"That is what I am here for after all," Nurse Stubley replied.

Jayne proceeded to question Nurse Stubley, in a manner like Nurse Sandy. Similar questions, similar answers: minus the jokes and sexual innuendos. Nothing that would help their investigation move along.

Jayne thanked Nurse Stubley. As the door closed, Jayne looked over to John.

"Holy shit, I thought I wasn't going to get through that one."

"Me too. I was glad you didn't start your questioning with "We have a prickly situation here Nurse Stubley"."

Jayne and John giggled like two school kids who have just noticed their teacher's fly is open.

5

"The package has been sent, Soul," Ruprecht Barren said. "Your Primera should have it by tonight. BMW's finest stock, express delivery."

"Thank you, my friend," Soul said. The next one will happen soon."

"Excellent. Once Primera re-confirms the methods, our soldiers all around the world will deploy. They are all ready."

"With my connections in North and South America, and yours in Europe and Asia, Project Oasis is close to eighty countries. We will reach our goal of a perfectly balanced ecosystem that we call planet Earth."

"Our contact at the United Nations is still in place?" Ruprecht said.

"She is. She has provided us with a list of targets that will ensure world leaders have the appropriate amount of interest in the matter. They will be motivated to come to an agreement. My contact herself will also prove convincing when the time comes."

"She is key to our success," Ruprecht said. "We are lucky to have her."

"We are. But mostly I feel fortunate to have you alongside with me, my dear Ruprecht."

"I am the lucky one to travel this journey with such a pure spirit. We will speak soon, Soul."

"We will. Once I hear from Primera, you will be my first phone call."

6

Thirty minutes had passed since Nurse Stubley left.

Detective Chandler and Constable Hunter had patiently waited for the arrival of Julian Northgate. Various clinic staff members had kindly poked their heads into the office and apologized. They each stated some form of "We're sorry. Doctor Northgate is in a procedure. He says he will be with you shortly."

Detective Sargeant Jayne Chandler did not like to wait. For anybody.

"I am really starting to not like this guy," Jayne said.

"I hear you. I feel the same way," John said, though for entirely different reasons.

As the door opened, they both rose with anticipation. No Dr. Northgate. It was Isabella and Michael, who were seizing the opportunity to provide an update.

"Wow, you can be seated!" Isabella said. "It's just us. Can we give you a report?"

"For sure, Inspector." Jayne said. She was embarrassed and annoyed at herself for giving that degree of deference to the man who was making them wait.

"We went through Lynne Nanton's file, Detective. I think you are interviewing the main players. Lynne and Don did interact briefly with many of the staff, but not in a manner meaningful enough to warrant you interrogating them. Michael and I can chat with a few of them if that is OK with you. One person that is not on your list that I would recommend adding is Ginny Fremlin."

"Who is she?" Jayne asked.

"She is the ultrasound technician. She would have been the last person from the clinic to see Lynne alive.

Lynne just had a twenty-eight-week ultrasound last Thursday, three days before the murder."

"Is she available now? We are waiting for the GREAT DOCTOR JULIAN NORTHGATE. Do you hear any trumpets for his parade into…"

"I'm sorry for being late, Detective," Northgate said. "Were you just talking about me, something about a parade? I have thought of lining my steps with red carpet, but would mean one more employee I would have to hire to cart the big rug around! Probably not worth the effort. Sorry for being late, was just getting another woman pregnant."

Inspector Isabella Lake and Detective Sergeant Jayne Chandler were speechless. While they had heard about Dr. Northgate's physical appearance, nothing can truly prepare someone for the first meeting with this Adonis of a man.

To rescue his colleagues, John intervened. "Welcome, Doctor. Thanks for taking the time out of your busy day to meet us. Inspector Lake, Captain Lahr, thank you. We will catch up with you later."

"Yes, thank you," Jayne said. Her face was visibly red from blushing. The Detective Sergeant was unusually flustered. "Please have a seat, Doctor, and we will get started."

7

After John and Dr. Northgate had engaged in idle banter to break the ice, Jayne had regrouped enough to start making eye contact with the Doctor. Jayne found her stride and started the interrogation process as she had done many times in her young career. Experience and competence fortunately permit people to find an autopilot that facilitates success, in any field of life.

"Doctor Northgate, you started this clinic three years ago?" Jayne said.

"That is correct, Detective. When I came back from my training in San Diego, I realized I wasn't suited to work in a garden variety fertility clinic."

"Why is that?" Jayne said.

"Because I thought I could push the envelope of fertility success. I think time has shown this to be true. After three years, our clinic is beating everyone else with our numbers. For example, the best clinic in the USA, the Western Fertility Institute, reports a live birth rate per embryo transfer of seventy-four percent. Conception Opportunities Calgary is pushing eighty percent in the past year."

"Yes. Conception Opportunities Calgary. I presume you came up with that name, Doctor?" Jayne said.

"I did. Do you like my COC? The name, of course." Northgate smiled as he stared directly into Jayne's eyes.

Detective Chandler uncharacterically hesitated. Just long enough for Constable Hunter to jump in.

"You chose the COC name. Did you also choose the clinic's symbol, the rooster?" John said.

"I did. The rooster is a great symbol of fertility. The cock is a walking symbol of manhood. Don't you think it's an appropriate symbol for my clinic, Constable?"

Is this guy for real? thought John.

"Not sure, Doctor," John said, "but it's certainly more appropriate in your case than the Dwennimmen, the African symbol of humility!"

Dwennimmen? Jayne thought. *Where did that come from?*

"Ouch. Touché Constable. My apologies for my lack of modesty. I feel, and I am sorry for this pun, that a cocky attitude is important to have in our clinic. It reassures patients and their families that someone is there for them at a time where they feel a great sense of desperation. People dream of having kids at a very young age. Most people get married for that reason. They speak of their future, which invariably includes children. With that taken away, they walk into this clinic feeling extremely vulnerable. We want to make them feel that everything will be OK, and their dreams are not dead."

It was difficult to know if this statement was the act, or the rest of the conversation was. This human side of Julian Northgate had changed the atmosphere in the room, and John's tone.

"Understood," John said. "What is the secret to your better numbers, Doctor?"

"I can't tell you that, Constable! Did you know that the rooster hides his reproductive equipment inside his abdomen, tucked near his kidneys? Like the rooster, we will keep our little reproductive secrets hidden!"

John laughed, every-so-slightly warming up to Northgate. Jayne was now ready to retake control of the interview.

"Doctor, is there anyone in your clinic that would have had issues with Lynne Nanton?" Jayne said.

"No, can't think of anyone."

"What about you?"

"Me? I can't see why?"

"I see that you are not afraid to be provocative, Doctor. Is it possible that you went too far with missus Nanton?"

"No, Detective. I did nothing wrong with missus Nanton, or with any patients or staff for that matter."

"Lynne's notes about your clinic mention issues like you standing too close to her, staring, fixating on her cleavage. Would it surprise you that she was considering reporting you to your College?"

"It would and it wouldn't."

"What do you mean?" Jayne said

"It would surprise me because my interactions were fine, and I have never been reported to the College. You can check that yourself, Detective. It wouldn't because of the well-known phenomenon of transference."

"Transference? As in Freud's concept?" Jayne asked.

"That's right. Falling in love with your therapist, or in my case a Reproductive specialist, is a common phenomenon, Detective. Maybe that clouded this patient's view of our relationship. Maybe she felt guilty, and it was easier for her to shift that guilt on to me and report me to the College, rather than report herself to her husband."

"That's quite a theory, Doctor," John said. "Do you have a side major in Psychiatry?"

"I don't. But medical school Gold Medal winners usually know something about all areas of medicine, Constable. At any rate, I go back to my unblemished record. Nobody has ever complained about me, or had a reason to, including Lynne Nanton."

Northgate got up, took a bottled water out of the fridge, and downed a huge gulp over several seconds.

"Have you questioned her husband?" Northgate said. "He struck me as being a little strange."

"We have," Jayne said.

"And all the clinic staff? I know that she had an ultrasound just last week. Did you talk to Ginny Fremlin? She could tell you what state of mind the patient was in."

"State of mind?" Jayne asked.

"Maybe she just had enough of living with her loser husband and killed herself."

"That would have been hard to do," Jayne said. "The victim was anesthetized with a rag then had a perfect surgical incision applied to her carotid. I would say that is tough to do alone, don't you think, Doctor?" *Take that you son of a bitch!* thought Jayne, who was finally back to herself.

"Maybe true."

"Which brings me to my final question, Doctor."

"I appreciate that, Detective. They are waiting for me in the clinic."

"Do you have access to anesthetic agents here?"

"We do."

"Inhaled ones?"

"No. We only use an intravenous drug. Propofol. The 'milk of sleep'. During our retrieval of the eggs. I see where you are going with this. We don't use anything that you can place on a rag."

"Thank you, Doctor. That's it from my standpoint. John, any more questions?"

"No, I am good, Detective."

With that, Julian Northgate stormed out before the customary handshakes. Jayne closed the door behind him. She could see someone outside the door, that she presumed to be Ginny Fremlin, and raised her index finger as the universal sign for 'one minute please'.

"He is a piece of work. I can see what Sandy was talking about. This guy is infatuated with himself."

"You got that right, Detective."

"It's Jayne, John."

John was caught off guard.

"You did well, John. Thanks for bailing me out with Northgate. I wasn't quite prepared for his forwardness."

"No worries. Pleasure to help. This is fun."

"Where did you come up with that African symbol of humility?"

"Not sure. Dug down deep for that one. Must be all those National Geographic magazines hanging around the house as a kid!"

8

As impressive a physical specimen as Julian Northgate was, Ginny Fremlin held her own alongside her boss. She stood at least six-foot tall. Ginny had long brown hair that flowed well past her square shoulders. Her white lab coat was open, revealing a white tank top with tight blue clinic scrub bottoms, both of which accentuated her strong features.

"Come on in, missus Fremlin," Jayne said. "Sorry to almost slam the door in your face before."

"No problem," Ginny laughed. "Please call me Ginny. Doctor Northgate can sometimes distract the best of us."

Jayne let that one go. "My name is Detective Chandler from the Calgary Police Department."

John sat stunned. *I must get a job here,* he thought. *I can see what Northgate values in his hiring practices. How did Stubley slip in then? Stop, focus John!*

"Are you going to introduce yourself, Constable Hunter?" Jayne said, snapping John out of his trance.

"I'm sorry, yes. Hello, Ginny," John said. "I am John Hunter. Please call me John. So sorry for staring…you just remind me of someone."

"I get that a lot, John," Ginny said. "I must just have a pretty generic look."

"Yes, that must be it, pretty generic indeed," Jayne said, grinning at Ginny, who smiled back knowingly.

"If you don't mind, Ginny," Jayne said, "I would like to get started and ask you a few questions."

"No problem, Detective."

"You saw the victim, Lynne Nanton, last Thursday, when she had an ultrasound?"

"I did. Her husband was with her."

"How was their state of mind?"

"They were ecstatic. When I showed them the twin boys, they were overwhelmed with joy. They cried for what seemed like ten minutes!"

John detected a surprising sense of impatience, rather than happiness, in her voice.

"You must see that a lot. The tears I mean," John said. "Must be the best part of the job?"

"Don't get me wrong, I get why people react that way, but the drama makes it challenging to get through my list of cases some days. I would say the best part of the job are the people I work with. And the pay is very good, better than most places. But overall, it boils down that the people here, including Doctor Northgate, are great to work with. We have a good time, and great parties. Our Christmas party is coming up next weekend. You should come!"

"No thanks, Ginny," interrupted Jayne, "that probably would not be appropriate. You didn't get any sense that there was trouble between Don and Lynne?"

"Not at all. Much the opposite."

"Or that either of them was depressed?" Jayne said.

"Not even a little bit, Detective."

"Thanks Ginny. I don't have any more questions," Jayne said.

"I have one, if I may," John said. "I have seen ultrasound pictures and have always wondered how you can make heads or tails from them. Seems to me you must have a lot of imagination."

"It is just a matter of being properly trained and having experience. I would not consider imagination as a part of what I do. In my view of the world, imagination is a very powerful force for humans, but also a dangerous one."

"You are telling me that imagination is dangerous?" John said. "And the movie Shawshank Redemption tells me that hope is a dangerous thing. What is left?"

Ginny laughed.

"I just think that imagination leads us to false views of the world, and down the path of error."

"That seems dark," John said.

"Maybe, but I think it is true," Ginny said. "Take this lab coat for example. What do people think of when they see a lab coat?"

"A figure of authority and knowledge," John said.

"Exactly. But I could be someone off the street who just bought a lab coat at Walmart. Their imagination led them to trust me instantly, because of an article of clothing."

"Two points of correction," John said. "For one, I don't think Walmart sells lab coats."

Ginny laughed. Jayne was getting tired, in general, and certainly tired of this pointless discussion.

"And two, in the example you gave, their imagination led them to the truth. I am certain you are someone who can be fully trusted."

"Yes, I can. Maybe not the best example. Imagination can lead to the truth, but in many instances, it leads to faulty assumptions about simple things, but also important areas like happiness and justice."

John sat staring at this stunning woman. *Beautiful,* John thought, *athletic, intelligent, deep thinker. If this girl plays the bagpipes, then she is truly perfect!*

Ginny broke the silence, sensing a look in John's eyes. "Sorry to ramble on about this stuff. It drives my husband crazy!"

That cuts like a knife, thought John.

John regrouped, and took a serious, professional tone. "No rambling at all, missus Fremlin. It was a fascinating discussion. Thank you."

Jayne saw an opportunity to cut in and end the session.

"Thanks, Ginny. That will be all. Have a great rest of your day."

9

"Let's head home for a few hours, John," Jayne said, "I'm hungry and tired. Doctor Vista just texted me and he will be ready to give me a preliminary autopsy report in the morgue, at seven PM."

"Seven PM tonight?" John said.

"Yes, John. Vista works very fast. Guaranteed results in less than forty-eight hours. He shares my love for dead bodies."

"Is it OK if I tag along?"

"Sure, that would be great, John." This time Jayne meant it. John had been quite useful at the clinic. More importantly perhaps, while Jayne respected Dr. Beau Vista's Pathology skills, she was not fond of the non-stop up and down movement of his eyes, and his constant snorting and grunting as he talked. It gave her, and every woman he met, the willies."

"Do you want to discuss your current thoughts on the way back to the station?"

"Not especially, John. I am quite hungry."

"Want to hear mine?"

"Not right now, John."

Jayne was tired. She needed to process all of this. But she then remembered her first investigation, and how she was dying to give her impressions to her senior partner at the time.

"I'm sorry, John. Please go ahead."

"I found most of the people we have interviewed thus far to be genuine and beyond reproach. I think the book is closed on most of the curlers, and almost all the clinic staff. However, in the context of attributing potential means, motives and opportunities to an offender, obviously Doctor Northgate is a prime suspect. He has access to anesthetics, he probably knew he had interacted poorly, and could easily have known where and when Lynne worked. Plus, he is an arrogant asshole, which makes me hate the guy, though his personality flaws don't necessarily make him a murderer. I am very intrigued by Doctor Richmond. She has the means for sure, and I thought she laughed nervously when you asked her about the rag. She had the opportunity, knowing that after her trip to the bathroom she may have been alone with Lynne in the rink. The problem is motive. But she tweaked something in me with her vague "personal reasons" comment and her knowledge that Lynne had twins. Those two are clearly at the top of my list."

"Holy shit, John," Jayne could not hold back. "That is an excellent summary and exactly what I would have said. I would only add at this point that Ginny Fremlin doesn't seem to have the patience to work with pregnant women or babies, but that makes her suspiciously in the wrong job rather than a murder suspect. I agree with you, though, everyone else seems clean."

As they drove into the police station parking lot, Jayne could not help but ask. "Are you as much of a Mimbo as you portray to be, or is that an act somehow?"

"Mimbo? Is that some another one of Doctor Richmond's Scottish farm animals?"

"Mimbo, male Bimbo!"

John was grinning wryly, leaving Jayne as perplexed as she was a few minutes ago.

As she drove home, Jayne found herself with a lot on her mind. Curiously, her first thoughts were not directed at the case itself, but her new-found partner. Not too many people surprised Jayne. With today's interview performance, and inciteful summary of the interviews, John had indeed surprised her.

I still think he must be a Mimbo, thought Jayne. *Maybe some days his stopped clock gets a bonus correct time.*

CHAPTER 6

THE BIRTH OF
PRIMERA

1

"Climate change is a hoax! Climate change is a hoax!"

The 2017 Bonn Climate Change Conference was no different than previous conferences. A great number of exuberant voices, placards, booths, on both sides of the argument.

"Miss, come over here. Miss! Climate change is a hoax. Let us show you the REAL science."

"I'm sorry, I don't really have time right now. I am supposed to be meeting someone."

"Until they get here, just listen. Greenland is fine. The oceans are fine. Doctor Judy Curry, a researcher in climate change, has shown that Greenland's ice levels were the same in the 1940s as they are today. Greenland melted, then froze, and is now melting again. Water levels also rose when Greenland melted in the 1940s. It's a natural cycle. By the way, Greenland melted in the 1940s without a change in atmospheric CO_2 levels. CO_2 has nothing to do with this!"

A chant of "Save our oil, save our oil", echoed from the booth.

"Speaking of glaciers, did you know that the United Nations report on climate change chose 1979 as a starting year to present their data? 1979 was the highest recent point of Arctic ice. If you choose a high point as your starting level, you will show what you want to show: the levels are dropping. The ice levels before the report's starting point were lower than what they are today. Antarctic ice levels are rising, and Arctic ones are falling. Contrary to what you are being fed at this conference, the glaciers are breaking even!"

"Save our oil, save our oil!"

"Thanks, but I really have to go! The person I am meeting will be here any minute."

"Have a great day, miss. And don't believe those pictures of the sickly polar bears. The bears are fine! Polar bear populations are healthier than ever. Look up research by Dr. Susan Crockford!"

"Thank you!"

2

Soul Fernandez reached out to grab the woman's left arm, and take her away from the mob outside the conference center.

"Hi there," Soul said. "Thank you so much for approaching me after my talk to arrange this meeting.

I look forward to escaping the hustle and bustle of this conference for a few hours."

"Hi! I wasn't sure how I would find you in this mob! These oil enthusiasts are really loud and pushy!"

3

Bonn would normally have been quiet on a Monday night, but with thirty-thousand attendees to this world conference, the streets were busting with energy. Looking around at the swarms of people filing through the downtown streets, finding a place at any pub would be challenging, particularly a quiet place.

"Let's go down this road," Soul said. We might have luck down this street. The Loud Woman pub is a part of that building complex down there."

"Loud Woman pub? That is your quiet pub, Soul?"

"Usually is. Maybe not tonight."

As they peered down the street and the word 'pub' was visible on the bottom right hand corner of a four-storey apartment. The building had three archways on the main floor, all three leading to a small restaurant and pub establishment. Above the archways were two floors with small, rectangular windows that looked like apartment rooms. The very top floor had three tiny triangular windows, right below the shallow slope of the triangular roof. The entire complex was made up of three attached buildings. An odd-looking complex, with two historical buildings flanking a center apartment block that looked like it could have been built in the last year.

The green, white and orange colors of the Irish flag became evident as they approached the door of the pub.

"An Irish pub, in downtown Bonn Germany, Soul?"

"You bet," Soul said. "There are several Irish pubs in this city. There is a surprising number of Irish expats in Bonn. I sure hope the people who live in the apartments have hearing issues. How can they possibly get to sleep?"

"I don't know how they do it, Soul. I would hate it. I need total silence. Even the slightest sound distracts me. And then I obsess and focus on it. Do you know what I mean? It drives my fiancé crazy! I would be a wreck living here."

"My guess is that the pub workers mainly live there. The apartments may be empty until closing time."

"You're probably right."

The pub was just as crowded as the streets on this Monday night. Fortunately, most of the patrons preferred to stand in the open area, or sit at the string of attached long tables, than tuck themselves away in the tables for two at the back. As they approached a small table, whose only light source was a dimly lit candle, Soul's new friend was chastising herself.

Come on, relax! Stop being such as fangirl. Probably right? Probably right? Of course, he is right, he is Doctor Soul freaking Fernandez. And stop with this sleep thing, you sound like a maniac! And what's with the "Do you know what I mean?" I hate people who say that. I never say that! Of course, he knows what you mean, he is a world-renowned PhD in Ecology!

"This OK?" Soul said.

"It's perfect."

"I'll go up to bar to order a drink. What would you like, Florida State University is treating us!"

"Great! I'll have a gin and tonic."

"An appropriate choice. Coming right up!"

The pub crowd was a very young one tonight. Undoubtedly a group of like-minded individuals who had invaded Bonn to change the world. Luckily, none of them had recognized the world-famous Ecology researcher walking up to the bar to order a couple of drinks.

4

"You mentioned your fiancé not being fond of your sleeping habits," Soul said, putting the drinks on the table and flopping to his cushioned chair. "Do you have a date set for your wedding?"

"Haven't picked the exact day, yet, but some time next summer for sure."

"He is a lucky man. Do you have kids?"

"No kids. And if you ask my mother, I never will. She loves to remind me that my manly features and android pelvis are not conducive to childbearing."

"Android pelvis. I haven't heard that in a conversation recently. Maybe never."

"I'm sorry. I don't know what I am saying. I am just a little bit freaked out by being here with…"

"It's no worry. Please, relax. You are a breath of fresh air in my stuffy world of University science."

The pub owner broke up their conversation with a loud announcement over the microphone.

"Ladies and gentlemen, you are in for a treat tonight. The Loud Woman pub is happy to host, for a one-week engagement, an exceptional group of musicians straight out of our dear Ireland."

Applause and roars emanated by the crowd, who had now mostly gathered closer to the small wooden stage.

"Thank you. We are proud and excited to introduce to you: Bobby ATM and the Limerick Shamrocks!"

More clapping and screaming from the crowd. Walking up to the stage was a group of five musicians. Bobby ATM went straight to the microphone. Bobby had the appearance of a man who had scraped together an existence of travel from pub to pub. He was extremely thin, a clue that the half a gram of protein in a pint of beer constituted his main source of the muscle-building nutrient. He wore torn, faded blue jeans, a white t-shirt, with an Irish flat cap partially covering a mop of wavy brown hair. Bobby had sparse, brown facial hair with a spot of grey in it, suggestive of a man who had not shaved in a while, but without the ability to grow a full beard or mustache.

Without an introduction, Bobby ATM broke into a melancholic a cappella version of the Irish classic Danny Boy.

The pub patrons were stunned. Out of this rugged appearing man emanated a beautiful voice that rivalled the most famous tenors in the world. The crowd that had gathered on the dance floor in front of the stage watched silently, arm in arm, soaking in the special moment.

Oh Danny boy, oh Danny boy, I love you so!

As Bobby ATM finished those iconic lyrics, his band jumped in and provided an engaging upbeat version of the classic, that had the entire crowd jumping and clapping.

"Soul, wasn't that amazing!" "Our quest for a quiet pub may be shot. Might be tough to hear each other!"

"We will manage," Soul said. "Makes it harder for others to hear us, also."

Whether it was Bobby ATM, or the alcohol, Soul's guest was starting to relax with the legendary scientist. The pair spent the next hour recounting their childhood, their current work, and the journey that had led them to this 2017 world meeting on climate change. By then, they were on their fourth drink, and getting very comfortable with each other.

"Thanks everybody, you are a great crowd! I am Bobby ATM, these guys are the Limerick Shamrocks, and we will be back in twenty minutes for our next set!"

"I do hope you manage to save this planet, Soul."

"It will take a team," Soul said. "When you approached me at the conference, yesterday, what were you seeking?"

"Just to meet you, and an autograph, really."

"We both know there is more to this," Soul said.

"You are right. There is. How did you…"

"I just do. You seek ideological clarity. And you have come to the right place."

"Ideological clarity. Interesting that you say that, Soul. I have been all over the place in my life. I started out as a young girl who attended church with my mother every Sunday, read the Bible regularly, but then her narrow-minded Evangelical Christian doctrines turned me right off from everything remotely religious. That's when I turned to Philosophy, which confused my religious beliefs even more when I read writings from Nietzsche that told me God was dead!"

"Unfortunate," Soul said.

"I went back and forth on my philosophical approaches. One minute I examined the world from my rationalistic, inner being, and the next minute jumped to an empiric view based on my life's experiences. Here I am, at a conference on climate change, meeting the world expert on the subject, yet my mind is filled with arguments from all sorts of staunch climate change deniers like we just met."

Soul stared across the table and took a long sip of his drink.

"The confusion in your mind is leaving you without a cause or purpose. You are seeking clarity in thought, because up to this point in your life you have slept with too many ideologies. This confuses you. It leaves you in emotional and spiritual turmoil."

Soul's guest was taken aback. After processing his words, and fighting back the tears filling her eyes, she restarted the conversation.

"I am not sure if I should be offended by that. But somehow, I'm not. You are right. My brain is full of these conflicting thoughts with my mother, my philosophies, my views of the world, my fiancé's opinions. Somehow, your words seem to be transporting this massive pile of confusion to a beautiful sea of..."

"Tranquility? Peace?" Soul said.

"Yes. Exactly."

"That is what you truly seek. Not an autograph, but the peace of mind and purpose that comes from commitment to a clear ideology. I am here to replace the darkness in your mind with light. To elevate your spirit and thoughts to a cause far greater than you can imagine."

Soul raised his glass, an act followed by his guest.

"Cheers to a new you. As the Good Book says, "You are the light of the world. A city that is set on a hill cannot be hid"."

On cue, Bobby ATM and the Limerick Shamrocks started into their second set. Soul's guest turned to listen, though she was more hearing that listening. Her thoughts were whirling.

But this time, a peaceful breeze had replaced the tempest in her mind.

5

After a few lively jigs, Bobby ATM started crooning a soft, Irish ballad, which lent itself to the resumption of their conversation.

"Soul, you mentioned a cause. I assume it is related to the environment?"

"It certainly is," Soul said.

"I have followed your career for so many years. I want to know more of what you have in mind. This is why I came to Bonn. This is why I sought you out. Meeting you and talking to you has erased any doubt I may have had."

"Clarity?" Soul said.

"Clarity, yes. It is a great feeling."

Soul inched closer to his friend, and asked her in a quiet voice, "What would you be willing to do to save the planet?"

"Anything. It's the most pressing issue facing human civilization now. Ever, in fact."

Soul took a long sip of his beer. He lowered his voice even more and got very close to her.

"Hypothetically speaking. Would you kill to save your planet?"

"Kill? Kill what?"

"Not what. Who?"

As Soul enunciated the word who, his proximity sent his breath over his guest's chest and face, and filled her with an overwhelming sense of reassurance, like a heated steering wheel kicking in on a freezing cold winter day. She was convinced the candle was burning brighter now, and with the darkness in this part of the bar, Soul's head looked like it was surrounded by a circular glow of light.

If I didn't know better, that looks like a halo around him, she thought.

"This conversation goes nowhere else, promise?"

"I do."

"I don't fault you, or anyone, for reading Philosophy works. But I prefer to read and study the Scriptures to find the measure of worth. For example, in Paul's second letter to Timothy, he says: "And that from a child thou hast known the holy Scriptures, which are able to make thee wise unto salvation"."

Soul took a sip of his drink and continued.

"The Good Book tells us that the Scriptures make us wise, the Scriptures lead us to salvation, and the Scriptures lead us to pursue work that has worth. Man is but an instrument that God uses to accomplish good deeds."

Soul's companion nodded in approval. Soul Fernandez was a difficult man to contradict, even if she wanted to. But she did not want to. The mood of the pub, the glow around this man, filled her with a feeling of comfort that she had never experienced.

Soul continued. "Are you familiar with the book of Revelations. The last book of the Bible, which predicts the return of Jesus Christ?"

"Not in great detail, no."

"Chapter seven of Revelations says: "And I saw another angel ascending from the east, having the seal of the living God: and he cried with a loud voice to the four angels, to whom it was given to hurt the earth and the sea, saying, hurt not the earth, neither the sea, nor the trees, till we have sealed the servants of our God in their foreheads"."

"It's beautiful, Soul. But what does it mean?"

"The four angels are trying to put an end to the Earth. They represent our world leaders, industries, machines, and people. I am the angel ascending from the east, sent by God, to stop this. And I am here to recruit a team of God's servants."

Soul's guest sat back to process this. If she saw this man on TV, or heard him on the radio, she would have assumed he was a complete quack. But here, in this Irish pub in Bonn, with the glow of the candle around him, it seemed all too true. Soul Fernandez had just doused her with a shower of spiritual liquor, and she was imbibing it fully.

6

"I have said a lot. We should go," Soul said.

"Soul," getting up from her chair, "do you need an answer from me?"

"Not now. I want you to think about this and come back to me when your mind is clear of the alcohol. I have a meeting with a colleague tomorrow night. If you are interested in joining our team, meet us at 5:45 PM in front of the Bonn-Düsseldorf train ticket window. If you decide you are not interested, I will fully understand. No hard feelings. I wish you well."

As they walked away from the bar, Soul turned and said. "My hotel is attached to the conference center. Yours?"

"It's just two blocks from the conference centre. I can walk there myself."

"I would like to escort you back. Though I have no doubt you could handle yourself if pushed into a conflict."

Both companions smiled at this moment of levity.

"And trust me, I am not walking to your hotel with hopes to go any further than the front doors. Angels of God do not partake in the fruits of the human flesh."

The thought that Soul was trying anything with his offer had not crossed her mind. Somehow, his declared vow of celibacy did not come as a surprise.

CHAPTER 7

BEAU KNOWS

1

After a simple meal and a fifteen-minute power snooze, Jayne summarized the day's interviews in her usual precise, well-prepared notes. It was dark outside as she hopped into her crystal blue 2017 Mazda-3.

I hate when we move the clocks back one hour, Jayne thought. *Why do we do this, anyways?*

The Mazda-3 is a simple, efficient, reliable car, for a simple, efficient, reliable woman. Jayne recalled the exasperated car salesperson desperately trying to sell her any additional features:

"Heated steering wheel?"

"No."

"Power seats?"

"No."

"Anything extra? Leather seats? Paint package? Tire Package?"

"No, no, and no. I told you, sir. Base model. All I want is a console with Bluetooth so I can listen to Spotify. Once I have that, I just need a car that takes me from A to B."

Jayne was not someone to dicker a whole lot on price. She was satisfied, having waited to 2018 to buy what they had left from 2017, that she must have gotten a reasonable deal. Exactly two hours after setting foot into the one and only dealership she would visit, she was off with her new 'A to B' car.

2

Jayne had agreed to meet John in the Pathology laboratory itself. In retrospect, on this dark December night, she now wished they could have met in her office and walked down to the lab together.

As one might expect, the Pathology lab was not front and center on display as you entered Police headquarters. It was quite an adventure getting there, and at seven PM, the adventure became a test of courage and inner strength.

After dropping her coat in her third-floor office, Jayne embarked on the journey. She walked through the now empty floor to the far end of the hallway, passed the darkened Police Chief's office, then took the stairs to the left of the men's bathroom. The stairs looked like they had been the first part of the headquarters that had been built, inspired by the architect's visit to the Paris catacombs. The area was poorly lit, had a musty smell, with brick walls that were exhibiting their age by way of multiple cracks and a faint brown stain. The stairs seemed to get worse as you moved from the main floor to the basement. They had clearly not invested the building budget into stair lighting below the main floor, and the Pathology area was in the sub-basement.

As Jayne landed on level ground after her last step, she saw a metal door with an entrance code panel to the right of it. Jayne now realized that she hadn't asked for the code.

Christ, if this is locked, and the stair door locked behind me, this is going to be one hell of a long night! Jayne thought. Jayne pulled on the door: nothing. She pulled again: nothing. *OK, back up again, Jayne. You will have to find this code.*

She slowly stuck out her left foot to catch the first stair. But before she set foot on it, she heard an unmistakable sound: the heel of a shoe on a metal stair, coming from above. Clump! Short Pause. Clump! Short pause.

"Hello? Is that you John?"

No answer.

"Doctor Vista?"

No answer. Clump! Short Pause. Clump! Short pause. Now getting closer. Jayne guessed that this person was on the basement level, moving her way. She instinctively reached for her holstered gun attached to her left belt buckle. *Shit, I left it in my office.*

Jayne squatted into the small, dark corner to the right of the last stair. She could just fit, squeezed right up against the wall.

As the stranger approached, Jayne could make out a pungent odor of dried sweat. This was not the type of smell from someone who had just skipped their shower that day. This was the smell of someone who methodically avoided all contact with soap and water. *Not John,* Jayne thought. *If nothing else, the guy is poster child for grooming and hygiene.*

The stranger walked past Jayne without noticing her. He approached the panel, entered four numbers, and the door opened widely. With the door open, a faint light from the lab allowed her to recognize Dr. Beau Vista.

"Doctor Vista," Jayne said. "It's me, Detective Jayne Chandler."

Still no response, and Jayne could now see why. She got close to him and yelled.

"Doctor Vista!"

Startled out of his trance, Vista turned to Jayne and said, very loudly, "I'm sorry Jayne, I couldn't hear you with my headphones on. Just regaling in Chopin's Nocturne Opus nine, number two. One of my all-time favorites! I hope I didn't scare you on the way down. Did you not know the code to get in?"

"No, I forgot to ask. I hope I didn't scare you either."

"I'm fine. Now follow me closely. You wouldn't want to get lost in the Pathology laboratory!"

3

Jayne had no desire to follow Beau Vista closely. His body odor was like nothing she had ever experienced before. *If this guy was enrolled in a clinical trial by Oil of Olay, he was certainly randomized to placebo*, thought Jayne, as she tried consciously avoided breathing through her mouth."

"Are you sick, Detective?" asked Vista. "You sound stuffed up."

"No sir, feeling quite well. Not stuffed up at all. I can assure you of that!"

4

As Dr. Beau Vista and Detective Sargeant Jayne Chandler entered the autopsy area, they were greeted by a warm smile and a cheery "Hello" from John Hunter.

The site of John was most welcomed by Jayne. She was surprised by feeling that way, and ascribed it to the dim working area, the frightening experience in the stairway, and Pathologist 'Doctor Pig-Pen' that she had just followed in.

"How did you get in here, Constable?" Jayne said.

"I wanted to make sure I got here on time, so I arrived at 6:45 PM to the lab door. I realized then that I didn't ask for the code. After some thought, I punched in..."

"7284," interjected Vista.

"That's right, 7284. P-A-T-H on an old phone keyboard. These codes are always four numbers!" John said.

Jayne felt a little nauseous. Maybe it was being outwitted by Constable John Hunter. Maybe it was the smell of formaldehyde permeating the air, which was better than the alternative of smelling the man who seemed to use Giorgio Armani's 'Skunk number 5' cologne.

Or perhaps Jayne's nausea was the site of Dr. Vista. Now that the laboratory lights had been fully turned on, his appearance was in full view. To say that Dr. Vista was not handsome was as obvious as saying that Justin Trudeau craves photo ops. He was a short, dumpy man in his fifties, dressed in baggy sweatpants and an old sweatshirt that was ripped in several places. His face was punctuated by deep scars suggestive of severe childhood acne. His nose was massive, with craters that navigated orange-tinged skin. Jayne would later learn with an internet search that Dr. Vista's nose situation has a medical term, rhinophyma, which was commonly a result of an untreated skin condition called rosacea. On that nose precariously rested dark-rimmed glasses that looked stolen out of the 1960's. With those distracting features, what stood out the most was Dr. Vista's hair. He was significantly balding, and had clearly attempted to rectify the front of his hair line with plugs. The plugs looked horrific. It looked as though someone had taken twenty toothpicks and stuck them just above his forehead. As much as they were trying not to, John and Jayne's eyes could not help but to fixate on the bamboo fence that was growing out of Dr. Vista's head.

"I'm sorry, Doctor Vista," Jayne said, "I haven't formally introduced you. This is Constable John Hunter. He has been helping me in this case."

"Nice to meet you, Doctor Vista," John said, reaching his hand out and now getting a full whiff of the Doctor. "Your first name, is it Beau?"

"That's correct, Constable. My mother was French."

"Is that spelled, B-O?" John asked, with a quick, wry look at Jayne, who was now fighting back an embarrassing laugh.

"No. It's B-E-A-U."

"That's a beautiful name, and very appropriate," Jayne said, with a big smile that allowed her pent-up laughter to come out. "It's French for handsome, isn't it?"

"Indeed, Detective. Very good. Thank you for the compliment!" Dr. Vista did not pick up on Jayne's brave attempt at sincerity. He had not gone into Pathology because of his keen instincts into reading people. "If you will follow me, I will take you to the body."

The trio walked into what looked like an operating room. In the center, under a circular light, was the body of Lynne Nanton, covered from neck to toe. Her face was visible.

"You are both OK with this?" Vista asked.

John and Jayne nodded. John was not super keen on this part, but realized it was a necessary part of Detective work.

"I won't elaborate much on the findings from the neck down. I will spare you the sight of the twin boys growing in her uterus. Suffice to say that the babies were perfectly normal for gestational age."

No argument was raised from Jayne or John on that point.

"Three relevant findings from the neck down. The victim had evidence of pelvic endometriosis, a diagnosis that had been made on clinical grounds."

"That is correct," Jayne said. "This had been uncovered in our investigation."

"Good, then. The second finding is a small collection of blood, or hematoma, on her left knee. Otherwise, not a scratch. Not any sign of struggle anywhere. No fingerprints. No DNA from the murderer. Not even a hair. The last finding is a puzzling one. The letters CC were written around her umbilicus, with what looks like a sharpie."

"Yes, we had noticed that too, Doctor," Jayne said.

"Any thoughts on what it means?" Vista said.

"Not quite sure at this point," Jayne answered.

"Alright then, I will have to think about that. Let's move on, shall we? There were two main findings in the neck and face. The first was evidence of an erythematous..."

"Excuse me Doctor, erythematous?" asked Jayne.

"Fancy name for red, isn't it, Doctor?" John said.

"That is correct, Constable. Well done."

Jayne's confusion about her partner mounted.

"There was evidence of an erythematous rash, around the victim's mouth. Pathologically, this had the typical appearance of contact dermatitis. It is an allergic reaction to many potential substances. This certainly supports the theory of an anesthetic agent that your investigation has proposed."

"Yes, the rash was noticed at the scene by Inspector Lake," Jayne said. "She is very sharp. We had supposed the murderer had doused a rag with an inhaled anesthetic agent."

"Inspector Lake is sharp indeed," Vista said. "But there is only one problem with that theory. I don't see any evidence of an anesthetic agent in the victim's lungs or blood."

"You can test for the agents?" Jayne asked.

"We can. And I did. I used a gas chromatography technique to look for halothane, isoflurane, desflurane and sevoflurane in the blood. When that was negative, I performed ion mobility spectrometry and cataluminescence testing for all usual inhaled volatile anesthetics, looking for evidence of these agents in the victim's lungs."

"Not sure what most of that was, Doctor," Jayne said, "but basically all was negative? No sign of inhaled anesthetics?"

"At least not those. I then dug deep and pulled out old testing for nitrous oxide and ether. Neither is commonly used today for anesthesia, but again struck out in this case. I also carefully looked for signs of a reaction to these anesthetic agents in her liver or heart. Nothing. Liver, heart, and all her other organs, were normal."

"Our theory is shot, then?" Jayne said.

"Not necessarily. First, no test is perfect. Second, there is one more agent that I haven't tested for. I have heard of its possibilities as an anesthetic agent, but have never seen it used."

"What's that?" Jayne said.

"Xenon. It's a great anesthetic agent, low risk. Just too expensive in our budget-constrained health care system."

"Xenon?" Jayne repeated. "Don't they make headlights out of that? I think that scumbag Mazda sales guy was trying to sucker me into paying more for these new fancy lights."

"That's correct, Detective." Vista said. "That's one use for Xenon. It is more expensive than normal halogen lamp. Comes standard in some of the fancier models."

"Not standard on my Mazda-3!' Jayne said.

"Xenon. Element fifty-four on the periodic table, right Doctor?" John said. "It's an inert gas. I imagine would be a very stable compound to use. Wouldn't react with anything."

"That is correct, Constable. Someone knows his Chemistry!" Dr. Vista said.

"What the fuck, John?" Jayne shouted. "Where did you pull that out of!"

"As a wise woman once told me. Read a book!" John made a fist and very lightly tapped Jayne's left shoulder.

"OK. Let's stick with the Xenon angle," Jayne said. "Can you test for it, Doctor?"

"Yes and no. There is a recent test for it that was published in a Forensic Medicine journal, in August 2018. I just don't have the test in my lab, but I have my staff working on making it available to us."

"Xenon. Xenon," John thought aloud. "Weren't there concerns that some countries might be using it to blood dope? Raises EPO levels, which in turn raises red blood cell concentrations, leading to better oxygen delivery?"

"Right again, Constable." Vista said. "It is now on the list of banned substances. Hence the recent interest in finding a reliable test for it."

"You seem to know a lot about blood doping, Constable," Jayne said. "Dabbled in a bit of illegal substances in your sports heyday?"

"No comment, Detective. They made it clear to me that it was Vitamin B12!"

The group shared a laugh. Jayne never thought she would be laughing out loud in the autopsy suite.

"Doctor, before we continue," John said, "could I take a quick bathroom break?"

"You can. Bathrooms are just outside this area, to the right."

5

As Ginny arrived home from a long day at work, she could smell an unmistakable scent permeating through her house.

"Homemade pizzas!" Ginny shouted. "Jonas Clavette, you are the best!"

"Nothing too good for my honey," Jonas said, as he gave Ginny a warm hug. "You are home late, busy day at work?"

"Crazy day. Tons of patients, cops delaying us with interviews of the staff, you name it."

"Cops?" Jonas said. "Is the clinic in some kind of trouble?"

"Not at all, I will tell you all about it after I devour this awesome pepperoni pizza!"

As they settled in for dinner, the BBC was reviewing the day's headlines.

"Greta Thunberg named Time 'Person of the Year' for 2019."

"You have to be kidding me," Jonas said. "That little runt knows nothing about climate change. She just regurgitates what her left-wing socialist teachers tell her. Person of the year? What a joke! I tell you, Ginny, it's all an anti-capitalist movement that opposes economic growth, but then turns around and profits from the economics of the climate change hoax. They are all hypocrites and liars."

Ginny interrupted her pizza feast, and looked up with daggers in her eyes.

"Jonas, please don't start this tonight. I am not in the mood to hear your fairy-tale stories about how climate change is a hoax. If you would prefer to ignore the evidence, bury your head in the sand, and take the easy road to life known as status quo, that's your decision."

"Not an ignorer, Ginny. Just a realist. I don't think both sides are being presented fairly by the media."

"Both sides? Both sides? There is only one side, Jonas. Our planet is being destroyed. And quickly. If you don't believe me, believe the ninety-seven percent of climate change scientists who agree that we are in a crisis, and man is the cause of it!"

"Are you sure about that, Ginny? We all keep hearing this "ninety-seven percent of climate change scientist agree that the earth is warming and that it is man made" statement. If you dig a little deeper, that statement is based on a poorly done review that misquoted a bunch of authors. The fact is only two percent of the scientists quoted made a clear statement that man-made greenhouse gases caused at least fifty percent of global warming."

"I am not sure how a guy who has never picked up a book can come up with that!"

"You are not with me twenty-four hours a day, Ginny. You are at work for most of the day, then start your two-hour workout. The book I DID read has data from a climate centre in the UK showing an increase in temperature of one degree over the last 150 years, which has tapered off in the past fifteen years. The USA is cooling, Ginny! Global temperatures rose in the first and tenth centuries, to levels which are like todays."

"I think you are being brainwashed by those who want to take the easy road, Jonas. Look at the amount of CO_2 we are firing into our atmosphere, should we just ignore that?"

"I am not suggesting we ignore that, Ginny. But we must keep our eyes open to all the facts. In this book, they show that CO_2 levels over the history of our planet don't correlate well with Earth's temperature. Plus, when the ocean warms up, CO_2 leaves the water and when the temperature drops, it goes back into the sea. If anything, temperature going up probably leads to increased water vapour, which is the most important greenhouse gas."

"I still don't see two sides to this one. When you're faced with a decision, you should think of the consequences of that decision if you are wrong. If I am wrong, rich countries lose a little bit of money. If you are wrong, the planet suffers, and all humans die. To me, and those I follow, it's a no brainer. And if what you are saying is true, why don't we hear it on TV?"

"The problem is that if you aren't an alarmist, you won't be funded, won't be published, and sure as hell won't be in the media. The blind are being led by magicians who are putting up smoke and mirrors around the actual data. I would rather look at all the information. To be in the media you must be an uneducated sixteen-year-old that is able to get uneducated socialists to parade on the street, based only on what they have been spoon fed by left-wing media. That is how you get on the news, and apparently how you win prestigious awards."

"Blind? Magicians? Uneducated? You are an asshole, Jonas. I can't believe I married a climate change ignorer. I should just come home and talk to our aquarium: the beta fish offer up more intelligent discussion than you do!"

"Fuck off, Ginny. I guess we can't have a reasonable debate on anything. So much for our nice dinner together. Enjoy your pizza. Don't choke on it. I am going for a walk!"

6

The break from the autopsy suite was much appreciated by Jayne who needed to sit down and process the flurry of information coming her way. A little break from the dead body and the many smells in the autopsy room did not hurt either. As John returned, the group reconvened around the body.

"We are almost done," Vista said. "I just want the both of you to have a close look at the victim's neck area."

"You mean the incision? It kind of looks like a smile to me, Doctor," Jayne said.

"Yes, it does. Very observant, Detective. The incision is twelve centimeters in length. It is mainly horizontal, but does have a slightly curbed appearance on each side. It appears to me to be made precisely with a surgical scalpel. If I didn't know better, I would say it looks like a perfect Pfannenstiel incision."

"Excuse me Doctor, can you repeat that and spell it out?" Jayne said.

"Of course, Detective. Pfannenstiel. P-F-A-N-N-E-N-S-T-I-E-L. It is a German word for a panhandle, which many people associate with the origin of the incision. It was invented in the 1900's by a German Gynecologist, Hermann Pfannenstiel. It has been used since then for many operations, but primarily

Cesarean sections. The incision is usually made a couple of centimeters above the pubic bone. I don't think Doctor Pfannenstiel had the carotid artery in mind when he invented the technique."

"Is it mainly used by Gynecologists?" Jayne thought aloud.

"Correct. I thought about it and confirmed it when I looked at the scar on my wife's abdomen."

"Wife?" Jayne said, meaning to use his inside voice. "I mean, Doctor, your wife had C-sections?"

"Yes, Betty had three of them. Poor woman, she is in bad shape these days. Betty is practically bedridden after her stroke."

"Stroke?" *Nice, Jayne. Don't I feel like an asshole!*

"Yes, big one. Middle cerebral artery. She has trouble getting words out and can't move the entire right side of her body. Happened one month ago. We were hoping for a better recovery in rehab, but to this point only minimal improvement."

Hopefully it affected her sense of smell and vision. Even as these spontaneous thoughts came to his head, John felt bad. *Jesus Christ John, the poor couple. Don't be such a dick!*

"So sorry, Doctor!" chimed both John and Jayne, almost in perfect synchrony. Though it was unclear how much of this was sympathy for the Doctor and his wife, or an apology for their hidden awful thoughts.

Putting his hand on Dr. Vista's shoulder, John said, "Hang in there, Doc. I have heard of many stories where people recover even years after a stroke. Don't give up hope." Jayne nodded in approval.

Dr. Vista looked at them both and was most appreciative. Life was lonely for him these days. The autopsy room was strangely the place he felt most comfortable and at peace right now.

7

After eating and "not choking" on her pizza, Ginny went upstairs to shower and hopefully wash off the events of the day, particularly her acrimonious debate with Jonas.

That wasn't a nice dinner, thought Ginny. *What a jerk! But then again, he did make me my favorite meal. I guess climate change should be added to the list of taboo subjects, right next to politics and religion.*

As she got undressed and walked to the shower, Ginny looked at her naked body in the mirror. She could easily have donned the cover of any fitness magazine, a career option that Jonas had encouraged her many times to take. Ginny was tall, slim, and rock hard with muscle throughout. Add to that her unnaturally bronzed skin and long dark hair, she certainly turned heads of men and women alike.

I'll make it up to him later the best way I can, Ginny thought, gently stroking her shoulders. *He will forget all about this!*

As Ginny stepped out of the shower, the lights in the entire house turned off.

"What the hell?" Ginny said in a low voice.

Ginny quickly put on her housecoat, and was now peeking her head out of the bedroom doorway. "Jonas, what is going on?"

There was no answer.

"Jonas, don't mess with me. You know I hate games!"

Ginny walked out of the bedroom into the hallway, and stood at the top of the stairs. The house was completely quiet. A tiny amount of light coming through the kitchen French doors from the neighboring streetlight thwarted otherwise total darkness.

"Jonas, I am going back to our room and getting out our gun. I will shoot you on the spot if you don't smarten up."

Ginny and Jonas did not have a gun. Her bravado was an act, in case this was not one of Jonas' pranks. They did keep a golf driver in their room for this very scenario, which is what Ginny was going to get.

Ginny sat in the quiet of her room, driver in hand, waiting to hear a sound.

That fucking idiot Jonas is going to make me call 9-1-1. This little prank will cost us a fortune.

Before she could get to her phone, she heard the loud sound of the basement door closing, followed by the creaking of their very old basement stairs.

Someone is in the house. Shit, I left my cell phone charging in the kitchen. Whoever this is, I am just going to take out his kneecaps with this driver.

"Jonas, last chance, I am not playing around here. You are going to get hurt." Her voice was up several octaves and decibels at this point.

The person was now walking on the main floor, heading towards the stairs.

Ginny could see a faint glow at the bottom of the stairs. The glow disappeared as the intruder began walking up the dark stairway. As he hit the fourth stair, a low, muffled voice that sounded like a bad guy in a Hollywood movie rang out.

"Ginny, beware of the angel of conception!"

What? Angel of conception?

The glow returned as the intruder was now halfway up the stairs.

"Ginny, beware of the angel of conception. It's coming to fill you up with a baby!"

Ginny, driver in hand, could now discern the features of the man walking towards her. As it became obvious to her that the glow was Jonas' cell phone flashlight shining on his neck below his chin, Jonas exploded in laughter. As he rolled around the floor, Ginny dropped to her knees and started punching him on both arms, then both thighs.

"You prick, you scared the shit out of me, what are you doing?"

Ginny started crying. Jonas grabbed her arms, to first stop the painful punches, and then to allow him to give her a big hug.

"I am sorry, honey. Sorry for my rant earlier. You know me and my pranks. I read in one of your journals that acute stress can induce ovulation in women."

"Did you read about the cardiac arrest it can cause as well? I hate you!"

"No, you don't." Jonas gently pushed Ginny to the ground and was now lying on top of her. "Because I am... the angel of conception!"

"What's with that voice? You sound like the bad guy in those new Batman movies."

"Voice changer app. It's great isn't it?"

Jonas started kissing the back of Ginny's neck, moved to the left side of her neck and ear, then slowly back across to the right ear. As he opened her housecoat and stroked her skin with his tongue, Ginny could feel the hair stand up at the back of her neck. Her body was covered in goose bumps. This was not the only physiological responses that Jonas was evoking. The long, pointy nipples on Ginny's fulsome breasts were now protruding proudly, like the angel at the top of a Christmas tree. Jonas started to kiss her right cheek, and moved toward her lips. Ginny tilted her head to help their lips and tongues connect.

"Where is the golf club? Or do you feel the driver head in my pants?"

"I do feel it. You obviously enjoyed all of this. You're lucky your shins are still intact."

"I love you, honey." Jonas lowered his voice. "You are incredibly hot, Ginny."

"Make up sex is the best," Ginny whispered. "Do me, my angel of conception."

CHAPTER 8

JOHN HUNTER'S COMING OUT PARTY

1

Jayne and John left Dr. Vista in the lab and marched the five dingy flights of stairs to the dark third floor. Jayne headed to her spacious office. John headed to his cubby hole.

Jayne felt exposed. Like nobody else she had ever worked with, fourth-class Constable John Hunter had been able to peel the harsh outer layers of the onion she had created for herself. Those layers had been her envelope during her entire life. Every relationship and every interaction she had experienced, whether personal or professional, had occurred with the shield of that thick external skin. With the protective coating gone, she felt vulnerable. With the peeling of her emotional onion came the physical response of tears filling Jayne's olive eyes.

Jayne was not sure why she was feeling this way. Was it the uncertainty of becoming someone different than who she had been? Was is a feeling of overwhelming joy, in finding a new life outside of her self-imposed cocoon?

Maybe her emotions had nothing to do with her inner confusion. Maybe the events of the last two days were catching up to her. Maybe the grotesque job of examining the corpse of someone who just forty-eight hours ago was alive and well, carrying two healthy boys, and who was now lying cut open on a steel bed in a Pathology lab, was finally getting to Jayne.

Before she got too far, Jayne turned around to face her partner.

"John?"

"Yes, Jayne?" He was anxious at what she might say. There was a distinctly different tone to her voice when she called out his name.

For a moment, she thought of showing John her new-found vulnerability, but she decided otherwise. Jayne managed to find another line of discussion.

"Do you really know people who recovered years after a stroke?"

"What?" Not what John had expected or perhaps hoped for.

"That's what you told Doctor Vista. Did you mean that or were you just desperate to find some way to provide him hope?"

"My uncle Tom improved after several months. Other than that, I might have seen a story about someone else on TV."

"You told him "many stories". One real story and one on TV now constitutes "many"?"

Jayne smiled. John could not help but think that even in the dark, she lit up a room with that smile.

"I heard that trick from a Doctor once. If you have seen something once, you can say "in my experience". If you have seen something twice, then you can say "many times". But if you see something more than twice, you can then say, "time and time again"."

"You are something else, Hunter." Jayne said with a laugh. "I guess I can say that "time and time again" you surprise me!"

"Thanks, boss."

"Boss no more, John. If it's OK with you, I will ask the Police Chief to make you my partner full-time as of now."

"Serious?"

"You're doing great. Now enough of this mushy crap, let's go get a drink. I think I am too tired to sleep! Do you know a bar that gives cops free drinks?"

"Unfortunately, not. But Tuesdays is ten-cent wing night at St-Hilda's pub down the street. The owner Julius might even cut us a deal if you make a fuss over his cheesy mustache!"

"Sounds good. I can do that. I will go home and change. Meet you there in an hour."

2

The Police Department Headquarters and St-Hilda's pub were not situated in the posh part of town by any means. You could probably argue that they were located in the dingiest area in the city. Each one of the narrow streets looked identical, with monotonous lines of tightly bunched small houses. Calgary became a city in 1894, and the houses in this area all looked like they were built around that time. Every street looked the same, and each house looked the same: square shaped, roughly six hundred square feet in size, each appearing as though they desperately needed to be torn down soon or else the moss-covered shingle rooves would collapse under the weight of the winter snow. Every small house had a single tall tree that took up the entirety of the front lawn. In the summer, these trees would soften the appearance of the neighborhood. In the dead of water, the leafless trees only added to the creepiness of the area, particularly at this hour of the night.

In the center of the neighborhood was the community's focal point: the four-business strip mall that also looked its age. Jayne thought of filling up her quarter-full Mazda-3 as she arrived at the mall, but decided against it for three reasons. Jayne liked the Air Miles she collected at Shell, and not only was this not a Shell but it was not a recognizable gas station chain. Second, the lighting was very low, to the point of wondering if the station and store were open. This light was not low enough to hide the five people hanging out in front of the convenience store, who appeared, as her mother would say, as "ne'er do wells". Lastly, and most importantly, the two old pumps did not have credit card paying capabilities, which was the death blow to her considering a fill up.

The parking lot had room for about twenty cars, and tonight was completely full. *People do love their ten-cent wings*, thought Jayne, as she maneuvered her car to the adjacent street. Unfortunately, the next four streets around the mall were all 'by permit only' streets.

No way, I am not walking alone in this area for six blocks without my gun! There is nobody on these streets. I don't usually do this, but if I get a ticket, I will just sweet-talk Jimmy at the Police Department parking enforcement office.

As she walked out of her car, Jayne could see an older man across the street, walking his dog very slowly. Even at a distance she could make out the man's very large nose.

I wonder if that is Doctor Vista walking his dog T-Bone? He would fit right in here.

Jayne walked briskly past the convenience store, then past 'Frank's Pizza' and 'Martha's Dry cleaning'. Tucked in a corner of the mall, as poorly lit as the rest of the area, was St-Hilda's pub. Like everything else in the neighborhood, the sign indicating the pub name was very small and hard to see. Beside the sign was a white piece of bristle board inviting people to 'Tuesday night wing night. 10-cent wings'. Only someone, maybe one of the "ne'er do wells", had inserted a piece of paper on the sign. Now everyone was invited for '0-cent wings'.

Funny. Maybe this neighborhood is not that bad. Explains the full parking lot, Jayne thought, as she smiled while reading the sign.

An inconspicuous red door, which could have used a fresh coat of paint, led to a small entrance, with nothing in it other than an arrow pointing down the eleven stairs to the pub. Contrary to the first door, the door at the bottom of the stairs was made of beautiful, dark mahogany wood. Carved in it were three coiled snakes, menacingly protruding their tongues and fangs.

Wow, fancy door. Unexpected! Jayne thought, as she opened it.

What was waiting for Jayne on the other side of the door was also a huge surprise. The inside of St-Hilda's pub was gorgeous. On the left-hand side of the pub were artistically finished wooden booths, with fresh stain that was resplendent as it basked in the glow of the multiple, fancy hanging lamps. The booths were filled with thick, comfortable-appearing brown leather seats, and tonight there was not an open seat in sight. As she walked to her left and got closer to the booths, Jayne once again saw the same serpent carvings on each side of the booths. Not seeing John in any of the booths, Jayne turned to her right where she saw the bar area, densely packed with people who were both sitting on bar stools and standing. Ten-cent wing night was obviously a standing-room only affair at St-Hilda's!

The atmosphere was as engaging as the pub's physical appearance. Between the booths and the bar was a small open area, where an older man sat on a stool with his accordion, pounding out a German polka that sounded to Jayne like 'Beer Barrel Polka', the only polka she knew, but not quite. Either way, it brought a smile to her face, which was noticed by the accordionist, who gave her a wink and knowing smile back. A few of the bar patrons could not help themselves in clapping along to the lively music.

"Jayne, over here," John said, from a small two-person booth quietly tucked away behind the bar and its standing crowd.

John had stood up, and as Jayne got closer to him, he shouted, "Don't you love this place? On a Tuesday night of all things!"

Jayne laughed as she they sat down.

"I have to admit, John, I am quite surprised that this even exists. I have driven by this area countless times and haven't noticed it. But to have it look like this inside? I am shocked!"

"Yes, it's beautiful. Harder to see the décor at night like this, but the owner Julius Marpole spared no expense."

"What's with all the snakes?"

"Legend has it St-Hilda, long before Jesus was born, expulsed the evil snakes from an area in England by throwing them over the cliff, and having them turn to stone on the way down. That has remained her symbol today. Isn't that right, Julius? The snakes are St-Hilda's calling card?"

Jayne looked over to see Julius Marpole, standing over her right shoulder. Marpole looked like he was fifty, but Jayne suspected he was much older. As he knelt beside their booth, Jayne could see some definite thinning of his curly black hair, and distinct wrinkles in his tanned face. Julius did have a prominent mustache, one frequently associated with 1970s adult film stars. He was grinning ear to ear, suggesting that he was a very friendly person, but also that he probably had started drinking many hours ago.

"That's right, John," Marpole said. "St-Hilda was a badass momma with those snakes!"

Jayne could hear him clearly, which made her realize that the music in the pub was no longer the live accordion songs, but rather softer, recorded, and less engaging tunes.

"I am Julius Marpole. Welcome to my humble pub." Marpole extended a warm hand to Jayne. "Let me tell you miss, you are with a great man here. John Hunter is a keeper in my books!"

"Oh, we are not toge…" Jayne tried to say.

"I have known this man for what, ten years John?" John nodded in agreement. "He is such a good kid. Everyone loves him. You are in our best booth, and people give it up for him every time he shows up!"

That was true again tonight. A couple that was in the booth offered it to John when they saw him, claiming they were leaving. That was partly true, but John could see that they were still not quite out the door.

"John Hunter, I love you like the son I never had!"

"Thanks Julius, that's not nece…"

"Anyways, I have to run. Have a great time. The staff are great here, but they still need Papa Julius to hold their hand!"

That was not true. The staff much preferred when Julius stayed away. Julius was borderline helpful when sober, which was typically before noon, but clearly harmful when he had been drinking. He was too kind. Business was more about making people happy then making money. Too many rounds on the house. Too many free wings. It was best when Julius sat and played his accordion, and they would soon send him back out there.

"What a nice guy. What a great place. Thanks for bringing me here John. What are you drinking?"

3

The drinks were flowing all around the pub that Tuesday night, and the Hunter-Chandler booth was no different. It struck John that he had always come to wing night with his male hockey friends. Eating wings was not easy to do cleanly and politely. *Note to self,* John thought. *Wings are not a first date meal. Not that this is date!*

John was notorious for his wing-eating technique. Most people eat one wing at a time, carefully wiping their mouths from the barbecue sauce after each bit. That was not John's philosophy on eating wings. John insisted that wiping after each bite, or even each wing, was futile. "Boys, better just to eat the whole plate, accept the few moments of disgusting goop dripping down your cheek, and just wipe once at the end. Way more efficient." The boys had grown to expect, and even like, John's less than perfect etiquette. Tonight though, John Hunter would eat his wings like the rest of the world.

4

After an hour of general chit chat, occasional hand clapping, and even singing, (yes, Detective Sargeant Jayne Chandler was singing at a pub! But who can resist Piano Man on the accordion?) Jayne felt comfortable and inebriated enough to ask John the question that had been on her mind most of the day.

"What's with you, Hunter?"

"What do you mean?"

"You come with a reputation of being this dumb guy who basically got a job because of his father. Yet the past two days have shown me a very different side of you. What's with you?"

"I like to set the bar low." John smiled widely.

"And that you certainly do. You started the day yesterday by insisting on using the wrong stairs in the curling rink. You follow that up with ridiculous observations about Lynne Nanton being pregnant and using a sharpie for your grocery list. With Doctor Vista, you follow-up with advanced Chemistry knowledge about Xenon. With Northgate, you were talking about that African humility symbol, the Dewey man or something?"

"Dwennimmen," John corrected.

"Whatever, I can't say that at the best of times much less after a few drinks. Why do you do that? Why do you let everyone think and say you are stupid?"

John hesitated. He looked around and realized that Julius Marpole was on another accordion break, probably to restock his personal booze supply. It was getting close to midnight. With the combination of the recorded music and people having left, he felt he needed to lower his voice.

"I decided long ago that I can't control, and won't care about, what people think of me or say about me. It's probably a combination of issues related to both my parents."

"What do you mean? By the way, you are OK talking about this, right? This isn't a police interrogation!"

"I know," John said, laughing. "I am fine with this, but I am afraid of boring you."

"Not at all," Jayne said.

"My mother was the hero in my life. She passed away when I was fourteen. Awful ovarian cancer."

"I heard about that, John. I am so sorry." Jayne put her hand on top of John's. "That must have been so hard."

John squeezed Jayne's hand, then let go. "When she died, my world was turned completely upside down. It was like the rudder on my sailboat had broken off, and I was just drifting through life without purpose. With the exception of when I played hockey, I became completely unmotivated. I just preferred to disconnect from society rather than face the world without her comforting presence."

"Was your dad helpful?" Jayne said.

"Not even a little bit. My relationship with my father was never great, but after mom passed it became worse. My absence of drive was in part some sort of teenager rebellion against him."

"That's too bad, John," Jayne said.

"My dad hammered away at me, probably a thousand times, that I should always "Aim high so that if you don't get there you are at least in the right ballpark. Aim for nineties John, and you will get 'eighties." I got sick of hearing his bullshit. I decided to take the opposite approach. Aim low, achieve low, so that anything higher looked great. Aim for fifties, get fifties, then astonish them occasionally with a sixty."

"Weren't you worried that once you managed to get over the loss of your mother, that you wouldn't get anything out of life with that attitude?"

"I guess it boils down to your interpretation of what you get out of life. This is where my mother's influence comes in."

Again, John looked around, then leaned closer to Jayne.

"This is going to get deep, you sure you want to get this serious?"

Jayne was fascinated by this conversation. It was such a new world for her. Such a different line of thinking. She was dying to find out where this came from.

"Absolutely. Maybe I will learn something from you, Hunter!"

"OK. Here we go. My mother was very religious. Every night, and I mean every night, even over the phone if I was away, we would recite the Lord's prayer together, and Psalm twenty-three. I hated it at the time. It was embarrassing to phone it in with your hockey buddies around. Now that she has passed, it is what I miss the most about her. I would kill to hear her voice again and recite them with her. I wish I had recorded her."

"She sounds like a great woman. You lost her too soon." John could see how genuine Jayne was by the tears in her eyes. "Can you refresh my memory about Psalm twenty-three?"

"Psalm twenty-three, Chandler. Read a book! Read THE Book!"

"I have to admit, I don't read my Bible as often as I should. Maybe never, in fact."

"I noticed. I am sure you will recognize it. "The Lord is my shepherd. I shall not want. He maketh me lie down in green pastures: he leadeth me beside the still waters..." It goes on."

"OK, I get it, the Lord is your shepherd. How does that relate to anything?"

"The key statement is "I shall not want". What our society associates with success: great marks at school, degrees, salary, rank, these are all related to satisfying our ego. Psalm twenty-three rejects that. My mother rejected that. I reject that. "I shall not want" means not yearning for material possessions. With my belief in God that I received from my mother, I fundamentally have everything that I, and every human being needs: a feeling of being loved, provided for, and protected."

Jayne had no immediate answer for this. John could tell the wheels were in motion in her brain. He had seen this many times during the past forty-eight hours. Julius Marpole had restarted playing. John steered his eye contact away from Jayne. He did not disrupt her thinking with idle words.

5

Jayne broke her few minutes of reflection. "But doesn't it bother you that people make fun of you? And not always behind your back!"

John smiled at her. Jayne smiled back. After a few drinks, his gap tooth was even cuter.

"It doesn't. Recognition and praise, just like money and possessions, are simply creatures of ego that weak humans have invented. They are included on my list of "I shall not want". Some of that comes from my mother's second favorite book, To Kill a Mockingbird. You must have read that one, Jayne?"

"Of course. A classic!"

"My mother's favorite line was Harper Lee's famous "Mockingbirds don't do one thing but make music for us to enjoy. They don't eat up people's gardens, don't nest in corncribs, they don't do one thing but sing their hearts out for us. That's why it's" ..."

"A sin to kill a mockingbird," interrupted Jayne. "I love that passage. It crossed my mind when people were talking about Lynne Nanton."

"I thought of that too," John said. "This may sound less than humble, but you can say what you want about me, I think most people like me. They may think I am simple, or even dumb, but when they get to know me, I think they see that I can bring joy to their lives. Just like my mother. Just like the mockingbird."

"Julius Marpole obviously feels that way," Jayne said, "and the nice couple that gave you these choice seats!"

As Jayne was reflecting on this conversation, and thinking that the last person who needs to worry about arrogance is John, John grabbed her by the arm and left her no choice to accompany her.

"Come on, Chandler. It's 'Beer Barrel Polka'. Polka with me!"

"What, I don't know what to do!"

"It's easy, just follow me. It's three beats. On one you move your left foot. On two you bring your right foot over. On three you stationary hop with your left foot. Just follow me and you'll have it by the end of the song, I promise."

And she did. What a forty-eight hours for Detective Sargeant Jayne Chandler. Smiles, laughs, philosophy, beer on a Tuesday, and now, polka!

John managed to keep Jayne out on the dance floor for one more song, yet another polka, but that was all he would get.

"I'm drenched, Hunter," Jayne said, wiping her forehead with her arm as they sat down. "What time do they close up anyways?"

"Great timing for that question," John said. "It's last call for alcohol. One more?"

"Sure, one more quick one," Jayne said.

As John ordered one more round, Jayne said, "I am having a great time, John. You are teaching me lots."

"Well you taught me a bunch during the last forty-eight hours, Detective. You are amazingly good at what you do. You deserve your great reputation!"

"Thanks. But I guess reputation isn't that important, is it?"

John laughed. "It's OK to seek out the ego things. You just can't let them dominate your life."

Jayne paused, as the server dropped the drinks on the table. "I meant what I said earlier, John. I will ask your dad to have you formally join me as a partner, and start the process of you becoming a Detective."

"Thanks, Jayne."

"It's still within your beliefs to get promoted, is it?"

"It is." John laughed. "But promotion is one of the 'dangerous P's'."

"What?"

"Oops. Didn't mean to get philosophical again. Let's leave it for now, enough deep conversation for one night."

"No, carry on, I would love to hear it."

"OK, but last serious thought for the night! My mother had a bunch of religious books lying around the house. One day, I just picked one up and started reading it. It was called 'Incarnational Christianity', by a pastor in Southern USA called Steve Meeks."

"Incarnational Christianity. That IS getting deep!"

"Agree. I don't remember all the details. In the big picture it is about embodying God in our lives and making Him and His principles the guiding force in our life. What I clearly remember, and live by, is a passage where Pastor Meeks talks about four 'P's' that should not define our lives, but unfortunately too often do: positions, pursuits, possessions, and people's opinions. I would add three more: praise, prestige and power."

"Wow. That sounds like me and what I value."

"I think you are being hard on yourself, Jayne. I have seen other values shine through your interactions in the past forty-eight hours. You warmed up nicely to Yves Lavallée and tried to put on a French accent for him."

"E really h-appreciated dat!" Jayne said, making both herself and John laugh.

"He did. And the clinic staff appreciated your warm offer for support. Doctor Vista was clearly moved by your genuine empathy towards his wife's situation. You have way more values inside than you realize. But the four 'P's are not necessarily wrong, I don't think. I think the message is simply to treasure and value your relationships first: with God, Jesus Christ, family and friends. Put the four or five 'P's' much lower down on your life's priority list."

"Another P. Priority!" Jayne said.

"Yes, exactly! Bottom line for me: after the fog lifted over my teenage years, I decide to live by only two 'P's. The one after the 'a', and the one before the 'i'."

"What?"

"Think, Detective. You like to solve riddles and codes!"

"The one after the 'a', and the one before the 'i'. Let's see." Jayne beamed. "I got it. Happiness!"

"That's correct, Detective. Great work!"

7

"You two seemed to have a great time tonight," Julius said. "Please come back, soon."

"We will Julius," John said. "That was a blast!"

"And bring your new girlfriend back, John." Julius said.

"No, Julius, it's not what you think." John said, waving both hands in front of his chest. "Jayne, I know you will fight me on this, but I will get this tab. You can get the next one."

"I have had too much to drink, John. You won't get a fight from me. I have sent for two UBERs and will take care of them."

Thumbs up from John, as he walked away from Julius and Jayne to the bar.

"He is a great man, Jayne," Julius said. "My son from another mother. I have known him for a long time. Superficial in appearance maybe, but quite profound in human qualities."

"I have certainly learnt that tonight," Jayne said. "We did have a great time tonight Mister Marpole. But just to be clear, John and I just work together."

"Whatever you say, Jayne. And please, call me Julius. Do come back, will you? I must run off and help the staff close. Pub owner's job is never done!"

As Julius stumbled away, John returned from the bar.

"What a great guy, that Julius," John said. "I don't know how he makes money. He knocked off four of our drinks from the tab, and half of our food. I think you got the raw end of the deal paying for the UBERs."

"Darn it," Jayne said, in an exaggerated fashion. "Let's head outside to catch our rides."

8

It was surprisingly warm outside for one o'clock in the morning. John and Jayne were huddled close together, but not quite making any actual contact.

"The neighborhood looks significantly more inviting and safer after a few drinks, doesn't it?" Jayne said.

"It sure does. It can feel a little sketchy when you are walking in," John said. "I could sure use a shawarma right now. No street meat vendor around?"

"Not that I can see," laughed Jayne.

"I have never had a shawarma sober. Not even a craving for one."

Jayne could see some headlights that were heading their way.

"Looks like the UBERs are almost here," Jayne said. "Thanks again for tonight." Awkwardly, she stuck out her closed right hand for a fist bump.

"That was fun," John said, returning her fist bump. "Let's do it again some time, Detective. You go ahead and get the first UBER."

"Thanks, John."

As Jayne was almost at the car, she turned around and looked at John, but said nothing.

"By the way, just to be clear," John said. "This isn't going to turn out like in the movies."

"What do you mean, THIS?"

"You and I."

"Turn out how?"

"Turn out like the old story where the girl and the guy don't get along at first, then grow to respect each other, then end up falling madly in love and being together forever."

Jayne laughed. "OK, got you. Not a good idea to date someone from work, is it?"

"Nothing to do with work. It's just that I am out of your league. Way too good looking for you. Relationships never work out when the guy is way better looking than the girl!"

John made himself laugh. Jayne had a huge smile as she opened the car door. A smile that made even this dingy neighborhood light up.

"Though when you smile like that," John said, "you certainly do level the playing field!"

"Ha! Maybe I will try to smile more then! By the way, I agree with your theory about the guy being too good looking. Brad Pitt is way more beautiful than Angelina, and look how that turned out. See you tomorrow, but not bright and early, OK?"

Another thumbs up from John, as Jayne got in the car and drove away.

CHAPTER 9

PRIMERA MEETS
LA FUENTE

1

"Achtung, Achtung. Der Bonn-Düsseldorff Zug fährt in fünf Minuten."

"She is not here, Soul," Ruprecht said.

"Attention, attention. The Bonn-Düsseldorff train leaves in five minutes."

"You scared her off, my friend. Come, let's get on our train. Doctor Mikhaël Leddy is not the type of person you keep waiting. What a waste of a ticket. First-class, too!"

Soul searched through the thick human fog scurrying through the busy Bonn train station. Announcements were being made from all directions for trains travelling throughout Germany and Europe. The same precision that applied to German engineering and manufacturing sector applied to their railway schedules. A 17:52 departure meant a 17:52 departure. Not one minute before, or after.

As he begrudgingly accepted Ruprecht's assessment, the figure of a lean, six-foot tall woman hasting towards them with perfect running mechanics emerged. She did not appear winded at all from her long run through the crowded station. This fact was not lost on Soul, who had suspected from their previous encounter that this impressive woman possessed a superior level of conditioning.

"There she is, Ruprecht. I knew she would come through. I read it in her soul."

"I am so sorry for being late. I got lost twice on the way here. I am hopeless with directions."

"No worries at all," Soul said. "Glad you can make it. My friend Ruprecht has started walking towards the train. Let's catch him. We have much to discuss."

This surprised the newest team member. She expected a coffee shop meeting at the station, not an actual departure from Bonn. She was not a naturally trusting person, and following these two strangers into a train was out of character for her. But Soul Fernandez was not your average person. With Soul, she felt an aura of belonging and reassurance that she had never experienced before.

2

As the trio settled into their private room in the first-class section of the train, Soul and Ruprecht passionately presented the background for their cause. They were very direct with her. A massive worldwide plan, involving multiple human casualties, all in the name of steering the world and its elected representatives away from words on the pages of agreements that make splashy headlines, towards real action that will have demonstrable impact in favor of our planet. Something dramatic had to happen to shake populations and their leaders out of their dreamworld and back to the harsh reality of this grave problem.

This group was going to provide the drama. Murders of pregnant martyrs, to be carried out simultaneously across many countries, repeated every forty days if concrete changes were not carried out that would alter the health of our atmosphere, our forests and our oceans.

As they completed their overview of the plan, Soul lifted his right sleeve to show the tattoo he had over his biceps and triceps area. A beautiful blue pond, surrounded by luscious green palm trees. Ruprecht moved closer to Soul's arm and pointed at the engraving on the top: 14U14US.

"Tell her what this means, Soul."

"One for you, one for us. This is the foundation philosophy of our plan. Humans are producing, on a yearly basis, a surplus of over fifty million people, and while the surplus is happening, there are 153 million orphans in the world. It's a travesty!"

"And because of this," Ruprecht said. "Soul, actually I should say we, not just Soul, will force government's hands to impose strict policies worldwide on live births. You can bring one child into this world. Your second one needs to be adopted. Until the situation stabilizes."

"One for you, one for us. That makes total sense to me. I can't stand these people who walk into my ultrasound area pregnant with their sixth child. Who needs that? It's egotistical. I just want to tell them to give their head a shake and take notice of the world they live in."

"You are correct," Soul said. "Our planet has a fixed limit of people it can accommodate. It is Earth's carrying capacity. And we have reached that number. There are enough people in the world."

The newest member of the team was about to say something, then paused. Soul and Ruprecht sensed this and waited for her to speak. Finally, she broke her silence, lowering her voice in their private train coach.

"So, what is my role in all of this?"

"We are giving ourselves two years to recruit all of our soldiers," Soul said, "and carefully plan out our method of handling our martyrs with dignity and compassion. You will be our first soldier. You will be our Primera!"

"Primera." She turned her head to Ruprecht, then smiled. "Primera. I like that name!"

Ruprecht and Soul looked at each other. Soul Fernandez was smiling more broadly than his customary fashion.

3

"Then our team is now three?" Ruprecht said.

"Yes. I want to be a part of this."

"And you are not concerned with..." Ruprecht lowered his voice even further. "The killing?"

"Humans and their governments sometimes have to make decisions that lead to the greatest good for the greatest number of people. This is one of those decisions."

"You are philosophical, my Primera," Ruprecht said. "That is good. I have only followed the works of one philosopher, my compatriot Gottfried Leibniz. He studied at my University, the University of Leipzig. On the wall, near his statue, a sign reads: "God understands everything through eternal truth, since he does not need experience." Tell me, Primera. You are not God. How do you know your decision to kill is a true one?"

Primera stared at Ruprecht. She was reaching back into her readings of Philosophy to summon a good argument.

"I can tell you, Ruprecht," Soul intervened, "that your friend Leibniz is correct. As I live through God and His Scriptures, I understand that what we are doing is the truth."

"I understand that, Soul," Ruprecht said, "But I would like to gauge the thoughts of our newest team member, on this difficult point. Primera, if someone were to say to you that "Philosophically, isn't killing always unjustifiable?" What would you say? As you can tell, this is the part of the plan that is taking me the longest to accept."

"That question is easy. You just have to inquire using the Socratic method of reasoning."

"Fire away."

"Ruprecht, is killing a person always unjustifiable?"

"Yes."

"Ruprecht, is killing a person for a given reason unjustifiable?"

"Yes."

"What if this reason were that someone was about to endanger your family and friends, would killing then be unjustified?"

"Maybe."

"What if the reason were that a group of people, during war, were about to endanger your family and friends, would killing then be unjustified?"

"I would have to say no."

"Then killing a person for a given reason is justifiable! Which calls into question the general statement about whether killing someone is always unjustifiable."

"Excellent argument, Primera. I guess I am sold now," Ruprecht said. "Thank you. This has been most enlightening."

"Rest assured, Ruprecht," Soul said. "Our martyrs will be well looked after. As will our team and our soldiers. Our mission is pure, and the Good Book tells us that "Blessed are the pure in heart: for they shall see God"."

"Amen, Soul. Amen," Ruprecht said.

4

"All that said, Soul and Ruprecht, I still feel a great deal of sympathy for all the people who will die."

"No need to worry," Soul said. "As the Book of Revelations tells us: "They shall hunger no more, neither thirst any more; neither shall the sun light on them, nor any heat. For the Lamb which is in the midst of the throne shall feed them, and shall lead them unto living fountains of waters: and God shall wipe away all tears from their eyes". Those martyrs will live in the ultimate oasis: they will bask in the oasis of heaven with God at their side."

"That's beautiful, Soul. You quoted me the Book of Revelations in the Loud Woman pub, yesterday. It's very inspiring."

"Soul, you quote the Book of Revelations to me all the time as well," Ruprecht said. "Is that the only part of the Bible you have read?"

All three laughed. It was a nice break in the otherwise tense train ride to Düsseldorf.

"Very funny, my friend," Soul said, "but I have read the entire Bible many times. I just quoted you Matthew's Gospel a few seconds ago. I do favor the Book of Revelations. Revelation means disclosure. And we have reached a time where our world must face the necessary truth of this divine disclosure."

An announcement interrupted their discussion.

"Achtung, Achtung. Der Zug kommt in zwei Minuten."

"Two minutes until we arrive," Soul said. "We can continue this discussion on our return to Bonn."

"Is Doctor Leddy part of our plan, Soul?" Ruprecht said.

"Let's just say he is our Plan B. Ruprecht, when we first met, I told you that our plan would take you to unimaginable heights. What Professor Mikhaël Leddy at the University of Düsseldorff is about to show is absolutely unthinkable!"

CHAPTER 10

DR. GEMMA AUGUSTINE

1

"Sorry I am late, gang," said Dr. Gemma Augustine. "Two drops of snow fall in this freaking city and it is completely paralyzed. I expected this in Vancouver, but you figure people out here would know how to drive in winter!"

It was Thursday evening resident teaching rounds and it was Gemma's turn to present. It was no easy feat for her to make it across the city for six PM. The teaching room for the rounds was at the medical school in northwest Calgary. Her Thursday afternoon endoscopy at the northeast hospital wrapped up just after five PM, and from there began her challenging trek across the city in a snowstorm.

"When are they going to make winter tires mandatory in this province?" said Gemma. "And would it kill the city to plow the roads?"

The group that had gathered in the small teaching room laughed. Gemma had only been in Calgary for three years, but she had quickly become a favorite faculty member amongst the trainees. She was a young faculty member, at the age of thirty-three, who was viewed by the trainees as funny, energetic and knowledgeable. Gemma worked very hard, but was not the type of faculty member to dump all the grunt work onto her trainees. "Let's divide and conquer" was one of her favorite lines, an attitude very much appreciated by her students and medical residents.

"And in a city that doesn't plow roads," continued Gemma, "do we really need people to dump the snow from their driveway onto to the streets? That should be a hefty ticket. You could ticket them three hundred dollars. One hundred for being stupid, one hundred for being lazy, and one hundred for being unkind!"

The small crowd that had gathered was loving this rant. As was typically the case for these teaching rounds, all six Gastroenterology residents were in attendance. While the forty-five faculty members in the city were all aware of the rounds, very few attended. Tonight, the turnout was even lower than usual amongst the faculty, with only two semi-retired doctors in attendance.

Stupid, lazy and unkind were three words that nobody would associate with Dr. Gemma Augustine. While she could be rough around the edges, at her basic core Gemma would be associated with profound empathy and exemplary work ethic. Her famous line, which was immortalized on a banner when she won the resident rookie teacher of the year award in 2017, is "when all else fails, as a Doctor you can always be two things: kind and diligent."

2

"Thank you for being here in... not very large numbers!" Gemma laughed. She was not one to care how many people showed up to listen to her speak. If one person showed up and learned from her, she had no problem with that.

"I thought tonight I would treat these like Christmas rounds and have a little fun. My intention is to spend the first fifteen minutes on a serious topic, then present a few unusual cases and endoscopy pictures. Everyone OK with that?"

The eight-member audience all nodded enthusiastically. The crowd was smiling in anticipation of what would undoubtedly be entertaining rounds. A break from hearing about chronic diarrhea, bloating and incontinence was most appreciated!

Gemma had inserted her USB and gotten her PowerPoint ready as she made her introductory speech. Slide one was now ready to go.

"My serious topic is a hot button topic. As you have probably heard, the Alberta government's recent budget has mandated that our inflammatory bowel disease patients will be changed from their current biological therapy, to the generic or biosimilar version. You will be getting a lot of questions from your patients with Crohn's disease and Ulcerative Colitis. For that reason, I thought I would give you a brief synopsis, over the next fifteen minutes, of biosimilars, their efficacy data, and the potential for relapse that this policy might bring. I promise, I only have ten slides on this. I will be done in ten to fifteen minutes."

Twenty minutes later, Gemma was done. Gemma had plenty to say about most topics, but was never at a loss for words on a topic near and dear to her heart like her patients' wellness.

"Sorry, I went over my ten to fifteen minutes, didn't I?" said Gemma with a beaming smile. "Any questions?"

There were always a few questions, usually from the second-year Gastroenterology trainees, who were always looking for an opportunity to impress in order to be considered for a job in a few months. One of the residents, Dr. Kenneth Sandringham, would go out of his way to ask a question, which was not a question, but a two-minute presentation on what he knew about the topic of the day. Some were impressed with Ken, but not all. Gemma was one of those who could do without him.

"Sorry, Ken, but is there a question in that ramble of yours?" said Gemma, to the immense pleasure of the seven others in the room. "I think your question, if there was one, was longer than my presentation!"

Ken stayed quiet. Gemma was a very kind person, one of the kindest around. But she had no patience for arrogance.

3

"OK, let's get to the fun part. I have four cases, each of them starts with an endoscopic picture. What's this?"

The crowd looked up and down, then side to side. Finally, an answer came forward, "It's a picture of a toonie."

"Correct, Ken." Gemma was feeling regretful at her tone with Ken, and was trying to make amends. "Unfair question, but where do you think it is lodged?"

"Tough one without being at the endoscopy, Doctor Augustine," said Ken. "But I don't imagine people would get a lot of pleasure sticking a two-dollar coin up their butt. I will guess the patient inadvertently swallowed the toonie, and it got stuck in the esophagus."

"Correct again, Ken! Nice work. Agree with you that coins are not the number one foreign body we find in patients' rectum! And I did most of my training in downtown Vancouver, which makes me quite familiar with rectal foreign bodies!"

Another round of laughter from the audience. Most weeks, at the half-hour point of rounds, people start looking at their watches thinking it is time to leave. Not today. Today, Dr. Gemma Augustine had a captive audience.

Gemma was familiar with the Vancouver scene. Born in White Rock British Columbia, she was admitted to Biochemistry at the University of British Columbia. Exceptionally, she was allowed into their four-year medical school after two years of Biochemistry. Gemma then went on to complete three years of Internal Medicine and two years of Gastroenterology training in Edmonton, at the University of Alberta, prior to coming on staff three years ago in Calgary, at the relatively young age of thirty.

"In the interest of time, I won't quiz you on how it got there. It was a Friday night. I had just started on staff, and I got a call from Emergency. "Doctor Augustine, we have a young man with a coin stuck in his esophagus. He and his drunk buddies were playing a round of penny football, with a toonie, and the extra point went right into his mouth and into his esophagus. I guess one of his buddies is an off-duty firefighter, and started the Heimlich on him until he realized the patient was breathing just fine. The patient is sitting here, stable, and ready for you to fish this thing out!" I hung up and got right in. I was looking forward to this case! All I kept thinking was the discussion at the National Mint when they decided to change the two-dollar bill to the toonie coin. "Now are there ANY possible downsides to this we haven't considered or explored? ANY others?" Bet you those public servants in Ottawa didn't consider this risk!"

By this point, the crowd was in stitches. Even Ken had loosened up and was laughing.

"When I arrived in the endoscopy suite, I met this young drunk guy who was babbling on with the Nurse about the prolonged and unsolicited hug he received from his sweaty friend. This was way more concerning to him than the toonie lodged in his esophagus! Anyways, I promptly gave him some Versed and Fentanyl and proceeded to stick the scope down and get the toonie out with a polyp net. As a matter of seriousness, don't try to grab something like this with a biopsy forceps: you are liable to drop it once you reach the patient's throat and could choke them."

"But then I could ask the firefighter to help me!" Ken said. Somewhat out of character, Ken seemed to be getting the greatest kick out this story.

"Great thought, Ken. Always thinking two steps ahead, I like it!" Gemma said. "You would think that would be enough weirdness for one night, but as I am wrapping this one up, Emerg calls me again. This time they have a woman who tried to harm herself by swallowing two batteries!"

"Wasn't getting enough of a charge out of life, Doctor Augustine?" Ken said. Ken was evidently proud of his humor.

"You are on fire tonight, Ken!" Gemma said. "Please call me Gemma, by the way. That goes for everyone here. We are all Doctors and colleagues, just at different stages of our journey."

All the trainees nodded.

"I felt so bad for this young woman. She looked so sad and apathetic. The two Energizers were clearly not doing the job! Two bits of good news from this case though. I got the batteries out, no problem…"

"With a net of course!" Ken said.

"Excellent, Ken, yes with a net. Second, she was admitted to Psychiatry and I saw her two weeks later in the hospital hallway and she looked like a new woman. Good thing her cry for help was with zinc and manganese rather than other more lethal means!"

Gemma paused for a moment, then continued.

"OK, I have two quick cases left. But I am sorry, momma needs a pee break. Into my third trimester and these two girls are pushing on my bladder!"

4

"Thanks for letting me do that. Two quick pictures and then we will be done. What's this?"

"Dentures?" This time from the entire crowd.

"You bet. Smile and the scope smiles back at you, I always say!"

More laughter. Most rounds are quickly forgotten by those attending. These ones were going to stick for a long time.

"This old man was brought into the Emergency room and the family asked me, "Doctor, we haven't seen dad's partial upper denture plate in a while. Could that be the cause?" Of course, being the all mighty Doctor, I said to them that this wasn't possible. How could someone swallow half a denture and not realize it? Well, guess what, jokes on me! What is the lesson here?"

At this point, one of the two grey-haired Gastroenterologists present chimed in. "As I always say to these young folks, always listen to your patients and families, they are usually correct."

"Bang on, Doc," Gemma said. "It's amazing how experience gets us all off our pedestal, isn't it?" Her colleagues nodded approvingly. "OK folks it's getting late, one last one for you. What's this?"

The picture was a black, T-shaped device.

"That's not a hammer, is it Doctor... I mean Gemma?" Ken said.

"No, shaped a little like one, but not a hammer. You are probably too shy to guess vibrator, but it's not that either. It's a prostatic stimulator. This man, who was well into his sixties, was visiting Canada from overseas. He was sticking the device up his anus for over ten years to compliment his meditation practice. He told me emphatically that he had never had a problem with it before: must have been our altitude! Apparently, it does vibrate a little, which he found very soothing. Lo and behold, it got stuck!"

A global "OOO" came from the crowd.

"As you can imagine, this one was a bugger to get out. Hard to get a T-shaped device out of a straight tube. Unlike the battery job, this one took me two hours. One and a half hours to remove the stimulator, and half hour to go over other options for stress release. Maybe try a little hot yoga instead?"

One final huge laugh. Then a round of applause that sounded much louder than what eight people should generate. Rounds were over time by about fifteen minutes, but nobody was about to complain.

5

Jayne had been true to her word. When she arrived at the office late in the morning Wednesday, she promptly headed to Police Chief James Hunter's office to update him on the case. She knew very well that the Police Chief would ask her about his son's progress. Jayne seized that opportunity to compliment John and suggest that he be promoted to Detective Corporal. She also proposed that John be her partner.

The Police Chief was visibly shocked at first. This reaction turned to joy and pride. After double and triple checking that this was truly what Jayne wanted, James Hunter promised he would complete the necessary paperwork.

"How long will that take?" Jayne said.

"Probably a week before it is official. I do have the authority, in a crisis, to instate someone to a position if it is clearly in the best interest of the public."

"I have a young woman and her twins lying on a slab in Doctor Vista's office. I am worried there may be more coming. I would say it is in the public's interest to solve this crime."

"Agreed. Give him a badge and weapon."

"Thanks, Jim. Anything more we need to discuss?"

The Police Chief looked at Jayne for several seconds. There was an incredulous look on his face. Jayne knew him well enough to know he had something to ask. Jayne broke the silence.

"What is it, Jim? What do you want to ask me?"

"Why?"

"Why what?"

"Why this quick turn around in your opinion of my son?"

"Jim, are you asking me if I slept with your boy?"

The Police Chief did not answer. Nor did he need to.

"Well I didn't. Not that I need to tell you if I did, do I."

Again, no answer needed. That was more of a statement than a question.

"He is smart, well read, and a surprisingly deep thinker. You should give him more credit, Jim. Sit down and engage in a meaningful conversation some time. It will open your eyes."

"Thanks for the family counselling, Sargeant!"

Jayne had heard this tone before. Police Chief James Hunter did not like to be corrected.

"Sorry, Jayne. You are probably right," James said, in a moment of unusual insight. "It has been a while since John and I have had a real heart to heart. He has never forgiven me for something I did."

"You mean screwing Georgy Brandle from communications? We all know about that Jim. And yes, that probably does piss him off. He adored your wife. In his eyes, she stood on a pedestal with a bright halo around her head."

"She was an angel. I regret that moment of weakness every day."

"Isn't it MOMENTS of weakness, Jim." Jayne rose from her chair and walked to the door. "There are no secrets around here. Which is why you don't need to worry about me dating your son."

"I am not worried about it at all. Either way. Goodbye Jayne, and thanks again."

6

Time for another pee break then let's get out of here, thought Gemma, as she slid her USB into her purse and grabbed her coat. Gemma had finally gotten through all the keeners' post-round questions. The last few stragglers were leaving the room, as she slowly got up and started walking. *This has been a long week! Thank God it's Friday tomorrow. My back is killing me. I hate being pregnant!*

Having children was not a lifelong ambition for Gemma. She and her partner, Jean Penhold, had married three years ago, with no plans to have children. The marriage had been very unpopular with Gemma's parents, who were staunch social conservatives. Because of them, Gemma had suppressed her orientation until her mid-twenties, when she met Jean and could not ignore her feelings any longer. Gemma wished she had a dollar for every time she heard, "The Bible says that marriage should be between a man and a woman, that's it." Her parents probably wish they had a dollar for every time Gemma answered, "What the Bible says, if you would open up to listen, is that you should fundamentally just be nice to, and respectful of, other people." Gemma sometimes thought that she carried part of her parents' attitude and restraint with her, which is why she chose a partner whose name on paper could be assigned to either a French Irish man or a woman.

As Gemma sat down on the toilet, she felt her babies kicking. This part she loved. The kicks and movements gave her a warm, maternal feeling. This made her think of her mother, and how Gemma regretted that her parents had chosen to disown her and not be a part of her life anymore. Sometimes Gemma wondered if she got pregnant just to annoy them, knowing full well how desperately they wanted to have grandchildren.

Gemma soon realized that her current needs were not limited to just a pee break. *Crap, I have to do a number one!*

Yes, a number one! Dr. Gemma Augustine was now legendary for her Christmas rounds from two years ago. Gemma had chosen 'Why pee should be number two and crap number one' as the topic for her very first Gastroenterology Christmas grand rounds presentation in Calgary. Her arguments ranged from Freud's development stages, where the anal stage comes before genital, to modern pop song lyrics such as Pharell Williams' song 'Number One', which clearly states "Number one …She may be nothin' to you but she the shit to me!" But she took down the house with her ancient Egyptian argument. In her declaration, Gemma argued that 1600 BC papyrus documents mention the enema as the Pharaohs' 'Guardian of the anus'. According to her, as it turns out, the length of the Egyptian enema tube was identical to the unit of measurement that ancient Egyptians coined 'number one'. The fact that only a very small part of her statements was factual did not matter to the attendees, who still talk about her unique and hilarious presentation.

As she started her 'number one', someone entered the two-stall bathroom. *Are you kidding me, can't I do this in peace!* Perhaps this explained the reason she chose Gastroenterology, but Gemma treasured her peaceful moment of defecation to an obsessive level. Jean knew that there was a severe penalty to pay for disrupting her moment of expulsion silence with non-urgent discussion. *Too late to wait for her to leave. I am literally pot committed!* Gemma made herself laugh, as she often did. She did not care what that would sound like to her intruder. Her unwanted company did not enter a stall, but just chose to wash her hands. She was still washing her hands when Gemma exited the stall.

"Hello," Gemma said, with no intention of starting a discussion, but only trying to dilute the awkwardness of the moment.

"Hi."

As Gemma washed her hands, she caught a glimpse of her new-found friend in the mirror. "Don't I know you from somewhere?"

"You do, Doctor Augustine. I work at the clinic."

"Of course. Well hello again. I won't shake your hand."

"Gotcha. That would be appreciated."

Gemma was not sure exactly who this person was, but certainly did recognize her from Conception Opportunities Calgary. *I should know her name. God I am bad with names!*

"You are far from work," Gemma said.

"Yes. I take a class here Thursday evenings to improve my skills."

Skills. What does she do at the clinic? Think Gemma, *think! You are pathetic.*

"Well, have a good evening," Gemma said. "Drive safely in this weather. I will see you soon at the clinic, no doubt?"

"For sure."

7

As they walked out of the bathroom, it became clear to Gemma that not only were they the only two people left in the building, but they would be undoubtedly walking to the parking lot together. *Now what,* Gemma thought, *how do I handle this? Do I walk beside her and continue talking, which I don't want to do? Do I pretend I forgot something? Do I walk really slow, or really fast, to create a distance between us where it is acceptable not to engage in idle chit-chat?*

"It's slippery out there, Doctor. I don't want you to fall, in your state and all. Are you parked far?"

"Please, it's Gemma. And no, I got lucky and parked in the first row of stalls." Gemma now felt bad for considering her anti-social options. "Are you parked close?"

"I have a little way to walk. I don't have parking privileges here. I just walked from the church parking lot across the street."

"Well, I won't hear of you walking all that way in this weather. Let me give you a ride."

"That is very kind of you, Gemma."

8

Gemma started the car while her hitchhiker brushed the snow off her sports car. *She is a very tall woman. How is she going to fit in here?*

"Sorry about the lack of head space," Gemma said, as the woman slowly got into the front seat, the only seat in fact, "my partner and I are very short people. All our friends laughed at us when we bought the Mazda Miata, but we love it."

"No worries. Luckily, it's a short drive."

"The car will warm up soon. God, I hate to be cold. Give me forty degrees anytime!"

Short drive, but slow one. Gemma was a little nervous driving in this weather, leading to very little conversation on the way. As they approached the church, Gemma broke the silence.

"What kind of a car do you drive? I guess I sound like the 'Park and Jet' attendant!"

"I am way at the end of the lot. You can't see my car right now, it's quite dark there."

"OK, let me know when I get close."

As they drove past one of two streetlights in the lot, Gemma slowed down even more and said, "I'm sorry, but I have to admit, I am blanking on your name."

"I can tell, Gemma. Are we friends?"

"Ah… yes," Gemma said, not exactly sure how to answer the unexpected question.

"Good. My friends call me Primera."

"Primera? I have never heard that name. It's lovely."

"It's a nickname. It refers to me being the first."

"The first at what?"

For the first time since being in the car, the woman turned directly towards Gemma. She stared her right in the eyes. Her eyes were wide open, and surprisingly dilated for the dim lighting from streetlight.

"Get me to my car, and I will show you."

Gemma was unsure if it was the dark, the questionable driving conditions, the woman's look, or the tone of her last sentence, but she was now scared. Very scared.

"You can stop here. That is my car."

Gemma followed the instructions and parked right beside the only car in this area. To her surprise and relief, the woman opened the door and slowly moved her frame out of the passenger side.

"Good night," Gemma said. She got no answer.

OK, Gemma, *let's get the fuck out of here. Jean will be worried.*

As Gemma backed up, she was startled by the warning signal coming from her rear backup camera. She looked up at her rear-view mirror. To her horror, the same look from a few moments ago was staring at her. Gemma was now shaking. She was getting cold, more from the frigid look of this Amazon woman than the outside temperature.

"Doctor, we have two problems."

Now fearing for her life, Gemma rolled down the window slightly. "I have to go now. You need to get out of the way."

"Doctor, we have two problems. For one, I have your key fob." Gemma furiously searched the coffee cup holder and realized the key was gone. "For two, you didn't ask me what I was first at. Roll your window down completely."

Whether it was because of the last sentence's softer tone, or the thought that she could not get far without her key fob, Gemma rolled down her window.

"Everything will be OK, Gemma. Just relax. Primera will look after you now."

As Gemma looked up, Primera grabbed the back of her head with her right hand, and forced it into a rag in her left hand. Gemma swung wildly at her assailant, but was feeling herself slowly slip away.

"Primera is the first who is taking care of women like you. There will be more."

Gemma was struggling, but less and less.

"It's OK, Gemma. You will be fine where you are going. I did meet you at the clinic. I saw your girls on my ultrasound. The three of you are blessed, as you are pure in heart. For that reason, you will see God."

Gemma took one last look at Ginny, as she drifted away. Ginny gently wiped the tears flowing down both Gemma's cheeks.

"I don't like forty degrees either, Gemma. That is what we are trying to prevent. Drift away, Gemma. Drift away. But don't worry, I will make sure you are warm."

Gemma had now passed out. Ginny took out her surgical scalpel, and proceeded to carve out her ten-centimeter, slightly curved incision over her left carotid artery.

Ginny next took out a sharpie. She exposed Gemma's abdomen, scratched out CC around her belly button, then buttoned up her blouse.

As promised, Ginny covered Gemma up with her winter coat, then went back to her car for a sleeping bag, which she gently wrapped around her victim.

"That will keep you warm. Sleep well, my darling."

9

"Did I wake you, Soul?"

"No, Primera. Still early here."

"The second is done."

"When?"

"A few minutes ago. I am calling you from my car. She is not far from me."

"Did she die well?"

"Yes, Soul. As per your instructions. She died peacefully, without pain."

"That is good. These victims must not suffer. They are soldiers in our war. They are now happy with God."

Ginny hesitated.

"Decisions need to be made to secure the most happiness for the largest number of people. Is that right, Soul?"

"I would agree with that, Primera. We need to stay strong in our difficult decisions. We shall not waver. Now go rest, Primera. You will be getting visitors tomorrow again. Your job is done for now. Sit back, and listen to the news. The world will soon be changing. They will have no choice but to take us seriously."

"Talk to you soon. 14U14US?"

"14U14US."

CHAPTER 11

DR. MIKHAËL LEDDY

1

As the trio stepped off the platform and through the sliding doors of the Düsseldorf train station, they were greeted by a chauffeur holding up a 'Doctor Soul Fernandez' sign. He was a tall man, with a classic black hat, and the fixed, frozen smile of someone who has no idea which of the passengers he is supposed to meet and be friendly to.

"No way, I have always wanted to be greeted with my name like this," Ginny exclaimed.

"You should have told me, Ginny," Soul said, "I would have put your name on the reservation. Then again, it would have been very presumptuous of me to assume you would join us."

"That's right," Ruprecht said. "That would have jinxed us for sure, Soul." Ruprecht reached over and placed his hand warmly on Ginny's right shoulder. "Ginny, we are thrilled you have joined us. Next time, I will see to it myself that your name gets on the card!"

Soul let the chauffeur out of his misery and identified himself.

"Welcome to Düsseldorf, Doctor Fernandez. My name is Hans Vonn Boechorstein. Doctor Leddy sends his regrets for not picking you up himself. Hopefully my presence will do."

"Absolutely," Soul said. "Do you need to see some identification?"

"I don't. Never have. Somehow people have never pretended they were someone else in this situation. Sounds strange in this world of excessive security and identity theft, doesn't it? Maybe the unwritten rules governing someone holding up a sign for transportation are the only sanctity left in the world!"

Soul, Ruprecht and Ginny all laughed as they opened the door to the fancy black car.

"We very much appreciate you being here sir," Ruprecht said. "But seriously, you drive a Volkswagen Phaeton? We need to get you in a real car, sir. A BMW 750i!"

"Company car, sir. I will have to pass along my suggestion to my boss."

As they pulled out of the train station and on to their fifteen-minute drive to the University, the affable driver was giving them a brief history of his beloved city.

"It is a beautiful city, Hans," Ruprecht said. "But that is what you would expect from a West Germany city, isn't it?"

"Are you referring to the economical discrepancies between what was once East and West Germany?" Hans asked.

"That is correct. Ginny, you may not be aware of this, but the unification of Germany, while great in many ways, has come at a price, particularly for the Ossis, or East Germans. East Germany trails the West in all aspects of income, prosperity and health."

"I have never heard this," Ginny said.

"An unfortunate truth, that has not hit the headlines," Ruprecht said. "Ginny, you look like a sports fan."

"I am, mister Barren," Ginny said.

"Again, please, call me Ruprecht, Ginny. OK then, what is Germany's national sport?"

"Soccer. Or football to you, I guess."

"Yes, football. I said it is our national sport. Probably better described as our national treasure. The jewel of this sport is our premier league, the Bundesliga. There are seventeen teams in the Bundesliga. How many do you think are in East Germany?"

Before Ginny could answer, Ruprecht spoke.

"One. One team on the East side, sixteen on the West. And the only reason we have this team is because an Austrian company, Red Bull, had to save us."

"It is an undeniable problem," Hans said, peering back at the group in the large rear-view mirror to his right.

"At any rate," Ruprecht said, "I digress. We can continue this another time. I see that we are fast approaching our destination."

"We are entering the University grounds, now," Hans said. "Doctor Leddy wanted me to show you this landmark before I bring you to his offices."

2

The driver made a left turn towards an imposing statue just inside the University's entrance gates.

"This is the statue of Christian Johann Heinrich Heine. The University is named after him. He was a famous German poet and writer."

"And somewhat of a prophet, correct?" Ruprecht said.

"That is right, sir."

"What do you mean?" Ginny said.

"Look at the words on the plaque," said Hans. "These were written in 1821, over one-hundred years before World War II."

"Dort, wo man Bücher verbrennt, verbrennt man am Ende auch Menschen," read Ruprecht. "Where they burn books, they will, in the end, burn human beings too."

"Prophetic indeed," Soul said. "Blessed are those who God touches with visions of the future."

"That is exactly right, sir," said Hans. "A plaque near and dear to Doctor Leddy. His mother escaped Germany as a baby. Unfortunately, his grandmother was not as fortunate. She was sent to Auschwitz and was never seen again."

"Oh my God, that is very sad!" Ginny said.

"It's a time we would all like to ignore, but can't," said Hans.

"Can't, and shouldn't," said Ruprecht. "Forgive, but don't forget."

"Forgive, but don't forget. Amen sir," said Hans. "Here we are. Doctor Leddy's offices are right through those glass doors. I will be here when you are done. Doctor Leddy knows how to reach me."

"See you soon," said Soul. "Thank you." Soul handed Hans a ten-euro tip, which Hans refused.

"Thank you, sir. Very kind of you. But the gratuity is included in Doctor Leddy's costs. Appreciate the gesture, though."

"We have appreciated your tour and lessons, Hans," Soul said. "Above and beyond the call of duty. I appreciate that in people. We will settle this later."

As Soul, Ginny and Ruprecht walked into the Biology department doors, Ginny spoke.

"How could the world let Hitler get away with that?

"The world has a history of ignoring the difficult problem, Ginny," Soul said. "It is our job now to make sure history does not repeat itself."

3

The University of Düsseldorf Biological Sciences building was quiet at this time of the evening. Most classes had wrapped up at six PM. Only a few students lingered in the lounge and stairs. A few were grouped in pairs, talking. Most were sitting alone, with headphones, deeply fixated on whatever information their laptops were feeding them.

"Doctor Fernandez, welcome." The voice came from the top of a small stairway in the right-hand corner of the vaulted lobby. The voice was low and scratchy, and difficult to hear. They would not have heard it in the busy rustle of the building's daytime hours."

"Hello, my friend," Soul said, hugging his host. "Great to see you. You are looking well."

'Well' would be accurate, from a health perspective. But if "well' was meant to equate looking good, it was far from true. Dr. Mikhaël Leddy looked like his mother's obstetrician used a vacuum to extract him, only the vacuum sucked his face down instead of out. Every feature on his tiny head appeared squished. He had very tiny eyes, covered with glasses that could not hide the swollen, puffy lower eyelids. Below his small and flat nose was a mouth that looked relatively larger than the rest of his face, only because his lips were curved, exposing the inner lining of his mouth. His small chin was covered with a scraggly, greying goat patch. Add to this his sickly pale skin color, and small, unfit body frame, and you had the picture of a man much more suited to life with mice in a dark lab than out in the bright world.

"Doctor Leddy," Soul continued, "I would like you to meet mister Ruprecht Barren, BMW engineer and Chairman, and missus Ginny Fremlin, ultrasonographer in Calgary, Canada."

"Mister Barren, fräulein Fremlin, pleasure to meet you. I hope I can call you by your first names." Ginny and Ruprecht nodded affirmatively. "Please call me Mikhaël. Welcome to Düsseldorf. I take it Hans took good care of you?"

"Hans was great," Ginny said. "Thank you for such a warm welcome to your beautiful city."

"Come, let's go downstairs," Mikhaël said, lowering his voice. "I am not ashamed of my visitors but would rather not attract too much attention at this time."

4

The group marched down one flight of stairs to the basement research area of the Biological Sciences building. The walk through this part of the building sounded like a Sunday stroll through the local zoo. Sounds of dogs barking, chimpanzees grunting, and cats yowling resonated throughout the many hallways that led to Mikhaël's office.

"Sorry about the noise levels," Mikhaël said. "The animals seem to wake up at this time of day. Seems like having important body parts missing only bothers them after six at night."

Mikhaël expressed a laugh that sounded like a quieter, harsher version of the chimpanzees' lamenting grunts. His guests smiled politely.

"Fortunately, the animals I work on are much quieter than these beasts. I have never felt the need to study these other animals. My mice are much quieter and cleaner. And cuter. And surprisingly close embryologically to humans."

The 'beep' of the keypad signalled their entry into Mikhaël's section of the building. Emanating from this very narrow, dark hallway were four rooms. To the left was a brightly lit office, equipped with a desk, several chairs, whiteboard, and the standard sprawl of disorganized papers, books, and journals. To the right, and straight ahead, were two rooms visible through a small glass portion of the door, with the word 'Labor' at the top of the door.

"Welcome to my humble laboratory. It is a very simple area, as you can see. Two laboratories and my office here on the left. This is where we will start."

Another keypad opened Mikhaël's office door. As they walked in and settled into chairs on the left-hand side of the office, Ginny noticed a solid metal door in the right-hand corner of the office that was mostly hidden by the whiteboard and hanging lab coats.

"What is on the other side of that door?" Ginny said, as she slowly walked towards it. As she moved aside one of the lab coats, she could see a sign with the yellow and black radioactive symbol.

"That is for later, fräulein. First, I need to prepare all of you with a lesson in Embryology."

"My apologies, Doctor. Or Mikhaël, I mean."

"It's OK, Ginny," Mikhaël said, smiling. "I appreciate the curiosity."

"Will we need a special suit for the radioactivity?" Ginny said.

"It's not radioactive. Let's just say that it is an area I would prefer to be visited only by certain people. The research I am about to describe to all of you is not…How would I put this? Is not formally University supported. But I trust Soul, I trust your group's mission, and so I am trusting you with something that nobody, and I mean NOBODY, else has seen."

The trio sat down and stared at Mikhaël Leddy. He now had their full, undivided attention.

5

"Let's see. Where do I start?"

"Start slowly, Mikhaël. You have a rookie audience," Soul said.

"Exactly. That is the challenge when you are an expert in a field. However, I will model my teaching after the great Doctor Soul Fernandez, and I will be fine."

"You are too kind, my friend."

"I will divide the session into two parts. Embryology 101, and Nutrition 101. I feel like I need to get through the Embryology part before I give you a sense of the bigger picture of project Pander."

"Project Pander?" Ruprecht said.

"Yes, named after the great German biologist and embryologist, Dr. Heinz Christian Pander."

"Sorry, Mikhaël. Please carry on," Ruprecht said.

"My experiments thus far have been on mice. You will see the results of these preliminary experiments in a few moments. I want to stress, we are at the bud stage of project Pander, but I feel optimistic it will burgeon rapidly. Admittedly, I am an eternal optimist."

"And a great mind. Which is why I have wanted you as part of my team," Soul said.

"Thank you. What I will describe will be in human terms, but there is no significant difference in this regard between the mouse and the human. For the Embryology part of my brief talk, I want you to remember one key word: gastrulation."

"Gastrulation? Sounds like something Jonas does in front of his porn-movie stash!"

"Not quite, Ginny," Mikhaël said, not quite as amused as Soul and Ruprecht. "Gastrulation is the fundamental stage of an embryo's development. Everything we have engineered starts at this stage."

Mikhaël grabbed a dry erase marker and starting writing on the whiteboard.

"We are all familiar with fertilization. The moment where sperm meets egg to form one cell. Some use the word conception."

"That is the name of my clinic. That is what we do for a living!" said Ginny.

"Correct. A key moment in the formation of life, but just the beginning," Mikhaël said. "That one cell then divides four times and becomes the morula, which gets to the uterus three to five days after fertilization."

Mikhaël had drawn the ovaries, fallopian tubes and uterus, and the journey of these early cells.

"The morula then becomes a blastocyst. Here is where it gets very interesting. The blastocyst is rapidly dividing. It grows what is called an inner cell mass, which points itself towards the wall of the uterus and starts digging its home there."

"Implantation," Ginny said. "Implantation is a good day in our clinic."

"That is right. That's when you start having a good chance of taking this process to completion. Now comes the key moment I told you to remember. In the second week of life, by day fourteen, the blastocyst changes. The inner cell mass flattens, turns into a disc, and from that disc three layers form: the ectoderm, endoderm, mesoderm."

"That is gastrulation?" Ginny said.

"Correct again. Gastrulation, just after day fourteen from fertilization, is when the embryo has formed the three primary germ cell layers that will develop into the major organs. The names of the three layers are key and worth repeating: ectoderm, endoderm and mesoderm."

"That is crystal clear, Mikhaël!" Ginny said. "I work in this area and was never clear on all of this. Can I take a picture of your drawing?"

"Absolutely, you can."

"Fascinating, Mikhaël, but how does this relate to our overall project?" Ruprecht said.

Ruprecht looked at Soul in a moment of worry. "I am sorry, Soul, I should have asked. Is Doctor Leddy aware of our plan?"

As Soul nodded yes, Mikhaël intervened. "I do know. We are considering this a Plan B for sure. I will get to how this relates to the overall plan in a minute. For now, I want you to digest what I have said so far, while I put on a pot of tea."

6

"Now to the second part of my introduction. Basic nutrition. What is the fundamental molecule of life?"

"Oxygen?" Ginny said.

"That is a correct answer, but I should have clarified. What is the fundamental molecule of life that we eat?"

"Sugar?" Ginny said.

"Glucose, to be precise. Glucose is key for several reasons. With oxygen, it is a reactant of cellular respiration, the process by which humans, and plants, make energy. It is the main source of energy for our brain. Also, the other important nutrients, fats and proteins, can be made from glucose."

"If our Plan A fails," Soul said, "and humans are struggling to survive, we need to find an alternative source of glucose."

"That is right," Mikhaël said. "And what organisms have solved their problem of glucose supply?"

"You're kidding," Ruprecht said. Soul and Mikhaël were now looking at each other, laughing. "Plan B is to make humans do photosynthesis? To turn humans into plants?"

"Partly true. Project Pander is to allow humans to synthesize glucose through photosynthesis in one specific human cell type. No matter what happens to our planet, the sun will still exist. That is how I will link the Embryology and Nutrition talks. But first, we must take a break. Think about all of this for a second, while I bring you all some tea. Anybody hungry?"

"I will help you," Soul said.

Ginny and Ruprecht sat, staring at the whiteboard, incredulous. Emotions of shock, dismay, curiosity and excitement were swirling around their bodies like an ocean jetstream. Eating was well removed from their mind.

7

"Milk in your tea? Sugar?" Mikhaël said.

The trio made their requests. As they were starting to sip, Mikhaël continued. He could tell that he still had an acutely captive audience. He was enjoying the moment intensely.

"Now, back to our three germ cell layers after gastrulation. What were they again, Ginny?"

"Ectoderm, endoderm, and …"

"Mesoderm," Ruprecht said.

"Correct. At this stage in the process, the cells in the embryonic disc are said to be pluripotential. They can develop into any of the three layers. This is what is generally referred to as stem cells, which I am sure you have heard about."

The three audience members nodded.

"The endoderm leads to internal organs, such as all the gut organs. The mesoderm develops into muscle, kidney and heart. Those two germ cell layers are not the best ones to turn into photosynthesizers. The ectoderm, on the other hand, turns into the outer layer of the skin, the epidermis. That layer is accessible to us with our microsurgery techniques. Because of this, we chose to intervene on the ectoderm."

"Makes sense," Ruprecht said. "The skin is directly in contact with the sun, the source of energy for photosynthesis."

"That is right, Ruprecht. Only one more obstacle. The ectoderm also develops into nervous tissue and the brain. We don't want to touch those."

"How can you become more specific to the epidermal cells?" Ruprecht said. The engineer was completely riveted by what he was hearing.

"Cell markers. As it turns out, the stem cells, the ones that can divide into anything, first divide into cells that can produce the ectoderm, and cells that can produce both mesoderm and endoderm. Those mesoderm/endoderm cells express a protein called GATA6. After gastrulation, we can isolate the cells that DON'T express GATA6, and those are the cells destined to be ectoderm."

"But that doesn't settle your problem of ectoderm turning into both skin and brain," Ruprecht said.

"Right. But we get lucky here again. The ectoderm cells that will turn into epidermal skin cells express keratins, the skin's protective protein. We tested for Keratin 18 or K18. Just to make sure, we excluded cells that express a factor called microtubule associated protein 2, or MAP2, which are ectoderm cells destined to be neural tissue."

"Let me just verify that I have this clear in my mind. You can find the ectoderm cells that will produce skin by finding GATA6 and MAP2 negative cells, and K18 positive cells."

"Yes, Ruprecht. We did exactly that. The mice you are about to see have had their ectoderm stem cells destined to be skin epidermal cells treated to be able to photosynthesize. There is a lot to that process, but let's maybe go see the mice now."

Mikhaël used a key from his chain to open a small drawer on his desk. In this drawer was a special key card that opened the large metal door.

"And no special suits needed?" Ginny said.

"No, all good. The sign works well to keep people out. You three are the first to see what you are about to see."

8

Mikhaël's hidden laboratory was clearly a redesigned storage space. As the light switch was turned on, a single incandescent light bulb, flickering as though it was on its last legs, illuminated the eight by ten feet area. As the three guests anxiously waited at the door, Mikhaël walked to the end of the room and turned on a very bright spotlight that was angled towards a cage sitting on a small wooden desk.

"I just turned on my sun for you. I keep it on a timer to mimic a normal day. Come, come, the animals won't bite!"

The view inside the cage was not settling. A total of eight mice shared the cage. Five of them looked healthy and happy as can be. These five mice, covered in lush white fur, were frolicking together, sipping on water, and taking turns spinning happily on the wheel in the left-hand corner of the cage. Tucked away in the right-hand corner of the cage were three small creatures that looked like direct descendants of Darth Vader after he took his mask off. Scrawny, grey, with scattered clumps of short hairs covering a layer of skin that was visibly bumpy, as though they had a blistering skin condition. The three were all spinning around aimlessly in circles. Even to the untrained eye, these mice looked unhealthy and completely oblivious to their siblings in the cage.

"I see you have all noticed a difference in our little friends here," Mikhaël said. "Mother mouse gave us a litter of ten offspring. Five did not have any intervention done: those are the five on the left side of the cage. Five had their ectoderm manipulated: one died at birth, one died two days after, but three of my little friends have survived, and are living on the right side of the cage."

Mikhaël was beaming with pride. Soul, Ruprecht and Ginny stared at the three poor creatures in shock.

Finally, Ruprecht built up the courage to break the silence.

"Are you a fan of Lord of the Rings, Mikhaël?"

"I am."

"No offense, but those three mice look like Gollum. On a good day."

Mikhaël laughed.

"No offense taken. Science rarely gets it right the first time, my friend. Or even the tenth time. This is very much a work in progress. But I am thrilled at the first iteration of project Pander."

"You are?" Ginny said.

"Indeed. What you see in those three little creatures is the result of a lot of scientific steps, which quite frankly involved a lot of educated guesses. Where do I start? The first step was to find a suitable plant that would donate its chloroplasts to the little guys."

"Chloroplasts?" Ginny said.

"Chloroplasts are the little structures in plants that are the engines for photosynthesis. After careful research, I chose to take them from *Arabidopsis thaliana.* It is a small plant related to mustard and cabbage. It is particularly well studied in the area of chloroplasts."

"Excellent choice, Professor," Ruprecht said, trying to lighten up the mood. "I love mustard on everything. I grew up to be the healthy man you see before you by eating mustard sandwiches."

"That's gross," Ginny said. "I was feeling a little bit sick before, but now I am close to throwing up."

"The next question," said Mikhaël, ignoring the condiment discussion, "was how many chloroplasts to inject in each ectoderm stem cell. Most plant cells have one-hundred chloroplasts. Incidentally, that is almost identical to the number of mitochondria each cell contains. Mitochondria are our cells' energy makers. They use glucose and oxygen to perform cellular respiration and make ATP, our body's energy engine. My initial thought was to inject one-hundred chloroplasts. But given that I am a scientist, I tried to be more scientific about it."

"Makes sense," Ruprecht said.

"A typical oak tree has two-hundred-thousand leaves. Each leaf has ten-million photosynthetic cells, each cell having about one-hundred chloroplasts. That came to about two hundred thousand billion chloroplasts in an oak tree!"

"Holy crap!" Ginny exclaimed.

"However, an oak tree grows to seventy feet, with a width of nine feet. That is a surface area about one-hundred times more than a human. That big number for the oak tree comes out to two-thousand billion in a human. The average human has thirty-five billion skin cells, that leaves us with about fifty chloroplasts per cell."

"Each of the little mouse K18 positive ectoderm cells received fifty chloroplasts?" Ruprecht said.

"Not quite. Remember, we are only manipulating the surface skin cells, the epidermis. The deeper layer, the dermis, comes from the mesoderm primary cell layer. If we are only using half the human skin cells, we need one-hundred chloroplasts per cell."

"Your first guess was right, Mikhaël!" Ruprecht said.

"It was. That's what makes science exciting. When your hypothesis is backed by facts!"

Mikhaël was obviously in his moment of glory. His visitors punctuated hours of time alone in his laboratory. To be able to share his pride and joy with such an interested audience was a welcomed distraction. After the initial discomfort of the makeshift laboratory, the artificial sun, and the unusual appearance of the little creatures, his guests were also warming up to his science.

"The problem now became that trying to inject one-hundred chloroplasts into each of the hundreds of ectoderm stem cells was virtually impossible, from both a technical standpoint and time point of view. I started a few cells but realized that the technique would take me years."

"Years that we don't have," Soul said.

"Yes. Perhaps more importantly, I was also tearing the cells apart by repeated chloroplast insertions. Then I got lucky. Six months ago, a group out of China published a study in Nature, the most highly regarded journal in the scientific world, showing very favorable reports with *Arabidopsis thaliana* plant cells that had been designed with only two giant chloroplasts within them. The plants performed as well on many of their research parameters, though did have about two-thirds the photosynthetic rates and efficiency. If two giant chloroplasts produce about two-thirds the photosynthesis, I landed on injecting three giant chloroplasts per cell. Much more feasible for me, and safer for the cell."

"Was there room for all those chloroplasts?" Ruprecht asked. "In our BMW engines, every time we want to add something, we have to take something out."

"Very astute, Ruprecht," Mikhaël said. "Only in Cell Biology, we can't take anything out. I had to add something, a filler, to expand the cells. That filler is cytoplasm, the little jelly inside our cells. That is why…"

"Their skin is so bumpy," Ginny said. Ginny was getting braver. "Can I touch their skin?"

"You can. You will see that one of the unfortunate consequences of adding cytoplasm is that it makes their skin cells bigger and spongier. It's not attractive, but I don't see another way around this."

"Attractiveness is not the priority when extinction is the only alternative," Soul said.

"Agreed, Soul. We left our teas outside. I will go get them. Get closer to the mice. They are very friendly. Put some gloves on and touch them. I will be back in an instant to give you a whole host of good news."

9

"Everyone getting acquainted?" Mikhaël said. "The more you see them, the more you reprogram your brain to what normal can be, and the cuter they become."

"You're right, Mikhaël," Ginny said. "They seem cuddlier than the others."

"I think that may be a function of the additional cytoplasm as well," Mikhaël said. "All body functions require proteins. To make a protein, the DNA in your cell nucleus gets converted to messenger RNA, which then travels out of the nucleus, through the cytoplasm, then to the ribosomes, the protein factory."

"More cytoplasm, more cell surface area, more time for all of this to occur?" Ruprecht said.

"That is right. I think your impression of them being cuddly may simply represent a slowness in their body function. Time will tell. Perhaps it is an unpredicted personality effect. I believe the absence of hair growth is a similar phenomenon. Hair growth requires very rapid protein turnover, and the engine just can't keep up."

"Why do they appear confused?" Ginny said. "They are just running around in circles."

"That surprised me, I have to admit," Mikhaël said. "But I think I may have figured out why. Chloroplasts are very similar to human mitochondria in many ways, but they are more complex. They can make the building blocks for proteins, amino acids. They can also make some fatty acids, the building blocks for our body's lipids. In our context, that is a plus, and may account for the positive anthropometric measurements I want to get to."

"Sorry Doctor, anthro what?" Ruprecht said.

"Anthropometric. Basically, how we measure body fat and muscle mass."

"Don't worry, Ruprecht. We won't do these measurements on you," Soul said.

"Thank you," Ruprecht said, grabbing his generous love handles.

"Yes, no worries, Ruprecht. Now back to our chloroplasts. They also synthesize ammonia from a substance called nitrite. I believe this elevated ammonia level in our little mice is mimicking a condition we see in humans called hepatic encephalopathy."

"My father had that before he died," Soul said. "He was very confused and somnolent from it."

"That is what happens," Mikhaël said, "and what I think is happening to our mice. The confusion from liver disease is thought to be due to increased ammonia levels from loss of liver ammonia breakdown. In the next iteration, I will add some lactulose to the mice diet from the beginning. It will lead to some extra loose stools, but it is the way we get rid of additional ammonia in humans with the liver condition. I have added some to these little guys' diet a few days ago, but too early to tell."

"I remember that also," Soul said. "My father was in the bathroom constantly."

"Those poor beings will be tiny, hairless, bumpy, confused, and have the trots?" Ginny said. "Sad existence."

"But they will exist, as will humans eventually. Life of any kind shines brighter than the darkness of death," Soul said.

"My dear Ginny, it is far from all gloom. We haven't gotten to the good news yet. I mentioned their anthropometric measurements. Without any additional fat supplementation, they have seventy-five percent of the expected body fat levels at this age. They have a little more than fifty percent of the expected muscle mass. This is despite the only supplementation, other than water of course, that they are receiving. I am giving them a mixture of nine essential amino acids. Those are the amino acids that our body can't make. In the next few days, I will add the other eleven amino acids to their supplementation to see if I can improve the muscle mass. It's a work in progress, but I am pleasantly surprised at our current results."

"The more I think of it," Ginny said, "if this evolves to creating humans this way, I think they might end up being happier than other humans."

"Why is that, Ginny?" Mikhaël said.

"It is a common thread in many philosophies that living in harmony with nature, which these beings will instinctively do, is the path to true happiness and fulfillment. Daoism and Buddhism were founded around this quest. They will have to be trained and guided, but I believe these new humans may find a state of Nirvana more naturally than what we currently see in our world."

Mikhaël was fascinated by this discussion. Working at the microscopic level, he had clearly not considered the philosophical line of thinking in his research.

"Trained?" Mikhaël said. "What do you mean by that, Ginny?"

"These new humans will look different. They will undoubtedly be teased by others."

"This is of course presuming that there are still others around, Ginny," Soul said.

"True enough. But if other humans are still around, it will be in their nature to mock these individuals. They will have to be trained to be resilient. They will have to be convinced that by their intense connection with nature, they are simple and humble beings. They will have to be taught the writings of the great humanists who remind us that the true virtues in life, like simplicity, humility and tranquility, will carve the path to happiness. These beings will need to be reminded that despite their physical appearance they are innately glorious in their creation. They are self-sufficient in their basic needs and thus desire and ambition can be cast aside. The writings of Daoism and Buddhism will remind them that glory, ambition and desire are the source of suffering, and by eliminating these, their lives will be free of hurt and filled with joy."

Ginny stopped talking. She stared at the cage with a sense of great love and admiration for the small, hairless and withdrawn mice in the corner to her right.

Soul, Ruprecht and Mikhaël were captivated by Ginny's knowledge and passion for this subject.

Turning to her audience, Ginny said, "I am sorry, I am rambling."

"You are not, Ginny," Mikhaël said. "This is fascinating."

"I hope I am around when the humans are born," Ginny said.

"You will be, Ginny, you will," Soul said. "Mikhaël is not that far from the next phase."

"That is correct," Mikhaël said. "Now I know exactly who I will hire to coach the Angiospermae."

"Would love to," Ginny said, "but who are the Angiospermae?"

Mikhaël laughed.

"That is the name I have given to the new breed. The plant classification system, initiated by your philosopher friend Aristotle…"

Mikhaël was now turned squarely to Ginny, who laughed appreciatively at the remark.

"puts *Arabidopsis thaliana* and all other flowering plants in the Angiospermae clade. A clade is a group of plants with the same ancestor."

Mikhaël got up and shut off the spotlight that was brightly illuminating the cage.

"Well, it's been truly invigorating, but I think that is enough Embryology, Nutrition, Botany, and now Philosophy for one day. It's bedtime for our little friends. And maybe for all of us. You still have a train ride to Bonn left in your day."

10

Mikhaël was wrapping up the tour for the night. He carefully replaced the key to his secret room in his desk, then proceeded to erase the pictures from his lesson on the whiteboard.

"Where do we go from here, Mikhaël?" Soul said.

"I still have some work to do on our Phase one animals in there. I mentioned the additional protein supplements, and the lactulose. I will also need to take a liver biopsy on one of the little fellows. I need to know if the glucose produced is leaving the chloroplasts and getting stored as glycogen in their liver. I am presuming that somehow this is happening, given their overall growth and measurements."

"Excellent. You have done amazingly well," Soul said. "I can't believe where you are at since we first talked about this two years ago. Working alone, after hours. You are a true soldier of our cause."

As Soul was releasing Mikhaël from his hug, Mikhaël replied. "Inserting the chloroplasts in the hundreds of stem cells of the frozen embryos takes time. Luckily for me, we are isolating just a small portion of the overall number of stem cells in the gastrula. I haven't even mentioned to you the meticulous DNA splicing I need to do to give the cells the ability to signal the chloroplasts to divide as the cells divide."

"Could you use some help?" Soul said. "We would have to choose this person very carefully."

"I have thought of that. You may be surprised to hear that the driver, Hans, was my assistant years ago. He was too social for this tedious work. He found himself dreadfully bored. I may be able to convince him. He would be sympathetic to our cause."

Soul nodded, looking intensely into Mikhaël's eyes, a look that conveyed the message of the necessary trust and secrecy involved.

"Is the DNA manipulation the reason why two of them died at or near birth?" Ruprecht asked.

"Possibly, could be a number of causes. Perhaps the immune system of the two that died rejected the foreign chloroplasts. Many unintended consequences can occur when dealing with frozen embryos in general, especially when you are doing what we are doing to them. If you thought our three survivors were odd looking, these ones were…"

"I get the picture, thanks," Ruprecht said.

"Mikhaël, I have one last question before we go, if that is possible," Ginny said.

"Fire away, fräulein."

"Why the secrecy? Shouldn't the world be aware of what you are doing, and fascinated by it?"

"Great question. Great question," Mikhaël said, looking at Soul. "What we are doing on the mice, I could probably get away with. Phase two over the next year will again be on mice, and probably would be not be adversely viewed. Phase three, planned for 2019, will involve human embryos. This will be controversial, never mind that according to the current rules, human embryos cannot be grown in a lab longer than fourteen days from fertilization."

"And you said gastrulation occurs after day fourteen," Ginny said.

A head nod and thumbs up concluded their session. Mikhaël led the group upstairs, where smiling Hans was waiting for them at the entrance.

To Ginny's absolute delight, Hans Vonn Boechorstein was holding up a sign that said 'Miss Ginny Fremlin'.

CHAPTER 12

COC FIGHT ROUND 2

1

"Well there he is folks, Detective Hunter! Two days on the job, and apparently some extra-curricular time at St-Hilda's, did the trick, right Hunter?"

A huge round applause erupted from the Friday morning assembly of police officers customarily gathered around the coffee maker and water cooler.

"What impressed her the most, Hunter? That you're a diligent fact checker, a bad guy wrecker, or simply your ten-inch pecker?"

"Easy boys, easy," John said, over the cacophony of laughter in the room. "I know it's hard for you to remember this, but I am more than just a pretty face."

"Hunter, we have to go," Jayne said, as she barged into the room. The gathered police officers immediately went dead silent. Had it been summer, a myriad of flies would have surely entered their gaping mouths. "Grab a coffee and we'll talk on the way to the car."

2

Isabella Lake, Michael Lahr, Jayne Chandler and John Hunter stood silent, trying to reconcile the grisly seen of a murder victim lying in the immediate vicinity of a holy church. It was Isabella who broke their silence.

"Looks like our same killer, Detective. Another pregnant young woman. Same incision, same lack of struggle."

Jayne had briefed John on the way to the church. Her statement to the Police Chief on Wednesday had unfortunately turned prophetic.

"I guess we now have a serial killer on our hands," John said. "Were you able to see…"

"The CC around her belly button? Yep. It is there again," Isabella said.

"I meant the erythema, I mean the redness, around the victim's mouth," John said.

"Good point, John," Isabella said. "That is not evident this time. Doesn't mean the killer didn't use a rag. The victim may not have mounted the same reaction."

"Any identification present?" Jayne said.

"Yes," Isabella said, "it is Doctor Gemma Augustine. She is a Medical Doctor. Gastroenterologist in northeast Calgary."

"A gut Doctor," Jayne said.

"OK, let's have a look," Jayne said, as she leaned in through the driver door. John went around the vehicle and inspected the passenger side. A ghastly site of dried, frozen blood everywhere in the front seat greeted him.

"This killer does have a heart," Jayne said. "He anesthetizes them, makes only one cut, then has this one all bundled up in a sleeping bag for warmth."

"I do get that sense also," John said. "It's almost like he is reluctant to kill them. Does he feel bad about it? Is he being forced?"

"Or this isn't personal," Jayne said. "This isn't about the victim themselves, but about a cause. Maybe that it what the COC is?" Jayne gently folded the sleeping bag over to see the incision.

"Speaking of which," Isabella said. "I made a phone call to Conception Opportunities Calgary. Doctor Augustine was also a patient of that clinic."

"That is strange. We should..."

"They are expecting us in two hours, Detective Chandler. Captain Lahr and I will meet you there. Just need to make sure the crew takes the body to the morgue."

"Next of kin?" Jayne said.

"A Jean Penhold."

"Isn't the 'n' silent in French, Inspector? You mean, Jean?" Jayne said, with her best French pronunciation.

"No, I do mean Jean. Like the pants. Jean is a 'she'."

"Well that explains why they needed Doctor Northgate's help," John said. "He seems more than willing to help out these pretty young ladies. We need to put the squeeze on that bastard today."

"Slow down, cowboy," Jayne said. "Inspector, can you talk to missus Penhold?"

"You bet, Detective. We will meet her on the way to the clinic."

3

"Ruprecht, my good friend, I have great news," Soul said. Soul had only met Ruprecht Barren in person a few times, but felt very close to his partner in his master plan.

"Primera has come through again?" Ruprecht said.

"You are correct. It went perfectly. Without a hitch. The martyr did not suffer. We are ready to unleash the army."

"I am ready from my end," Ruprecht said. "Packages have been sent to my contacts in thirty-nine European countries. For now, I have left out the five smaller European countries. I have acquired reliable assets in eighteen Asian countries, Australia and New Zealand, who all have packages. You?"

"Same," Soul said. "Packages sent to my soldiers in three North American, seven Central American, and twelve South American countries."

"A total of eighty-one countries," Ruprecht said. "I have assets in six German cities, given my close contacts here."

"Good idea. We will have two in Canada. The USA and China have been particularly behind in its climate change policies. They have completely ignored all warnings and continue their destructive behaviors. I have handpicked fifteen soldiers for my country, and eleven in China."

"That's 111 targets. You still sure about this, Soul? That is a lot of blood on our hands."

"I am sure, yes. They are 111 martyrs. They will bleed for God and His Earth. The Bible tells us, Ruprecht. Revelations Chapter seven says it. "These are they which came out of great tribulation, and have washed their robes, and made them white in the blood of the Lamb. Therefore are they before the throne of God, and serve him day and night in his temple". Our team, our martyrs, we will all be with God when our judgment comes. You still steadfast in our plan, Ruprecht?"

"I am, Soul. And the manifesto?"

"Almost ready. On the third day we will launch our soldiers into battle. On the fourth day the United Nations Security Council will receive our severe warning. I will remind them once again of their crimes against our beautiful planet. I shall give them forty days to provide a concrete response. They shall ignore us no more."

"I look forward to reading it," Ruprecht said.

"I look forward to living in a healthy and prosperous planet Earth. Speak to you soon, my friend."

4

"Sorry to be disturbing you again, Doctor," Jayne said.

"It's common for women to want more of me, Detective," Northgate said.

This guy is hard to take, thought John.

"Your staff seemed even more upset this time," Jayne said.

"We deal with life and death in our jobs, Detective, but not usually murder. And now twice in the same week. It's tough. Plus, all lives are valuable, but some are just more valuable than others."

"What do you mean?" Jayne said.

"He means that a Doctor's life is more valuable," John said. "Isn't that right, Doctor Northgate?"

"That is what I mean, yes. You don't agree, Constable?"

"It's Detective Corporal now, and no I don't agree with you."

"I guess it's less than humble of me, isn't it CORPORAL. I think you got me on some African symbol of humility last time."

"Yes, the Dwennimmen," John said.

"That's right. Excellent word. Congratulations on your promotion, Corporal. Were you promoted because of your mastery of the English language, or maybe," turning to Jayne, "due to other talents that your tongue possesses?"

"Let's get back to the issue of a second murder from a patient in your clinic, shall we, Doctor," interrupted Jayne. "Any more ideas on the link to your clinic?"

"None."

"I omitted to ask you this last time," Jayne said, "but both Lynne and now Gemma had the letters CC written into their umbilicus. Any thoughts on what that could be?"

"Are you thinking it means Conception Clinic?"

"It had crossed our mind. Or with the circle of the belly button, it could mean Conception Opportunities Calgary," John said.

"Not sure. I don't think anybody in my clinic is a murderer, if that is what you are getting at. I can't think of anything else those letters could mean. Our receptionist's name is Caren Calon, but she is the sweetest girl in the world."

"Thank you. We will add her to our list of interviewees," Jayne said. "Going back to our last visit, we mentioned Lynne Nanton was thinking of reporting you to the Alberta College. Did you have similar problems with Doctor Augustine?"

"I had no problems with Lynne Nanton, and none whatsoever with Gemma. Gemma and I go way back. We trained together at the University of Alberta. When she moved here, she and her lesbian lover approached me to help them with artificial insemination. Wasn't surprised that Gemma swung that way."

"Why is that?" John asked.

"I tried to hit on Gemma during our resident orientation. She wasn't interested. Sure sign. If a woman isn't interested in me, only three possible explanations. One: they want to stay faithful to their partners. Two: both their ovaries have been removed. Three: they are lesbians. The first two options weren't in play at the time, leaving only the third one."

"Thank you for the life lesson, Doctor," Jayne said. "By the way, where were you last night at the time of the murder?"

"What time was the murder?"

"Around eight PM."

"Right here then, Detective. We run our clinic from noon to eight PM on Thursdays."

"Who can corroborate that?" Jayne said.

"We run a skeleton staff on Thursday nights. So, last night I was with Nurse Sandy, and some other Nurse. I don't notice anybody when Nurse Sandy is around. What a body on her! Wouldn't you agree, Corporal?"

John smiled. Half from genuine amusement, half from wanting to kill him for objectifying the love of John's life!

OK, now I really hate this guy, John thought. *One punch, give me one fucking punch!*

"Thank you, Doctor," Jayne said. "That will be all."

"Good luck, Detective. Please get this guy ASAP. If word gets out, there will be another death on our hands: my business!"

5

Jayne and John decided to divide and conquer the rest of the interrogations. John of course immediately volunteered to interview Nurse Sandy, as well as Ginny Fremlin. Jayne saw right through his motives for picking those two to interview, but left it alone. Jayne was going to interview Nurse Stubley and the receptionist Caren Calon.

This time, John met with Ginny in the ultrasound area. John knocked and opened the ultrasound door a crack.

"Missus Fremlin?"

"Yes, come on in, Detective. It's still Ginny by the way."

Ginny sat alone in the dark room, at a small desk behind the ultrasound machine.

"Thanks, Ginny. Is it a good time for me to come in?" John said.

"It is. Though I will warn you to keep a distance. I have been sick all morning from a viral gastroenteritis. Seems like everybody in the clinic has had it."

John instinctively doused his hands in sanitizer. After sympathizing with her illness, John proceeded to ask Ginny some usual questions. He asked her about where she was on Thursday night, to which Ginny answered that she takes an ultrasound upskilling course at the University on Thursday evening. John asked Ginny about her relationship with Gemma Augustine. Ginny confirmed that she remembered Dr. Augustine very well. She had a normal ultrasound three days ago. She remembered them crying and hugging at the sight of the twins: two girls.

"Nothing out of the ordinary. Usual melodrama," Ginny said.

John was going to explore that last statement, but Ginny restarted.

"How is the investigation going?"

"It's going. Preliminary stages. No firm leads yet. But I feel confident we will bring this person to justice."

"Justice," Ginny said, starting at the still picture that was left on her ultrasound machine. "It's interesting, Detective."

"What is?"

"In a way you and I have similar jobs."

"What do you mean?"

"Remember the last time we met, you asked me how I could possibly look at this ultrasound picture and make an interpretation?"

"I remember it well. You told me that imagination was a dangerous thing."

"That's right. And it still is. But it strikes me as though both you and I are working in the great Greek philosopher Plato's cave."

"Pardon?"

"Plato had a famous analogy. He imagined men who spent their lives chained in a cave, and who only saw images as shadows on the cave wall. Those men would then have to interpret these shadows on the background of a set of forms in their brain."

"Go on. This is very interesting."

"My job is literally taking the acoustic shadows from the ultrasound signal, and then applying them to a form I have in my brain for what we call a normal fetus. I never truly see the baby, but through its shadows I decide if the baby has a perfect form or not."

"That is really cool! But how does that apply to me?"

"As a Detective, you don't see the murder. You acquire information, through your investigation, that allows your mind to create shadows of what might have occurred. I take shadows to decide something concrete: baby is normal or not. You take shadows and apply them to abstract concepts such as crime and justice. That is what Plato said close to 2500 years ago, and it still applies today."

"Smart guy! And you are a smart woman. How do you know that much about Philosophy?"

"It was my first degree. I started it for two years then stopped."

"Didn't like it?"

"You kidding me? I LOVED it! But to work in Philosophy you need a bachelor's degree, then at least a Masters, but more likely a Doctorate degree. Jonas and I just couldn't foot the bills for that. Led me to take my ultrasound technician course and start working."

"Shame. Will you go back to it someday?"

"Probably not. I have lots of other responsibilities. I am married, I work…"

"And starting a family soon?" John said.

"Maybe. Jonas and I have talked about it."

"A big one, I presume. You do work in a fertility center, after all."

"Definitely not a big one, Detective. That would be irresponsible in our current climate situation. There are enough people in the world already."

Before John could speak, Ginny continued.

"Detective, could we continue this discussion some other time? I think I am ready for a bathroom trip. So sorry, Corporal. Maybe we can talk at our clinic Christmas party tomorrow?"

And with that, Ginny raced out of the room. John doused for a second time in sanitizer, and rejoined Jayne.

6

"What do you have?" Jayne said, as they reconvened in the main office.

"Nothing much from Nurse Sandy. She is…"

"Perfect, yes I know!" Jayne said.

"OK, maybe, yes she is perfect. But I was going to say that she is devastated, and has an alibi. She was here last night, and she confirmed that Northgate was as well."

"Go on, what about Fremlin?"

"That was an interesting conversation. She didn't know Doctor Augustine very well, but curious that Doctor Augustine had an ultrasound on Monday, three days before being killed. Same time frame as Lynne Nanton. I would normally just call that a coincidence, but..."

"But what?"

"You said it when we debriefed after our last visit with her. She seems to have a chip on her shoulder about pregnant women and their emotional reactions. Just seems odd. I didn't get a chance to fully explore it as she wasn't feeling well today. She looked much paler than last time we saw her. Apparently caught a bug floating around the clinic. Other than that, we had a great philosophical discussion about our respective jobs, and the climate situation."

"Climate situation? How did that come up? Don't answer that, I don't want to hear about her philosophy. Does she have an alibi?"

"Yes. She takes a course on Thursdays. I can confirm that later."

"Interesting about her impatience with pregnant women but that still doesn't make her a murderer, especially with that alibi, if it holds up. If she is sick, you should take more of this stuff."

"Agree," John said, rubbing his hands in the blob of sanitizer that Jayne squirted him with. "What about you?"

"Not much. Nothing new from Nurse Stubley."

"Still Stubley, will always be Stubley?"

"Yes, for sure," Jayne said laughing. "Glad you weren't there with me for that one. Would have been tough. I then met with Caren Calon. She is a very nice person. Couldn't stop balling the whole time. Plus, she was away on holidays until last night, just flew back late.

One interesting coincidence though, I ran into one of the curlers."

"Who?"

"Doctor Patricia Richmond, the Anesthetist."

"The one with the means, opportunity, but no motive. What was she doing here?"

"Correct. Still no motive by the way. But she does work here once a week, helping give the intravenous anesthesia before the egg retrievals."

"The Propofol?" John said.

"That's it," Jayne said. "She strikes me as an odd duck. Was very vague on where she was last night. But doesn't strike me as the murdering type. Where does that leave us?"

"Not sure. Though I didn't tell you that Nurse Sandy invited us to the clinic's Christmas party on Saturday."

"That's tomorrow!" Jayne said.

"I think we should go. She said she ran it by Northgate and he was fine with it. It will give us a chance to see folks like Ginny Fremlin and Patricia Richmond in another light."

"What, people in the clinic go to their office Christmas party?"

"Apparently they all do. Northgate hosts, in his, as you would have guessed, ostentatious home. He hires a live band and everything. We should go."

"OK. Not sure your motives are entirely work-related, are they, Corporal?" laughed Jayne.

"Oh no, Sargeant. One hundred percent work, always work, you know me! By the way you'll need a costume."

"What? But it's tomorrow! I am hating this even more now. I like sitting in my pyjamas on Saturdays. Now I have to hang around creepy Northgate in a costume?"

"Yes. It's a twenties theme. Twenty-twenty for 2020! You like it?"

"Great, a short skirt around Northgate!"

"Sandy in a short dress? Oops, did I say that out loud?"

A firm punch to his right shoulder followed, as Jayne and John exited the office back to their car.

CHAPTER 13

THE CHRISTMAS PARTY

1

The Northgate home would have been a comfortable and cozy abode, for about thirty people. For one man, it was a ridiculously-sized mansion. The house was situated just outside of Calgary, on a two-acre lot overlooking the Rocky Mountains. After passing the entrance gates, a two-hundred-meter driveway approach left ample room for visitors to park near the palatial house. Jayne was able to park very close to the home's sizeable garage.

Six-car garage? Car collector probably? Woodworker? Doesn't strike me as a pottery maker.

"Come in, Detective," Northgate shouted. "Glad that you could make it. It feels like you are a part of the clinic now."

"Thanks for the invitation, Doctor," Jayne said. "You have a lovely home."

"Thanks. Please call me Julian. I will show you around later, once the flood of guests has finished arriving. Where is your partner in crime?"

"You can call me Jayne. We are no longer in an interrogation, Julian. John is on his way. He texted me about a half hour ago. John and I are not always together."

"Oh. You are not together, together?"

"Not in the way you mean it, no. The police force discourages such relationships."

"Well that's the best news I have heard all day. Oops, more people arriving. I must greet them. Tough gig being the 'host with the most'! We will talk later. Please, take a number for the games, and grab a drink in the bar set up in the kitchen."

Julian handed Jayne a hat filled with cardboard squares of different colors. She pulled one of the squares out of the hat. She was on team number six.

Whatever that means Jayne thought. *Why did I get here this early?*

2

As Jayne stood in the entrance, she could not help but stare with wonder at the massive chandelier hanging from the second floor, encircled by a majestic wooden staircase. At quick glance it looked as though there were at least five bedrooms upstairs.

Is Northgate planning on adopting a small African country? Jayne thought.

Jayne made her way to the main part of the house. She first walked to her right, in the spacious living room, where several guests were already seated in two cushy, white sofas. The living room flowed to the dining room, which was a complete set, including a beautifully finished wooden table surrounded by eight chairs, a small decorative hutch, and a very ornate dining room buffet with glass doors revealing a fancy white china set.

Wedgwood dining set. Of course. Must hand it to this guy, he does know what he is doing with house décor!

As Jayne walked into the kitchen and living room area, she could see a team of four caterers dressed in black pants, white shirt, and black bow tie, busily getting appetizers from the grey-haired chef, who looked much less frantic and nervous than the servers.

"Good evening, madam," said a server with black hair, dark brown eyes, and a dreamy Spanish accent. "Can I interest you in a smoked salmon appetizer?"

"Sure, thank you," Jayne said. "But mostly I could use a drink!"

"Of course, madam, the bar is set up right over there. Where everybody is congregating!"

Jayne should have known. Two sure-fire areas where people group together at a party: the bar and the kitchen. In this case, they were both in the same place, making it by far the most crowded area in the house.

"Detective Chandler, hi! Come get a drink?" Nurse Sandy looked particularly good tonight. She had gone all out with the 1920s theme. Her outfit was exactly what you would imagine from the era. A silver flapper dress, with only one strap on the left side, exposing her slim yet muscular shoulders and arms. The dress was short, significantly above her knees, with only transparent fringes covering most of her legs. The outfit was perfectly accessorized with silver high-heeled shoes, neck choker and headpiece, which made her look like she was pulled right off the stage of the Chicago Broadway musical.

"Hi Sandy, please call me Jayne. You look great!" *John is going to lose his shit!*

"You look great also, Jayne." That was very nice of Sandy to say, but Jayne had not done much to get ready for the 1920s theme. Fairly standard long black dress and shoes, but she had gone to the effort of acquiring a red cloche hat for the occasion.

"You are too kind," Jayne said. "Sort of prepared at the last minute. I will take you up on the offer of a drink. Are there any coolers?"

"For sure, Smirnoff vodka cooler coming right up!"

Sandy was surrounded by four other clinic staff, all female. "Is John going to make it tonight?"

"Yes, he is on his way."

"Good. Glad you could both be here," Sandy said, with a knowing look to the excited-looking staffers around her. "Do you know everyone here?"

"I don't. I am Jayne. Jayne Chandler." Jayne shook hands with everyone, who in return gave her their names. This was probably a futile exercise, both by the sheer volume of new people she was going to meet, and that Jayne had a nasty habit of not quite listening to people when they introduced themselves.

One of the group members was Louise Agat. Louise was a more senior Nurse in the clinic, but was very popular with everyone. Louise was funny when sober. She became extremely funny with a few drinks. Add to the many drinks a few joints, and Louise Agat definitely straddled the fence between appropriate and inappropriate office party humor.

"Jayne, did you see Julian on your way in?" Louise said.

"I did."

"Good, then he knows you are here. He will be REALLY happy you came. I mean dropped by. Well maybe I did mean came."

As usual, Louise got a hearty laugh from her captive audience.

"Sandy, maybe Jayne here can continue the yearly party tradition?"

"Ignore her, Jayne. Louise, you are such a potty mouth!" Sandy said, laughing. "Jayne, her nickname is Loo Loo Louise!"

A chant of "Loo Loo" from the growing assembled crowd.

"Potty mouth, maybe. But every party needs some spark, chicky! That's my job."

"What tradition?" Jayne said.

"You don't know?" Louise said. "Every year Northgate hooks up with somebody at the Christmas party. Male, female, small animals, doesn't matter. Someone must be a target. My money is on you this year, Detective!"

Louise started a "Jayne, Jayne, Jayne" chant, that became mainly a solo effort.

"#metoo hasn't made its way to Doctor Julian Northgate and our clinic," Sandy said. "Louise, that's enough. Let Jayne settle into the group, will you?"

"That's exactly what I am trying to do!" Louise lifted both arms to her side, and looked up at the sky, in apparent exultation. "Jayne, welcome to the ultimate sausage party, and tonight I think you are the main course."

"Sausage party?" Jayne said. "But there are more girls than guys here." Jayne was downing her drink, which helped her start to warm to the rowdy Louise.

"Not that kind of sausage party, silly. Don't you know where you are? This is a COC fest!"

A "COC fest, COC fest" chant spontaneously erupted, this time with more participants than just Louise.

"Wow, what kind of party have we joined, Jayne?" John said.

"John!" said both Jayne and Sandy in harmony. Jayne with a somewhat relieved look. Sandy with a decidedly more excited look.

John had also made significant effort for his costume. Black hat, black shirt, black stripped pants, contrasted with white tie, white suspenders, and white shoes.

"Nice look, gangster John," Sandy said. "And I love the fake mustache. Just missed Movember!"

"What kind of party you ask? It's a COC fest, Detective, with lots of traditions," Louise said. "They will fill you in. One of those traditions is that Loo Loo Louise needs to go out for some 'air'. Anyone joining me?"

A few of the staffers nodded affirmatively, as Louise made her way out of the kitchen.

"By the way, be careful, Stubley just arrived," Louise said. "Stay at a safe distance or you might get jabbed. If Julian comes in Monday morning with puncture marks all over his face, we will know for sure who carried on the tradition!"

Louise believed in the first rule of comedy. Say a joke and get out leaving them laughing and wanting more.

3

"You have two minutes to finish the quiz, then you will have to put your pens down, teams," Northgate said.

The six teams were furiously finishing up Julian Northgate's twenty-five multiple-choice question quiz about the 1920s. Jayne had become the leader of her Team six, which included Loo Loo Louise, who was too stoned and drunk to be of much help. Nurse Sandy had taken control of Team two. This included a pre-game trade of Nurse Stubley to Team one, in order to acquire the services of Detective John Hunter. John was feeling blessed by this move, though could not be sure if Sandy's motivation was to get him on her team, or ditch her boss Stubley.

"OK, time's up! Hand in your sheets to another team for correction. Here is the grid, team captains. Four points per questions. The quiz is out of one hundred."

As the team captains furiously corrected the questions, another yearly tradition was unfolding. Loo Loo Louise was getting rowdy.

"Julian, can we just stop with these fucking games!" Loo Loo Louise shouted. "We all hate them! Let's get the band going and start dancin'!"

"Take it easy, Louise," Northgate said, "we are almost there. Results are in. A first, I think. A tie! Teams two and six are both tied with ninety-two points! Time for a showdown!"

"Jesus Christ," Louise said, "just give it to them and get on with it. They can just have my prize. Box of Toblerone again, Julian?"

"No way, Louise," Northgate said. "What we need is a good old fashion overtime shoot out for the win! Teams two and six, pick a representative for the showdown."

"John, you go ahead," Sandy said.

It was clear who was to be selected from Team six.

"OK, we have our very special guest Detectives going head to head. Hunter vs Chandler! Let's give them a huge round of applause!"

The crowd, except Louise, loudly cheered the two combatants.

"And to boot, it happens to be a police-related question. Here we go. Three parts. Write out your answers. Quiet please, crowd. Lots at stake."

The crowd quieted. Louise kept talking, to nobody in particular. "Fuck this, I am going to the pantry to look for Doritos."

"The question is: which famous gangster was first captured May 17, 1929? In what city? And what were the charges?"

On cue, the brass band, which had just finished setting up in the monstrous family, soon-to-be dance, room, piped in with the famous Final Jeopardy jingle.

"OK. Hand me your answers. Let's see. Very interesting. The first part of the question answered correctly by both Detectives. Of course, it was none other than the infamous Al Capone!"

A loud cheer drowned out the sound of Louise munching on her Doritos.

"For the next two parts, we have one fully correct answer, and one fully wrong answer."

Drumroll from the band. Northgate was clearly enjoying this.

"Detective Jayne said he was arrested in Chicago, for tax evasion. That is true!"

Loud cheer from Team six.

"But true, only in 1931! Making that a wrong answer!"

Loud cheer from Team two.

"In 1929, he was arrested in Philadelphia, for carrying a concealed weapon. Detective John Hunter is correct! Team two wins!"

High fives all around for Team two. Hug for John from his favorite Nurse. Loo Louise was correct: Northgate proceeded to hand out the winning Toblerone bars to Team two.

"Thanks for humoring me everyone," Northgate said, "I realize the game is probably more fun for me than everyone else! Everyone is looking forward to hearing the band and getting to their best Charleston. At least we know Louise is! If she can stand up that long, of course."

The audience loved Northgate's burn on Loo Loo Louise.

"But I do want to take this opportunity to remind you of how great you all are. This is the best clinic in the world, and it's because of you all. Cheers to you and your families for a great holiday season."

"Cheers! Best COC in the world!" Louise shouted, now slurring. "Come on everyone, say it with me, WE LOVE COC, WE LOVE COC!"

Nobody said it with her.

"Thanks for that, Louise. Seriously though, it's been a very hard week. I want to honor our two patients who lost their lives this week. Such tragedy. I also want to thank our two Detectives, Jayne Chandler and John Hunter, who treated the victims with dignity and treated us with respect. I am fully confident that you will catch the bastard who did this! Cheers to Lynne, cheers to Gemma, and cheers to the Detectives!"

After a heartfelt "Cheers" chant from the gathered crowd, the music started. Sandy lead the way to the dance floor. She grabbed John and gave him no choice but to head to the dance floor. Jayne stood mesmerized by the speech she had just heard. There was a distinct crack in the voice when he mentioned the victims. Was this the real Northgate? It was certainly a charming and humble side of the man.

I'm confused, thought Jayne. *Maybe Lynne Nanton did misread him? I am usually better at figuring people out. No question he is gorgeous, though. But you're a Detective, Jayne, and your job description doesn't include keeping Christmas traditions going!*

4

"Doctor Vista?" Jayne said. "Sorry to bother you late on a Friday. I wanted to catch you before the weekend. I have John Hunter with me on speakerphone."

"Hello, Doctor," John said. "Thanks for taking the call."

"No problem at all. Where are you both? Sounds very loud where you are!"

"We are at a mall, Doctor. We have to find a costume for a party we are going to tomorrow night!"

"Costume? That sounds like fun!"

"1920s theme. Can you help us out?" John said.

"I am not that old, Detective!" Vista said, laughing.

"Sorry, that's not what I meant!" John then whispered into Jayne's ear, "That is kind of what I meant!"

After Jayne mouthed "Stop" to John, she addressed the Doctor. "Any news on the new autopsy? And the Xenon?"

Vista proceeded to a very detailed report regarding Gemma Augustine's autopsy findings. John was feeling giddy and excited about the party, and found it hard to concentrate. He whispered to Jayne, "This is a much better way to talk to him. Avoids the disturbance of your visual and olfactory senses!"

Jayne once again mouthed "Stop", as she was killing herself laughing. Luckily, she had lots of time to compose herself as Vista went through each organ system in detail.

"Bottom line is," Vista said, "the findings for Doctor Augustine are identical to Lynne Nanton."

"Thank you, Doctor," Jayne said. "What about the Xenon?"

"Now that is very interesting. You will recall that I didn't have the test for this inert gas, but I did manage to contact the authors of a recent article who allowed me to courier a sample of missus Nanton's blood to them for testing. They are in Switzerland. They got back to me today."

"And?" asked Jayne.

"They use a very interesting technique for measuring the gas. It's gas chromatography coupled with tandem mass spectrome…"

"Doctor, I am sorry," interjected Jayne. "But positive, or negative?"

"Right, of course. You may not be that interested in the technique. Anyways, we were right. Positive. It is Xenon. I will send them Doctor Augustine's sample today."

"Where would you get the Xenon, Doctor?" Jayne said.

"That is an interesting question. Xenon was linked to Russian doping theories. But in my email exchanges with the authors of the testing paper, they seem to think that the main car manufacturers would be the most likely source. Problem is that many car manufacturers make Xenon headlights. Ford, Kia, Mercedes, BMW, and many more."

"Anywhere in the world then?" John said.

"Maybe. But the second author in the paper comes from Aachen, Germany. On the border with Belgium and Netherlands. He has heard through the grapevine of unusual shipment quantities going to the BMW headquarters, in Munich."

"Maybe making Xenon headlights standard for all their models now?" Jayne said.

"That's one possibility of course," Vista said.

"OK, we will have to keep that in mind. John and I appreciate the call. All the best to you and Betty, Doctor Vista."

"Thank you, Detectives. Have fun tomorrow!"

"For all his physical challenges," John said, "he is a super nice guy. I have to stop making fun of him."

"Ditto. Now let's find this stinking costume. I am telling you right now, nothing too short, and nothing too extravagant!"

5

"Let's get out of here, Jonas," Ginny said, "I think I am the only sober one here." Ginny had offered to be the designated driver this year. After two years of attending her husband's Christmas functions, she now fully appreciated that the only way a spouse can tolerate their significant other's office Christmas party was to get blitzed.

"But I was just starting to have fun, Ginny," Jonas said. "I even liked Northgate's game this year. The food is amazing. Have you tried the potatoes? Loo Loo Louise and her marijuana maidens are on fire this year. The band is awesome! Normally I hate this party, but the music is great, the costumes are great, the dancers are great, Nurse Sandy is looking great. Oops, did I say that out loud?"

"You did. And I don't blame you at all. But I am tired." Ginny lowered her voice. "And I am really horny."

"OK, no argument from me, let's go."

As they were putting their coats on, John Hunter caught the couple out of the corner of his eye and raced to the door.

"Leaving so soon?" John said. "I was hoping to continue our philosophical chat outside of the confines of your ultrasound room, missus Fremlin."

"It's Ginny, Detective. And time for me to go home. I'm exhausted. It's been a long week."

"It certainly has," John said. "I am getting pretty tired myself. Chasing down a double murderer takes a lot out of a guy."

John was staring Ginny directly in the eyes for a reaction. Ginny stared right back, emotionless.

"What has made your week tiring, Ginny?" John said.

"Work has been busy. Having two of our patients die is not exactly a boost of energy. And the GI bug I talked to you about didn't help."

As John searched for another question, Ginny continued.

"How rude of me, I haven't introduced my husband. Detective Hunter, this is my husband Jonas. Jonas Clavette."

"Hello, Jonas," John said, as he shook his hand. "Ginny, Jonas and I have met several times tonight. We were just in the middle of a heated cornhole game when he said you wanted to leave."

"John is the best, Ginny. We are tied two-two in our cornhole series," Jonas said. "We will have to play our tiebreaker some other time. Great party wasn't it? Best one ever!"

"It's been a lot fun," John said. "More fun than I expected, that is for sure. Let me tell you, Ginny, Jonas has quite an arm. Must have been quite a pitcher in his days."

"I had the second nastiest slider in Okotoks baseball in my day, that's for sure," Jonas said. "The only better right-hander was our very own Ginny Fremlin!"

Ginny grinned and swatted away Jonas' comments.

"But getting back to the party," Jonas said. "Hard not to have fun when you have been staring at Nurse Sandy all night, right John?" Jonas half covered his mouth like baseball players on a pitching mound. Jonas was too drunk to realize that this degree of discretion only works when you are not shouting at the top of your lungs.

"She is an awesome person indeed, Jonas. This is a great group. A lot more fun than the police department gang!"

"They are," Ginny said. "We are lucky to work with such a group."

"Come on, John," Sandy shouted. "Time for a foxtrot!"

"I guess the party is not done for me, Jonas," John said.

"You better go, Detective," Ginny said. "Great seeing you. Let's go, Jonas."

As Ginny and Jonas, left, John was already doing the 'slow walk, slow walk, quick side, quick together' of the Foxtrot.

6

"I promised you a tour, Detective Jayne," Northgate said, "shall we start now?"

"Sure. I am definitely curious to see why a single man needs a six-car garage."

"No problem, let's go."

Julian took Jayne by the arm and led her to the basement. Jayne did not resist the friendly gesture, nor did it go unnoticed by the party attendees. Louise would have been particularly interested, had she not been outside sprinkling the front lawn with undigested Doritos.

After a quick tour of the basement, including an eighty-inch television that looked like a movie screen, Julian escorted Jayne upstairs and showed her the fully furnished, five bedrooms on the second floor.

"Why this many rooms, Julian?" Jayne said.

"I wanted to make sure I was prepared for any future family size. I am a fertility doctor after all."

Jayne was still puzzled by the abrupt personality change she was seeing in Julian. The narcissistic prick that she had visited in the clinic had been completely replaced by a genuine and affable person.

"Now time to show you why I need six garages. It's a little hobby of mine that I just started."

The garage looked like a perfectly minted showroom of a very fancy automobile dealership. In it were five shiny sports cars, all red. The sixth car looked more like her little simple Mazda.

"It's a silly, pretentious hobby, but walking in here every day warms my insides. When I feel stressed, I just stroll between these beauties, and I feel my blood pressure drop by thirty points. It's expensive, but cheaper than a heart attack or stroke."

"I am not a car connoisseur. What are these?"

"The silver Toyota is my day-to-day car. The others are all sports cars that I drive infrequently. As you can tell, I like red. That is an Alfa Romeo. I like it because the emblem has a snake that looks like the medical symbol. The others are a Mustang, Ferrari, Corvette, and my first baby, the one that I do drive a little more, the BMW-335."

Jayne stared, stunned by the impeccable cleanliness of the garage, and the scintillating collective shine from the five cars.

"Can I look inside them?" Jayne asked.

"Sure. Look away, Jayne."

As Jayne got to the fifth car, the BMW, she could tell that Julian was getting very close to her. As she opened the door, he placed his hands over her shoulders, and slid them down her arms. He grabbed a hold of the back of both her hands. She could feel his breath on the back of her neck.

"I see that you are enjoying yourself," Northgate said. "Can always use another set of headlights in here."

If Jayne had any thought of responding to Northgate's advances, the mention of the headlights jarred Jayne her back to the reality of the week.

Headlights. Xenon. Jayne, what are you doing, you are a Detective on a murder investigation from this guy's clinic?

"This is wrong, Julian. I am a Detective, investigating two murders from your clinic."

Julian pulled away from her, smiling.

"I totally get it. This was presumptuous of me. My apologies."

"And I can't figure you out. One minute you present yourself as completely narcissistic and self-absorbed, and the next you are genuine and caring. Who are you?"

"A complicated man, with a perhaps misguided persona aimed at reassuring worried couples that someone has their back. But Jayne, I am not a murderer. I sometimes stare at people too long. But that doesn't make me a murderer. You have to believe that."

"I am starting to believe that. I really am. Perhaps we could meet at another time, in different circumstances?"

"You bet, Jayne. I hear the band blaring out a classic. Let's head back to the party."

7

Ginny walked upstairs to their bedroom. She removed her 1920s outfit in front of her bathroom mirror with just a black bra and panties on. She cut a very impressive figure, which she recognized, as did countless others she had encountered over the years.

If only I had a nickel for every head I have turned, I might be able to retire from that boring job, Ginny thought. *Looking good, but feel like shit! Could this really mean what I think it means?*

As she stood gazing at her reflection, Ginny took a long look at her abdomen to see if there were noticeable changes.

Your period is three weeks late, Ginny. You're not going to show for a while.

Ginny was having trouble grasping how she and Jonas could conceive naturally. Ginny's periods were erratic, a problem she self-diagnosed as an ovulation dysfunction. To add to their difficulties, Jonas had an undescended testicle requiring surgery at age one. She and Jonas had never used birth control in the five years they have been together. Ginny believed her mother, who repeatedly told her that her body features were too manly to conceive.

But this time it was different. She had been vomiting all week. Her breasts were noticeably tender. Tomorrow, she would take a pregnancy test. But right now, she was going to focus on Jonas, and reward him for being a good sport at the Christmas party tonight. Jonas always had somewhat of a social phobia, making these get-togethers a difficult task for him.

"Honey, I'm in bed," slurred Jonas. "Someone is ready for a little visit!"

"On my way, Jonas,".

I hope it's a short visit, Ginny thought, *I think I am close to another puke session!*

As Ginny crawled into bed, Jonas immediately rolled over to her and put his arms around her.

"I had fun tonight," Jonas said. "Now for the real fun. Now let's make a baby. The angel of conception is back!"

"I'm all yours, my angel." *But* we *may already have a baby.*

Jonas was too drunk and involved in his fantasies to realize that Ginny was just going through the motions. The angel reference had caused her mind to drift to Soul Fernandez, and their first meeting in November 2017.

How much has happened in two short years, Ginny thought. *Just go through the motions with Jonas. It will save you the embarrassment of shouting Soul's name again while you orgasm.*

"Almost there, Ginny, almost there!" Jonas shouted.

Good, he is almost done. For me, things have just started. I am the trail blazer that will lead the planet to safety and glory. I am the first. I am Primera!

8

Ginny was unable to sleep that night. Jonas passed out very quickly, and soon after, unbeknownst to the man in his deep vegetative state, Ginny had raced to the bathroom to vomit for the fifth time that day. She concealed her sickness, not that she needed to, by racing to the downstairs bathroom and flushing repeatedly to drown out the sound of her retching.

Jonas' snoring was mild and tolerable at normal times. When he had been drinking, it sounded like a yacht idling at the marina dock. Adding to the disturbance from her husband were thoughts racing through her head. She was reliving in her mind the whirlwind that had been her last two years. Her first encounter with Soul, and then Ruprecht. Their life-altering train ride to Düsseldorff. Professor Mikhaël Leddy's ground-breaking experiments. Their subsequent meetings in Katowice and Madrid, at the next two climate change conferences. The finalization of their plan. Her clear and ever-growing conviction that the team was on the correct path.

Ginny thought of all the knowledge she had gained over the past two years. The climate state of our planet. The Bible. Xenon. Pfannenstiel incisions. Then there were thoughts of Lynne Nanton. Gemma Augustine. She envisioned them basking in the sunlight of God, underneath one of the palm trees on Soul's oasis tattoo.

Once she got over the frustration of the snoring, of not being able to fall asleep, the thoughts of Soul and their mission filled her with an inner joy and peace that she had rarely felt.

Could he really be the angel from the east?

Her rational side would argue that he was just another man, maybe a narcissistic man, whose charisma could move people to do whatever they wanted.

Is that what Jesus Christ did?

But Soul Fernandez had awakened the spirituality that Ginny had buried deeply inside her. He had moved her to pick up and read the Bible, for the first time in her life.

Jesus Christ moved his disciples to continue his teachings after his death, even in the face of intense persecution and horrible deaths. Jesus was for real. No human would have faced what his followers experienced for a normal man. Soul is the same way. And I, Lynne, Gemma, the entire team and all the martyrs are repeating history. Jesus and his disciplines saved humanity from certain death. Soul and his disciples are saving the planet from certain death.

Ginny almost drifted to sleep from the peaceful feelings evoked by her deep convictions. Then, thoughts of her mother grew inside her head. These were far from peaceful visions. Soul Fernandez equated to an opium-induced bliss. Ginny's mother equated to nails on a chalkboard hell.

You're pregnant? I can't believe it. Gosh, how is that kid coming out of that pelvis? Who is going to be the female influence in that baby's life? Jonas, I guess. I always knew that every rag finds its dirty towel. In your case a tomboy found its effeminate man!

Enough, Ginny, enough. Get that woman out of your head. Your period is just late, as it often is. You're making up symptoms. First thing tomorrow, I will head to the pharmacy. Shoppers opens at seven AM.

She once again thought about Soul and their first meeting in the Loud Woman pub in Bonn. She now relived the relaxed, clairvoyant feelings that she experienced that night. Ginny was breathing slowly again. She felt calm and at peace. This was a true serenity that only Soul could elicit.

CHAPTER 14

THE WORLD AWAKENS

1

It was a typical December Monday morning in Calgary. After four days of minus twenty-degree Celsius weather, a warm Chinook wind had blown in from the west to raise the temperature by twenty-five degrees overnight. The little bit of snow on the ground and roads was turning into water. The reflection of the sun on this beautiful white painting was blinding. Nobody would complain about the strain on their eyes this morning. Putting on sunglasses in the dead of winter was a welcomed reprieve, and a reminder that at some point soon it would be spring again. As usual, the Sunday night curlers would wake up with memories of their shots, mostly missed shots, from the night before. Dr. Warren Mcallum would be dwelling on another loss, with the euphoria of his win over Dennis Parkwood a short week ago long gone from his memory banks. Dr. Paul Riverside would undoubtedly be feeling fine, like a bag of salt.

What transpired next was far from typical.

What transpired next was the sort of event that turns the entire world upside down. An event that sucks the life out of everyone, paralyzes leaders, brings workers and companies to a halt. 9/11, JFK, space shuttle Challenger. Events permanently engraved in the human psyche. We all remember where we were when news broke of those events.

Jayne Chandler received a sneak preview that something was coming. Her phone rang as she was stepping out of the shower. This was not a common occurrence so early on a Monday morning.

"Detective, you have to get in here, pronto," said Police Chief James Hunter. "There have been developments on your two recent murder cases."

"Developments? What do you mean, Jim?"

"This is huge. Way bigger than you, I and our two dead bodies. There are reports coming in from INTERPOL, the FBI, the Moskow politsiya. You name it, there are reports of similar murders coming from seemingly everywhere in the world."

"What?"

"It's mind-blowing, Jayne. I don't know where to start. Just text John and get the hell in here!"

2

Jayne hurried to get her clothes on. A thousand thoughts were racing through her head. Visions of Lynne and Gemma multiplied by who knows how many more victims overnight. She felt simultaneously that she had a bigger role to play in the world, but somehow also that her little department was now insignificant in the grand scheme. She felt bonded to the hundreds of officers, investigators, Pathologists around the world who were now scrambling to solve these crimes, just like her team had done over the past week.

Lynne Nanton was only a week ago? How is that possible?

No time for your hair Jayne, just get going. The wet look will have to do.

I wonder if they were all pregnant?

Better text John.

Did they all have CC on them?

Come on, answer, John.

Did they all have the same incision?

John answered, good he is heading in.

Better get Vista going on this, need to test for Xenon.

Stop texting me back, John. Just get going!

Who would do this?

Jayne turned on the television.

Surely this will be all over the news, she thought.

To her surprise, the station was currently on commercial break. An advertisement for a new hair loss agent was on, showing men at various stages of balding frolicking happily with their families on a sunny beach.

Don't they look happy? I guess alopecia trumps an international crisis this morning, Jayne thought.

She turned away from the screen to continue her morning ablutions, but couldn't help listening in on the advertisement.

Chromedomera is a revolutionary agent, that sends an antibody to target the hormones known to cause your hair loss. Common side effects include rash, vomiting, arthritis, bleeding from orifices, depression, testicular atrophy, impotence, and stimulation of dormant hair follicles in unsightly places. Ask your doctor if Chromedomera is right for you. Tell your doctor if you have a history of immune diseases, infections, exposure to tuberculosis, bleeding, feeling sad, or ever had to see a doctor in the past before for anything.

Wow, thought Jayne. *Sign me up for that drug!*

As Jayne was about to turn off the television, the chilling sound of: *We now interrupt regular programming to present you this important message,* was being transmitted simultaneously by all the channels.

Every morning news station. Every breakfast television show. Every weather report, every traffic update, every lame chit-chat over who was wearing what on which awards show had stopped. All eyes were being turned to the United Nations.

The President of the United Nations Security Council, Marie-Hélène Beaudry, sat solemnly behind an oak desk to deliver a somber message. This Canadian woman had come a long way from her start in life, in a small suburb of Shawinigan, Québec.

"Dear Citizens of the world. The world is a different place this morning. We are receiving news from at least seventy countries of victims, all women, found dead in what appears to be very similar, if not identical, circumstances. The thought that these are random events was always improbable. I have now received the following message by an untraceable email address, <u>angel111@guerrillamail.com</u>. This email confirms our suspicion. I will now read you this email, with a warning that the message it contains will be unsettling to many of you."

President Beaudry paused to gather herself. She was noticeably shaken by what she was about to read. She cleared her throat, then began.

"The message reads:

President Beaudry. You are now undoubtedly aware of the hundreds of victims that police forces have found overnight. I will get back to honoring these brave soldiers later in my letter.

You are likely scrambling to try to determine exact numbers, because that it was the United Nations is good at: numbers and statistics. Let me clarify this point for you. Eighty-one countries, 111 martyrs. What the United Nations is less good at is action, and this is the purpose of our cause.

President Beaudry, in times like this we need to turn to the only important source of information: The Bible. The Book of Revelations, which predicts the future of mankind, says:

"Babylon the great is fallen. For all nations have drunk of the wine of the wrath of her fornication, and the kings of earth have committed fornication with her, and the merchants of the earth are waxed rich through the abundance of her delicacies.

And the kings of the earth, who have committed fornication and lived deliciously with her, shall bewail her, and lament for her, when they shall see the smoke of her burning.

And a mighty angel took up a stone like a great millstone, and cast it into the sea, saying, Thus with violence shall that great city Babylon be thrown down, and shall be found no more at all. And in her was found the blood prophets, and of saints, and of all that were slain upon the earth."

President Beaudry, Babylon is our planet. The world leaders are the kings of the earth, the organization that you represent. The merchants are the world's industries and people. You have all fornicated with this planet. You have lived deliciously with her, ignoring any consequences to her.

Look around you: temperatures are rising, gas levels are climbing, oceans are rotting, forests are disappearing, weather is chaotic, and animals are dying.

But like teenage boys, you are dilettantes who pretend to care about your planet, pretend to talk to her, but continue your only true desire to fornicate with her.

You will also undoubtedly be focused on who I am. Who I am shouldn't matter. What I stand for should. For now, let's just say I am the mighty angel, here to give you one last chance before your planet is thrown down and burns for eternity.

President Beaudry, these are my initial demands to your organization. In forty days, you will stand in front of the world, and provide explicit policy changes undertaken by ALL the world's countries, including and especially the USA and China, to meet or exceed the Paris agreement targets. This is not new, and long overdue.

Second, will be an update to policies that will drastically change the human arrogance towards their increasing population numbers. Our planet can no longer tolerate increasing population. It has reached its carrying capacity. Yet world leaders have allowed unregulated births. In 2019, you have grown human population by a staggering eighty million humans. And this happens while over one-hundred million children are orphaned on our planet.

The policy is simple: women can have one child of their own. Any further children will need to be adopted through one single planetary agency. You can call it the 'one for you, one for us' policy.

President Beaudry, you will soon find out that all the victims were pregnant women who were contravening the above policy. It is normal for the world to mourn and sympathize with them. Rest assured that they died comfortable, peaceful deaths. But you should not think of them as victims. They are 111 martyrs. They are soldiers in the mighty angel's battle to restore Babylon. Remember them like you remember your fallen soldiers. They have bled for God and His Earth. My martyrs are blessed, as they now sit with Him in the glory of His kingdom. Those who mourn are also blessed, as they will be comforted by the Heavens.

You have forty days, President Beaudry. Should your response be unsatisfactory…"

President Beaudry's lip quivered as she was visibly choking up after reading the troubling message. She took a deep breath and collected herself.

"Should your response be unsatisfactory, project Oasis will be again unleashed, and you will find the blood of 111 new martyrs on your and your fellows fornicators' hands."

President Beaudry put the message aside. She paused, then started to speak, making infrequent eye contact with the camera, "I hope you can understand that given the gravity of the message, and its demands, I cannot officially comment any further at this time. I will convene an urgent meeting of the Security Council. We will proceed with a press conference as soon as possible."

She paused again. This time, she stared directly into the camera.

"President Kennedy famously said, "Our most basic common link is that we all inhabit this small planet. We all breathe the same air. We all cherish our children's future." Perhaps like no other moment in our planet's history, these words ring true. These words must bind us together. Today, we must break down our borders and act like one big country of eight-billion people.

Thank you all. We will speak soon."

3

"I just heard the message from the United Nations on ZDF. Very well written, my friend."

"Thank you, Ruprecht," Soul said. "Everything went as planned with your soldiers?"

"They have all emailed the secure channel. All are reporting comfortable deaths, exactly as Primera had executed. And your soldiers?"

"The same. All report perfect execution."

"What now?" Ruprecht said.

"We wait," Soul said. "No further communication or packages need be sent until President Beaudry delivers her message in forty days."

"Feels strange and difficult to wait now."

"While we wait for the next round of Project Oasis, Project Pander is moving along very well. Do you have plans for March 2020?"

"Not that I know of, Soul. Why?"

"I would like to offer you an all-inclusive trip to La Perla, Puerto Rico."

"That sounds nice, why?"

"Do you remember our last visit with Doctor Leddy in 2018?"

"How can I forget. Seeing the lab would have been exciting enough. But the flight from Katowice to Düsseldorf was the worst flight I have had in my life!"

"Poor Ruprecht, you looked shaken. Don't like flying in thunderstorms?"

"My intestine is still in my throat from the turbulence. My breath stinks like holy scheisse since then!"

Soul laughed. It was a refreshing distraction from this highly charged day.

"It wasn't all bad, though," Ruprecht said. "Ginny. Excuse me, Primera held my hand during the worst moments."

"She is a soothing sight for sure, my friend."

Soul paused, then continued.

"Flight aside, you remember the progress Mikhaël was able to make, now that Hans was on board?"

"I was. The little mice in Phase two, while still tough to look at, were more robust looking, and much less confused. The addition of more amino acids and lactulose seemed to help the little guys significantly."

"Agree. Based on those advancements, Mikhaël has now moved on to Phase three."

"Humans?"

"Yes."

"Why La Perla, Soul?"

"Let's just say that extreme poverty makes a significant amount of money go a lot farther. Easier to keep secrets. Easier to recruit volunteers. Easier to, how would I say it, circumvent the usual research ethics barriers."

"Wow. Do you mean that by April we will have…"?

"Yes. It won't be mice playing in the cages."

"Book my flight. This I have to see."

"With Primera beside you again?"

"Of course."

4

Ginny did manage to settle herself down Sunday morning, enough to drift in and out of very light sleep. At the first indication of sunrise, she headed out of the house to the pharmacy. Jonas was still comatose. He would be for a while. After picking up the pregnancy kit, she made several stops for items of variable urgency to acquire, as though unduly delaying her testing would somehow change the result.

As she returned home two hours later, she settled into the downstairs bathroom for her testing.

"Blue line," Ginny whispered. "I can't believe it, there's a blue line."

Ginny cried. They were not tears of joy.

"I don't want this. Not now, not ever!"

Ginny paced frantically in the small bathroom. Four paces to her right, four paces to her left, repeatedly, thinking.

"Who should I tell? I certainly can't tell my mother. I don't want to tell Jonas yet. I don't want tell anybody."

"Ginny, honey, are you on the phone?" Jonas said, with a gentle knock on the door.

Ginny regrouped and stepped out of the bathroom.

"You look like hell, Ginny. What's wrong? Who are you talking to?"

"I was just reading out loud. Ignore me. You don't look well either, Jonas. Twelve beers got to you?"

"I feel horrible, to be honest. I am never doing that again!"

"Yeah right. Come into the kitchen, I will put on a pot of coffee and make you some toast. That will settle your stomach and head."

5

The Calgary Police Department headquarters was bustling like the opening of a department store on Black Friday. The main phone lines were jammed with calls from the public, media outlets, reporters, and police units from all over the world. This little Canadian city was now in the spotlight. Even its federal Liberal government, who had long ignored the city and its province, was now paying attention.

"I need our communications team in here, now!" shouted Police Chief James Hunter. "This is a nightmare! We look like we have never done this before!"

"But sir, we never have done this before!" answered a junior Constable who was now assigned to phone duties.

"Shut up, Constable. Just answer the God damn phones!"

As the head of communications, Georgette Brandle, and her two assistants jogged up the stairs to the third floor, the Police Chief barked orders at them.

"OK, listen, Georgy. 9-1-1 calls are still 9-1-1 calls, and they take priority. Anything else that looks like the public, don't answer. Granny will have to call 9-1-1 if kitty won't come down from the tree. Maybe the fire department can hold off on shaving their oversensitive faces today and help us out. Anything from the media needs to be deflected. Write up a standard statement, like "Fuck off, we are busy, and the Police Chief will address all of you when he can." Or something like that. Maybe you can leave out the "Fuck off" part.

Anything from nosy police stations not currently involved in one of these murder investigations, you can deflect as well. Tell them to listen to the press conference. You can include the "Fuck off" part with them. Critical in this is that calls from a credible investigative unit, whether INTERPOL, FBI, DSGE, MI6, or local city police investigating a similar murder get access to us. Once you have verified their credentials, you need to patch them through to someone who knows what is going on with our investigation."

By now, the entire department had gathered to the third-floor central area where the Police Chief was directing the team. The Police Chief was still shouting, not only because he was agitated and wanted to promote his authority, but to be heard above the symphony of ringing phones.

"Chandler, Hunter, Lake, Lahr. You are now our official spokespeople on this matter. But only to credible, verified agencies. If you don't have a private office, you now do. If you have a private office and you aren't named

Chandler, Hunter, Lake, Lahr, well you don't have one until this dies down. Welcome to the cubicle world."

Grumbles were heard from the crowd.

"Stop your whining. Would you prefer being on a metal gurney with your carotid slashed? We have a serious issue here. Get your ass in a cubicle and try to be helpful. That is how I started. It's good for you. Builds character."

The Police Chief turned to Georgy Brandle.

"Georgy, once you have verified who we are talking to, you patch them through in the order that I discussed. Did you get that. It's…"

"Yes. Chandler, Hunter, Lake, Lahr. Got it. By Hunter, you mean John?"

"Yes, John. But that is a good point. Chandler, you will need to fill me in so I can be a part of this team, and not sound like a retard when I talk to important folks. I will start by joining in on as many calls as possible. You now have an office buddy, Chandler."

"Great, sir," Jayne said.

"OK, let's go. Wait, one more thing. We need to get Vista out of his dungeon and into one of these offices. He needs to be available to talk to his nerdy friends around the world. Just make sure het gets an office that is well aerated."

The Police Chief did not mean to ridicule his only Pathologist in public. Jayne knew her boss well enough to read his facial expression.

"Good call, Chief," Jayne said. "Doctor Vista gets very warm easily and needs a cool breeze at all times."

As the crowd dispersed, and they headed into their respective offices, or for some, cubicles, the Police Chief whispered to Jayne.

"Thanks, Detective. I didn't mean to publicly humiliate Vista. But you know what I mean."

"I certainly do, Jim," Jayne said.

"He is a great at what he does, but it would be nice if he got over his soap and water allergy!"

"Agreed, Jim," Jayne said, laughing. "Let's roll up our sleeves. It's going to be a long one!"

6

"Good morning, Soul," Ginny said. "I just saw your message on the news. This is really happening!"

"It is, Primera," Soul said. "You should feel very proud of your key role in this."

"I am, Soul, I am. I feel solidly entrenched in the mission and satisfied with my place on the team. Somehow, it feels like decades and minutes since we first met in Bonn."

"That is true, Primera. I am happy to hear you are pleased and have no lingering doubts."

"None, Soul. I am so grateful for what you have given me."

"Clarity?" Soul said.

"Clarity and peace," Ginny said.

"Thank you for the call, Primera. I must run to take another call from a team member. Was there anything else you wanted to discuss with me?"

Ginny hesitated. She had wanted to discuss her news, but at that moment she thought twice about starting a discussion about her pregnancy.

"There was but it slipped my mind. I think maybe I wanted to ask you about Project Pander."

"There is great news on that front as well, Primera. We should discuss that in detail on another day."

"Sounds good. Will talk to you soon, Soul. 14U14US, always.

"Always, Primera. Thank you for the call, it's nice to hear your voice."

7

It was a quiet day at the clinic. The gravity of the events and impact of Soul's statement had led to many cancellations from shocked, and in the case of a fertility clinic, frightened patients. Patients who had time-sensitive procedures such as egg retrievals and implantations showed up, questioning whether they should go through with the procedures.

Soul's statement was already having a major impact.

For some, the statement raised safety concerns. For others, it raised questions about the Earth's population and their moral obligation to think twice about a larger family.

For others, it raised economic concerns. "This guy is bad for business," Northgate said. "He seems obsessed with fornication. I would like to fornicate a metal rod up his ass! This is ridiculous!"

The events monopolized almost every conversation around the world. The Conception Opportunities clinic was no different. There was occasionally room, with all the down time, to rehash the memories, and in the case of some, absent memories, of the wild Saturday night affair.

"That was the best party ever!" said Nurse Sandy. "Too bad you missed it, Louise."

"I wasn't that drunk, Sandy," said Louise. "I remember clearly enough your great escape with Detective John Hunter. Strictly business of course? Rehashing the evidence?"

Sandy laughed. "Louise, let's just say that I had a close examination of the entire body of evidence. It was both exhilarating and illuminating!"

"I am jealous, Sandy," said Louise. "He is a real cutie. Some of us ended the evening with yet another round of self-interrogation. In the case of Sandy, the Detective sliced her open with something way nicer than a scalpel!"

A raucous laugh from the group echoed in the almost empty clinic. Louise may be a little too wild at parties, but she always gathered a crowd around her. And she rarely disappointed.

"Inappropriate, Louise," Sandy said, smiling, "completely inappropriate. Let's get back to work, everybody."

8

Ginny had spent most of the Monday alone in her ultrasound room.

She furiously scanned comments from social media following the worldwide release of Soul's manifesto. The opinions were of course wide ranging.

"Who is this madman?"

"Is this the second coming of Jesus Christ?"

"This group has to be stopped!"

"It's about time someone demands action."

"I think this makes a lot of sense."

It does make a lot of sense, Ginny thought. *14U14US.*

The internet was buzzing with information leaked from police sources about the state of the body. Already, rumors were circulating about the consistent findings of a left carotid incision and the mysterious CC letters on the victims' abdomens.

"CC: Christ coming?"

"CC: Carotid cutter?"

"CC: Contrived cooling?"

"Fools. It's in the United Nations message. Carrying Capacity."

You have got them talking, Soul, Ginny thought. *Well done.*

Ginny looked around the room at the equipment.

OK, Ginny. You have all this time today. About five weeks into this pregnancy. Should I scan for the little guy?

Ginny had come to terms with the pregnancy, and was even allowing herself to get excited, mostly for Jonas.

I do get one for me. This will be the one.

After locking the door, she hopped on the bed, removed her top, and lowered her hospital greens to her pubic bone.

This might be a little tricky. Never done this before. Might be a little early to see the yolk sac. Usually visible at six weeks for sure. But Ginny Fremlin is the best in the business.

Ginny applied the ultrasound gel then began to run the probe. After a few iterations across her lower abdomen, she saw something that brought a tear to her eye.

Oh my God. There it is. A yolk sac. This is really happening, Ginny!

With a quick clockwise turn and increased pressure on the probe, Ginny was able to better see the entirety of her uterus.

What she saw brought tears pouring down her face. Her neck hairs were standing on end. The nausea which had settled returned with a vengeance.

No, it can't be. A second yolk sac!

Ginny rubbed her face and eyes, cleared her mind, and restarted, trying to pretend she was objectively scanning a random person.

No doubt about it, Ginny. Two sacs. Fuck no!

Ginny dropped the probe, which now dangled loosely off the stretcher. She stared blankly at the wall in front of her, trying to process what she had just witnessed inside of her.

CHAPTER 15

A PHILOSOPHICAL DEBATE

1

Ginny did not tell anyone about her pregnancy. Two weeks ago, she had carried out another self ultrasound that had confirmed two fetal heart beats. Ginny knew very well that once an ultrasound detects a heartbeat, a miscarriage is very uncommon. She was close to ten weeks into her pregnancy, and six weeks away from being able to definitively declare her babies' gender. Her intuition, helped by her excellent ultrasound skills, was quite certain that she was carrying two baby boys.

Ginny was clear on several fronts.

She was clear that she would continue the pregnancy.

She was clear that she would not tell anyone, including Jonas, until she absolutely had to.

She was clear that she had to carry on with her mission.

She was clear that the team's mission was the true path.

She was not clear, however, on who should be her next target.

2

"Two days away from the second wave of targets, my friend," Soul said.

"We are ready," Ruprecht said. "The Xenon packages have been delivered to our soldiers. They were once again delivered in a gift box, all under the disguise of team jersey presents."

"A brilliant plan," Soul said. "Discretion is of paramount importance. The soldiers are all still as firmly resolved to the cause?"

"They are," Ruprecht said.

"Did you remind your soldiers of the escape plan?"

"I did, Soul. They are all aware, and willing to ingest the suicide pill if need be."

"As are mine, Ruprecht. Including Primera. She is fully willing to die for our cause."

"Let's hope it doesn't come to that," Ruprecht said.

"We will talk soon. I will let you know when we officially are set to execute our successful plan."

"Yes, we will talk soon. Success is key, Soul, but remember, it's just life and death after all."

Soul was waiting for the message from the United Nations. He was optimistic that progress would have been made, but not in the desired and necessary magnitude. The message from the Security Council would be couched in multiple vague terms such as "We have formed groups looking into", "We are exploring", "We have started the process", "We need more time".

Time was not on the group's side. Time was not on the planet's side. Action must be clear, decisive and unbending.

Soul was certainly going to be clear, decisive and unbending.

3

Ginny sat alone on a sub-zero and dark night, on her favorite park bench overlooking the bright lights of downtown Calgary. Ironically, her favorite bench was near the South Mountain curling club, where Lynne Nanton had come into her life less than two months ago. A few weeks ago. Weeks that simultaneously felt like a few short weeks, and the longest weeks of her life.

Ginny had long johns underneath her track pants, and a turtleneck covered by a sweatshirt and parka. These layers were all wrapped in the same brand of sleeping bag that had covered Gemma Augustine at the end of her life. Thoughts were racing through her mind at fervent speed, trying desperately to be guided towards the correct decision.

Ginny had lived her life fervently adherent to two guiding principles. The first was consistency.

"Consistency is better than excellence" is a motto she had heard from a Calgary Nephrologist, Dr. Kevin McLaughlin, when he gave her class a session on kidney ultrasounds. Dr. McLaughlin may not have been as famous as some of her favorite philosophers, but was equally as smart and wise.

Ginny had taken those statements to heart in many aspects of her life. She tried at all turns to be consistent in her effort for her sports teams, consistent in her personal relationships, consistent in her dealings with patients, and consistent in her diligent attention to every ultrasound she performed.

14U14US. I have lived by this statement for two years. I believe wholeheartedly in what it says. I believe that it is a necessary step for our planet, and for the children of the world.

If I am to be consistent with this, shouldn't I be the next target?

The second principle was loyalty. This was something she had felt since she was a little girl. She was a loyal friend, a loyal teammate, a loyal community player. This guiding principle had been reinforced by her favorite philosopher: Kong Qiu, better known as Confucius, whose wisdom is as true today as it was in China, five-hundred years before Christ was born.

Loyalty, faithfulness, sincerity. These were crucial to Confucius' thoughts and existence. These values were how humans could transform themselves and society.

Confucius said, "Only he who is possessed of the most complete sincerity that can exist under Heaven, can transform."

This whole project was about transforming. Soul and Ruprecht have been sincere to this project. As have I. How can I abandon that sincerity now and not complete the journey by being a victim myself?

4

Ginny was in the process of unwrapping her sleeping bag and getting up from the park bench when thoughts crept into her head and stopped her. She sat down again to rethink her dilemma.

I have already accomplished so much with this project. I started all of this. I am Primera for God's sake! Why can't I just enjoy my newfound family with Jonas? Soul and Ruprecht would understand. Maybe. But maybe I shouldn't care what they think?

Ginny's thoughts turned to John Stuart Mill's description of two major desires in life: the desire to fulfill a sense of duty, and the desire that will give us pleasure.

Why do I have to be a martyr? Would I be doing this just to fulfill a sense of duty to Soul? I have already done more than what he could expect from any other woman. Why can't I just ride off in the sunset and enjoy the pleasures that life has to offer?

She had once again bundled herself into the sleeping bag and was staring at the red glow from the Calgary Tower lights.

Certainty is more pleasant than doubt. Am I just deciding to follow my convictions because I don't want to shed doubt on my lifetime convictions of consistency and loyalty? Is the certainty of following my convictions the path of least resistance?

Ginny looked up at the starry sky, searching for an answer.

Where are you right now, God? Do you even exist? Or have I just been programmed to believe your existence by religion and the great philosophers? Is my belief in You just a low-risk, rational human choice based purely on playing the better odds of an afterlife?

Ginny continued to set her sights on all four quadrants of the beautifully lit heavens.

I don't feel you right now, God. I don't hear you. Things that are exterior to our minds, like You, can't be known. Nietzsche says that if You can't be known, then you are dead! Are you really dead, God?

If there is no God, there is certainly no angel from the east. If there is no angel from the east, why am I following this man Soul to my death? Why don't I just listen to Nietzsche, and stop putting value to a life to come, at the expense of this one?

5

As usual, Detective Sargeant Jayne Chandler was the last to leave the police station. On this night, she was not alone in the third-floor offices. John Hunter knocked on her door as he was getting ready to leave.

"Jayne, I am leaving," John said. "You look exhausted. Come with me, you need a break."

Jayne realized that John was right.

"Yep. Nothing more I can do here tonight. Let me get my coat and I will walk with you to the parking lot."

As they walked down the stairs and to their cars, Jayne discussed the details of their cases, her communication with the rest of the police agencies, and the lack of progress they had made in their investigations.

"Jayne, I think you need a night out," John said.

"Probably, but I think I am too tired John. Thanks though."

"Come on, Jayne. Nobody is too tired for a little bit of Julius Marpole's accordion music. It will re-energize you for sure!"

"You're going to St-Hilda's tonight?"

"You bet."

"Alone?"

"No, Sandy is coming, and she is bringing a whole group of her friends, guys and girls."

The look on Jayne's face made it clear what she was thinking.

"Sorry, Jayne, I don't think Julian will be there. I saw you walk away with him at the party."

"He's a prick," Jayne said. "Or at least might be. I am really not sure. Either way, nothing happened: he is a suspect in a murder investigation. As is Nurse Sandy, by the way!"

"I'm sorry, Jayne, I never thought of that. I should have waited until this is all over, it just never crossed my mind that Sandy was still on our list of..."

"She isn't a suspect, John. Just pulling your chain. Don't worry about it. If Nurse Sandy is our murderer, then I just flat out give up!"

"For what it's worth, and I never thought I would say this, but I am just as unsure about Northgate as you are. Truth be told, he is starting to grow on me a little bit. The arrogant prick façade threw me off at first, but I think that's what it is. A façade. Deep down I think he is a decent guy. Maybe Sandy will have some insight. Come with me."

John grabbed both of Jayne's hands and gently pulled her arms as he repeated several times, "Come with me!"

Jayne eventually laughed and caved to the request.

"Stop! You are a bully. OK, let's go. But I do need to clean up a little."

"Great! I will swing by your place in an hour. We can share an UBER on the way home."

Jayne got into her car and headed home. She was still amazed about how first impressions had let her down about several people during this investigation, most notably her now cherished partner John Hunter.

6

Ginny sat back on her bench. Her thoughts were still whirling in her brain. Still unsure of her decision, she did what she had done many times in her life: she shut her brain off, other than her visual pathways. Her eyes took in all the beauty around her. The full moon, the bright stars, the snow-covered trees, the downtown lights, the cool wind, the pure snow, the white hares, the symmetric row of houses. It was a perfect blend of nature and human activity.

This can't be random. Something must control this. God is here. I feel it. I have always felt it. Look at all this beauty, all intertwined. Humans, animals, plants, air, sky, all bound together by one eternal presence in the universe. Maybe Rumi was right: when I cease to exist in one form, I will resurface in another way. That is all fine with me. It is all filled with beauty.

Ginny was breathing calmly and deeply now. The same breathing pattern that had been inspired many times by Soul Fernandez.

I have felt it with every strand of my intuition. Just like painters create works of beauty then imprint their signature, God creates beauty and leaves His signature in our innate thoughts. I have also felt it with all the connections in my rational brain. We know God exists just by the fact that we think about Him. Seems simplistic. But it's not. It's Aristotle's perfect syllogism. If A leads to B, and B leads to C, then A must lead to C.

Ginny brought her feet up to the bench, and curled herself into a ball, snuggled by the warmth of the sleeping bag. She now felt hugged by a divine presence.

I think, therefore I am. I am, because God exists. And so: I think, because God exists.

Tears flowed down her cheeks as she realized the path that was before her. As the tears flowed to her lips, her tongue reached out and trapped them in her mouth. These tears tasted differently. They tasted divine.

As Ginny drank, she felt an overwhelming feeling of balance and serenity.

God, I asked for your help, and you bring me water. Water. The essence of life. The omnipresent substance described by Thales, the father of Philosophy.

These tears taste like wine. It's now gone full circle. From Philosophy to the Scriptures. From the Scriptures to the virtuous angel, Soul Fernandez.

God, thank you for giving me absolute clarity. I am now righteous, and will be blessed by the kingdom of Heaven.

Ginny's face was enlightened with the type of smile one only gets from a profound realization. She got up again from the park bench. Only this time, there was no going back.

CHAPTER 16

THE AGREEMENT

1

The former President of the United Nations Security Council, Marie-Hélène Beaudry, was ready to deliver her speech. She stood confidently at the podium of the United Nations General Assembly. The Assembly was teaming with delegates from all 193 United Countries, and reporters from the world's major news agencies.

"Ladies and gentlemen, if I could have your attention please."

Marie-Hélène Beaudry stood motionless as the room settled.

"Thank you. I will proceed to read my message. My hope is that it will lead to communication and open dialogue with those behind the murders six weeks ago, at which point I will be happy to organize a press conference in a more suitable location."

Marie-Hélène Beaudry cleared her throat and proceeded to read her statement.

"Dear Citizens of the world. I stand here as the former President of the United Nations Security Council. The position of President rotates on a monthly basis. However, as I was the initial point of contact with the perpetrators, and hope that I will continue to be, the Council decided that I should represent them here today.

Six weeks ago, a day now known as December-111, the world woke up to hear of 111 murders. 111 murders of innocent women from a total of eighty-one countries. To this day, none of these crimes have been solved, despite the intense work from police forces and agencies from around the globe. I would like to take this opportunity to thank the men and women who tirelessly work to solve these and unfortunately many other heinous crimes. The men and women who protect our existence and way of living.

I would also like to take this opportunity to remember the 111 victims. We think of you, we pray for you, and hope that the global unity displayed since these events transmits peace and love to your families and friends. I would now ask that everyone in this room, and anyone listening across the world, bow their heads, place their right hand towards their hearts, and remember the victims in a minute of silence."

The room fell deathly silent. Even the sound of this many people breathing was not heard. Everyone in the room happily acquiesced to the request. Everyone except one captivated spectator in the second-floor gallery, who took this opportunity to catch a glimpse of those who were in attendance.

"Thank you. You will remember that the Security Council received demands, via encrypted email, relating to updates and policy changes in our climate change fight. The United Nations has been a leading organization in this battle and will continue to be moving forward. A full, detailed report will be made available to all of you later today, but I am happy to report that eight of our 193 countries are currently meeting Paris agreement targets, and another thirteen will achieve the goals by the end of 2020. By 2025, 109 countries will meet the targets, with 191 countries meeting them by the date that was set in Paris: 2030. Two countries are currently falling behind the target, but plans are underway to rectify this situation.

The second part of the demands dealt with policies surrounding population control. As you can understand, these are not easy issues to tackle in such a short period of time. However, I am happy to report that talks have been very encouraging regarding a unified vision and policy regarding capping family size, promoting adoption, including a worldwide adoption agency to streamline this important process.

To the person, or should I say persons, behind December-111, I say this. Your demands are being taken very seriously. The United Nations is committed to halting climate change and saving our planet. We share the same views. We do not share the same morals, however. Violence is never the way. Killing is the never the way.

Let us come to a peaceful conclusion that will satisfy us all. We just need a little bit more time."

As she finished that sentence, Marie-Hélène Beaudry was startled by the vibration of the Apple watch on her left hand. An email was coming in.

The distraction was obvious to the audience. They could tell something was distracting madame Beaudry.

The timing was too coincidental to ignore. As she reached to her watch, she saw that the message was coming from the same angel address.

Looking down, she read the brief email in her head.

Not good enough, madame Beaudry. You should stop talking and start warning your police agencies.

Marie-Hélène Beaudry looked up to the crowd with an expression of horror. If this was her best effort at a poker face, it was not good at all.

The room was now buzzing with excited and worried discussion.

"I am sorry, everyone. I must end this meeting. I will address the media later, but for now I will ask that all media equipment, including cameras, phones and recorders, be turned off. Please do this immediately. Security, please ensure that this is done."

Security personnel responded rapidly, filing through the media area, asking in less than polite fashion that madame Beaudry's order be followed. Understanding the potential gravity of the situation, and the need for continued unison, the media representatives followed the order without protest.

"Thank you, everyone, and again my apologies for the chaos. Country representatives on the main floor can stay, but I will ask everyone else, including the media, to please exit the room at once."

Marie-Hélène Beaudry saw the looks of fear and horror starting back at her.

"The ushers will escort you out, calmly. Nobody here is in immediate danger. I repeat, nobody here is in immediate danger. But I have received a concerning message that the Security Council will have to address urgently. Please trust that I cannot share it with you now, but will communicate with you at the earliest possible opportunity."

The noise from the room had reached deafening levels. Doors had swung open. Instructions from security and ushers were bellowing. Agitated conversations abounded from all corners of the room. Reporters were shouting "Madame Beaudry, madame Beaudry!"

The exit of the room proceeded in a remarkably ordered fashion. The throngs of visitors were leaving the headquarters peacefully and quietly. As the last people cleared the room, Marie-Hélène Beaudry's phone vibrated again. Another email.

Nobody HERE is in immediate danger. Not exactly accurate without the word HERE, is it madame *Beaudry?*

Marie-Hélène Beaudry froze again, staring at her watch. She was now surrounded by fellow members of the Security Council.

"Are you OK, Marie-Hélène? You don't look well. Are you in danger? Are we?"

"Not here. Not right now. I will explain…"

Marie-Hélène Beaudry looked up at the now empty balconies.

"Holy shit, he was here?"

"Who?" said a colleague.

"The guy behind this. He was here. How else would he know that I told everyone here they were not in danger? All the media equipment was turned off. Get me the head of security, or the police, or the FBI…Just get me someone God damn it!"

2

"Did you see her face?" Jayne said. "She read something that bothered her. That's not good, Jim."

Police Chief James Hunter was pacing around the lunchroom, which had filled with onlookers hopeful for a peaceful resolution to this crisis.

"OK, folks, these guys are going to strike again. No telling if this time it will be even more violent. I can't imagine it would be tonight, but we need to be ready. For the next seventy-two hours, this department will be on high alert. Every woman, man, dog who is not dead or hospitalized needs to be available to us sixteen hours a day. I don't care how much this costs us. Any task that is not life threatening goes on the back burner. For the next three days, I don't give a shit about speeding in a thirty zone, texting while driving, or jaywalking. Priority is to this portfolio."

"Anything you want us to communicate to the public, boss?" Georgy Brandle said.

The Police Chief hesitated.

"Only that we are taking this matter with the utmost seriousness. We will be looking and will be seen. We will hit the streets with cops flying, walking, biking, driving, crawling on their hands and knees if need be. Every security camera and satellite that we have at our disposal will be on and monitored."

Georgy nodded as she wrote feverishly.

"The eyes of the world are on Calgary, everyone. Time to shine. Let's show them what we have been well trained to do."

The group scattered, buoyed by the energetic words of Police Chief James Hunter.

"Thanks, Jayne. All eyes on us. Feels like the 1988 Olympics again."

"I wasn't born, but I will take your word for it, Jim."

"Wish I was watching Eddie the Eagle soar today instead of our entire fleet of surveillance helicopters."

"Yes, would have been something to be there," Jayne said. "Wish I could have seen it."

"It was an amazing experience. Would have been nice to repeat it in 2026. Have a good day, Detective. Bring me back a killer."

"Along the lines of finding the killer, Jim, I was hoping you would allow me to investigate a lead that is outside of our jurisdiction."

"How far outside?"

"Munich, Germany?"

"What are you talking about, Jayne?"

"Doctor Vista confirmed that the anesthetic agent used in the murders was Xenon. He also found that an unusual amount of Xenon had recently been shipped to the BMW headquarters in Munich. Might be because they are making it a standard feature in their headlights, but seems to me too much of a coincidence to ignore."

"I agree, but not up to you to investigate. Let the local authorities know. I can't lose you at this point, not for a minute. And don't look at me that way. That's an order, Detective, and I am not in the mood right now to have my orders questioned!"

As the Police Chief turned and walked away, Jayne darted towards her office.

"Woah, there, Jayne," John said, racing after her, "are you training for Olympic race walking? If you are, I highly recommend against it. It looks ridiculous. I mean, what are they doing? Just get into a light jog while you are there!"

"We need to pursue this Xenon angle in Munich. I think we should be doing it. It's our case!"

"Then let's go!" John said.

"The Police Chief, in his infinite wisdom, has ordered me not to. He wants me to turn it over to the German police. Fuck him, I am going to go anyways. I'll take the redeye on my own dime. He can't tell me what to do on my weekends!"

"Detective Chandler. How you have changed! Scorning authority, ignoring direct orders! This may cost you your promotion to Lieutenant!"

"I don't care, John. We need to find these pricks. And who cares about promotion. A wise person once taught me to be careful about 'P's like position, power and prestige. There is more to life than the title before your name."

John Hunter was speechless. The only reaction he could muster was a proud smile.

3

"Settle down, Marie-Hélène, settle down," Marie Meadows said. "Come with me for a minute."

Marie-Hélène Beaudry and the Secretary of the United Nations Affairs Division walked down the hallway, turned left, and hurried into an empty meeting room.

"We knew this was coming, Marie-Hélène. This is good. Soul and his team made sure to take out a dozen relatives and friends of key heads of states. I have been getting calls day and night since this started, frantically asking me to influence the Security Council. I think we are there, Marie-Hélène. The Security Council will support this. Especially when the next wave hits even closer to home for these politicians. We get a lot more done when important leaders have skin in the game."

"I don't know about this guy Soul Fernandez," Marie-Hélène said. "I have never met him, but he seems a little creepy and narcissistic to me. But I do believe in what you are doing. What WE are doing. It still makes it unsettling when events are happening this quickly and lives are being lost."

"Think about all the lives that will be lost if we don't succeed, Marie-Hélène. We have to stay strong and see this through. But when we go back out there, it is totally normal for us to show the outside world a rattled side. Appearing calm with everything happening around us would look strange."

"I understand, Marie," Marie-Hélène said. "Let's head back out there. We have work to do to get this to the finish line."

4

Ginny stared at the Xenon package on the patient stretcher beside her ultrasound equipment. Today was the day for phase two of the plan. Yesterday's United

Nations speech was couched in vague terms, just as Soul had predicted. And so, the plan was initiated.

Ginny had thought of hundreds of different places to do this. This one was harder to plan than the other two. Any public place would be more difficult today with the increased police surveillance. She did not want Jonas to find her at home.

Last thing Jonas needs is to be grieving me and having to clean up my mess!

She had made herself laugh at this thought. She was about to leave this Earth, and had managed to consider housecleaning issues. Ginny had taken this thought as a good sign. A sign of her comfort with the decision. A decision that had included all the people in her life that she admired, and had made her who she truly was.

The clinic seemed the perfect place to do this. It felt like the right place. The place that was bringing children, too many children, into the world, would be the site of her well-planned departure. The choice made for a surreal day of work today. Couple after couple streaming in, as usual worried about a million things. Today these couples had the additional worry of a killer "out there". Only little did they know that the killer was actually "in there".

The room that was giving couples reassurance of bringing children into this world, would be the same room giving Ginny the reassurance that the correct path was to take her children to another world.

The clinic space would also help with the additional technical difficulties to consider. She would have to carefully plan her steps to mimic the death of Lynne and Gemma. These technical challenges would best be addressed in a heated environment, with her tools immediately accessible.

Ginny had to resist the temptation of extended farewells to the clinic staff as they were leaving. She had told them that her classes were demanding additional work that would best be done with her equipment handy.

As she sat alone in her room, Ginny went over the plan once again.

You will douse the rag with Xenon. You will then lie back on the stretcher, with the rag in your left hand and the scalpel in the right. Lynne and Gemma seemed to need about twenty seconds of inspiration to be fully out. After eight seconds, I will grab the scalpel and do the deed. I may feel a bit of pain, but it shouldn't be long.

The noise of a door slamming startled Ginny away from her thoughts. She rushed out her door, and yelled down the hallway. "Hello, is anybody there?"

There was no answer. The clinic was completely dark and silent.

Must have been the last of the cleaning staff.

Ginny looked around her ultrasound room one last time. She took a deep breath. Just as she had done many times in her competitive sports, an intensely focused look had taken over her face.

Ginny no more. Welcome back, Primera.

Primera sat on the edge of the stretcher. Her gloved hands reached for the sharpie on the desk. She scratched out the CC letters over her now showing abdomen.

Maybe it was the feel of her belly. Perhaps it was the heightened significance of the CC letters over her two babies. But something jarred her out of Primera mode and back to Ginny.

Should I see them one more time to say goodbye?

Ginny grabbed some gel and as she had done thousands of time, she ran the probe over her abdomen.

There you are little guys. You are so cute! I would have loved to play shinny on an outdoor rink, race you to the next stop sign, or wrestle with you on our basement floor. But Charles and Codey, momma is taking you on a big trip, now. We're going somewhere nicer, to make this world a better place. I love you. See you soon.

After wiping her tears with her forearms, Ginny placed the equipment on her desk. She doused the rag with Xenon, and lay back on the stretcher.

Taking big breaths into the rag, she started to count her last seconds in her head.

This stuff works fast.

Five. Breath. *Six.* Breath. *Seven.* Breath. *Eight.* Breath.

Wait. Wait. All my stuff will be lying around. How did I not think of that?

Ginny tried to remove the rag from her mouth. She felt a resistance over her mouth and right hand.

"I will take care of everything, Primera. Just keep breathing."

Ginny kept breathing. She had stopped counting. She felt weightless. She was drifting away. She desperately looked up to see the source of the resistance.

Soul? Is that you? Am I dreaming?

"Sleep, Primera. Sleep. You have been a good soldier. The angel will take care of you."

The light of the ultrasound room was now replaced by a new light. Something completely unfamiliar to Ginny. It was a glow that could not be man-made.

Everything is good now, little guys. Buckle up for take-off.

As Ginny Fremlin drifted away, the scalpel was taken from her right hand. In one smooth cut, her left carotid was severed.

Ginny, Charlie and Codey had left this world.

"You were the BEST of soldiers. I will see you soon, my sweet Primera."

The angel tenderly kissed Ginny's forehead and proceeded to carefully cover her up. After emptying the room of all incriminating material, the angel was gone. As swiftly and mysteriously as he had arrived.

5

Detective Chandler put down her phone, grabbed her car keys and raced into the station. Another early morning. Another startling early morning phone call. She rapidly headed to John Hunter's office.

"Another body has been found, Hunter," Jayne said. "Guess where."

"Our dead body tour has taken us to a church parking lot and curling rink," John said. "I don't know. Can I try bowling alley?"

Jayne was not in the mood to mimic John's laughter.

"It's in the Conception Opportunities clinic."

John's expression changed immediately.

"Is it…"

"I don't know, John. Isabella and Michael are on site. They didn't give me a name. It's another visibly pregnant woman. That is all I know. Let's get going."

John's first emotion was great relief. He had not yet heard from Sandy this morning. Since they started dating, he had become accustomed to an early morning text from her. It was the best way to start his day. Sandy could not be pregnant. John's mother's beliefs had permanently influenced his approach to pre-marital relations.

His second emotion was concern that for the first time in his Detective career, he would have met the victim beforehand. He was not certain he was prepared for that experience.

John and Jayne did not exchange much communication on the way to the clinic.

"Do you at least know if she works there?" John said.

"I don't know that either. I suspect yes, by the tone of Isabella's voice."

6

Marie Meadows was racing through the United Nations headquarters building to the Security Council's private meeting room. Marie-Hélène Beaudry was receiving calls from all over the world, with the news of another wave of murders. The pattern seemed very similar to the events of eight weeks ago.

As she approached the meeting room door, she was stopped by two hulky security guards. They had converged from opposite sides of the door to intercept Marie as she reached for the handle. The most imposing of the two security guards blocked the access to the door with his tree-trunk sized right arm. Meanwhile, his left hand had reached over to inspect her badge.

"I'm sorry, ma'am," said the guard in a deep, menacing voice. "They specifically said that no one can interrupt them."

"But I have the guy on the phone," said Marie.

"Which guy?" said the second guard, who had a surprisingly high voice for someone of his physical stature.

"THE guy. The guy behind all of this. I have to go talk to madame Beaudry."

"Yes, you do," said the first guard. "I will walk you in."

7

As they approached the building, Jayne and John were greeted by Inspector Isabella Lake and Captain Michael Lahr. Jayne could see that the clinic staff had been quarantined in the front lobby.

"Are they all waiting there for us?" Jayne asked.

"I kept them there, away from the body, thinking you would want to question them," Isabella said. "I should really credit Nurse Stubley. She had taken control of the situation and was already gathering the staff when we arrived. She strikes me as someone you would want around when the 'you know what' is flying around!"

Jayne and John looked at each other, regretful of their previous behavior with Nurse Stubley.

"Have you talked to any of them?" Jayne said.

"Just the one who found Ginny."

From the stunned look on their faces, Isabella realized that she had not told Jayne or John the identity of the victim.

"I'm sorry, I forgot to tell you over the phone. You know all these people well, now. It's Ginny Fremlin, the ultrasound technician. She was found in her ultrasound room this morning."

As Jayne and John opened the doors, the already quiet group became silent. They turned their full attention towards the two Detectives, who now felt as familiar to them as the rest of the clinic staff.

"I'm very sorry to greet you like this," Jayne said. "The previous two victims hit close to home but this one hurts even more. Ginny was a great woman, and a key member of your team. We won't be interrogating anyone today. If it's OK with Doctor Northgate, I would suggest you all head home. We will be in touch with you tomorrow."

Julian Northgate walked up to the front of the group, right beside Jayne. "I agree with the Detective. We will cancel clinic today. I will stay here to talk to any of the patients that arrive. Doctor Richmond and I will be here this afternoon for the retrievals and transfers."

He stood and stared out at the gathered crowd. He wanted to say more, but wasn't sure he would be able to get through it. He decided that he had to try.

"We would all agree that the best part of our work are the colleagues around us. Today, we lost a key member of our team. A key member of our family, I should say. Ginny was of course a great ultrasonographer. But she was way more than that to us. She was kind, diligent, fiercely loyal, and deeply intellectual. I will miss her reassuring presence, her warm smile, and most of all our lunchtime philosophical discussions about the world around us. Stay as long as you need, get some hugs and love from the rest of our family, then please head home to be with your other friends and family. We spend our lives looking after others. Now is the time to look out for ourselves, individually and as a group. Thanks, all."

Nurse Sandy was the first to break out of the group and approach Julian with a warm hug.

"Thanks, Julian, beautiful words. You will need help this afternoon. I am fine to stay. I would rather be here anyways."

"Thanks, Sandy," Julian said. "You are the best. A gift to this clinic."

As Nurse Sandy walked over to John, another person had made her way to Julian.

"Nice speech, Doctor," Jayne said. "You never cease to show us a new side of yourself. It was heartwarming. The staff needed to hear those words."

"Thanks, Jayne. Listen…"

"Nothing needs to be said right now, Julian. Maybe we can be in touch when the dust settles on this whole thing?"

"I would like that," Julian said.

Jayne hugged Julian, then got right back into her Detective mode.

"Now on to a murder investigation," Jayne said.

"You have to get this guy, Jayne," Julian said.

"I know, I know. Bad for business."

"This time that had not crossed my mind. This has become personal now. Ginny deserves to look down and see her killer behind bars."

"I will do my best."

Jayne took one more look around the room, then signalled to John to follow her down the hall. As she made her way to the ultrasound room she reached out and softly put her hand on Louise Agat's shoulder. Louise was sitting, arms crossed across her knees, with her forehead resting on her hands. Jayne did not need to ask who had found the body: Louise's face told her all she needed to know. Jayne started to speak but decided that her warm touch said everything. At some point, she would need to talk to Louise, but this was not the time. Knowing Isabella Lake, the details of the horrifying discovery had surely already been deposed.

8

"Madame Beaudry," Marie Meadows said, as she barged into the room, already well ahead of the security guard. "He is on line three. He wants to talk to you. He wants to talk to all of you."

"You mean."

"Yes, madame Beaudry. The Angel."

"The Angel 'mon cul'! You mean the devil. Put him on."

Marie Meadows was about to patch Soul Fernandez into the Security Council room when she was interrupted by Marie-Hélène Beaudry.

"Wait!" said Beaudry, "Can you trace this?"

"That will be tough. He is on a burner phone."

"Burner? What do you mean Marie?"

"Disposable. We can trace it, but it takes our nerds a little longer."

"How long?"

"You have to keep him on the line for a minimum of three minutes. Probably no more than five minutes. It varies."

"Minimum. Probably. Varies. Can't you get a little more precise in your language, Marie?"

"I will let you know when we have him. FOR SURE!"

Marie-Hélène Beaudry picked up the phone.

"Hello?"

"Who do I have the pleasure of speaking to?" The soft voice left no doubt to the audience that the man on the other end of the line was a cool customer.

"It's Marie-Hélène Beaudry, sir. I am surrounded by all the members of the UN Security Council. What should we call you?"

"Good morning to you all. Angel will do, madame Beaudry. Nice to speak to you again. We almost met the other day, madame Beaudry."

"Angel? That will be difficult for me to do, sir. Especially when I am talking to a serial killer."

"Serial killer? That is interesting, madame Beaudry. You seem to forget that the countries you represent have on multiple occasions committed serial killings. Only they carry it out under the glorified pretense of war. You and I are very similar, madame Beaudry. We both want to achieve the same goals."

"We are not alike at all, mister Angel of death."

"My war, which is identical to the UN's war, is against climate change and the death of our planet. You have been outstanding in your support for this war, madame Beaudry. Our war, madame Beaudry, is the most justified in the history of all wars. The most altruistic of them all: neither you nor I profit from this war, madame Beaudry. It is also the war with the lowest cost of casualties: 222. To this point."

"OK, mister… Angel. What can we do for you?"

"You can start by updating me on where you stand with my demands."

Marie Meadows signalled to Marie-Hélène Beaudry to slow down.

"Mister Angel, making sweeping changes takes time. I don't know if you are aware of how things work at the United Nations. You are talking to one arm of the organizational chart. The Security Council needs to receive a formal recommendation by the 193 members of the UN General Assembly. Once that recommendation comes to us, it can get complicated. We have fifteen countries represented here. Ten are non-permanent, voted in for two years. Five are permanent, with the power of veto. Those five are France, USA, China, United Kingdom, Netherlands, Russia. Getting everyone to agree…"

"You are stalling, madame Beaudry. Probably under the direction of your Affairs Division Secretary, Marie Meadows. Please give her my regards. Now let's get to the point or I will hang up and continue with phase three of my plan."

Marie-Hélène Beaudry followed the direction and got right down to business.

"We are pretty close, Angel. I think a proposal of a two-child limit, followed by adoption, would pass."

"That is not what I asked for, madame Beaudry."

"Angel, please. You must be reasonable. Trying to move this many representatives, this many countries, this many governments, is near impossible over years, much less in months."

There was a pause in the conversation. Soul Fernandez was breathing deeply, directly into the phone. He was trying to mathematically assess the impact of this modification on the planet's carrying capacity.

Soul also was changing his tone. The death of Primera, an original team member in the master plan, had hit him hard. He was ready to turn his attention away from seeking death, and towards Mikhaël Leddy's creation of life.

"You can make that work in timely fashion?"

"Before summer. Though I will need some leeway in how we enforce the two-child limit. The devil will be in the details with that one. No pun intended, mister Angel."

"And follow through with your previously mentioned Paris Agreement targets?"

"Yes."

"What about the USA and China?"

"They are here beside me. They are right at this table. I have seen a much more conciliatory and earnest effort from these two superpowers in the past weeks. And that comes from a Canadian. I can be objective in my dealings with these two countries."

"And trustworthy. I am a big fan of yours, madame Beaudry, and of all Canadians."

"Do we have a deal?"

Soul understood that his conversation was reaching the three-minute limit of traceability.

"I need to hang up this phone, madame Beaudry. Sorry, miss Meadows. I will call you back, on a different phone of course, in fifteen minutes."

"Did you get his location, Marie?"

"Two minutes, fifty-five seconds," said Marie. This guy is good."

9

Jayne and John walked past Inspector Isabella Lake and Captain Michael Lahr, and stood at the foot of the stretcher, trying to come to terms with the reality of a third murder in their small city. Only this time it was somebody that they knew.

John wiped away a few tears, then broke the silence. "I feel terrible that I suspected her in the murders of Lynne and Gemma."

"You and I both," said Jayne. "There were some irregularities that you picked up on. You were just doing your job."

"Maybe. Or maybe I jumped the gun as an excited first-time Detective."

"It's OK, John," Jayne said." It's part of the job. We have to cast the net wide."

"Everything is exactly the same," Isabella said. "Same cut to the left carotid, same CC. No evidence of a struggle. No evidence of assault or other injury. Ginny was definitely starting to show."

"Her husband was a nice guy," said John. "I talked to him a lot at the party. He looked completely infatuated with her."

"I will go talk to him right after," said Isabella. "Unfortunately, I am getting to be a kind of pro at these conversations."

"Thanks, Isabella," Jayne said.

"Ditto. Can you tell Jonas that I will drop by to see him later today?" John said.

"Will do, Detective. We will see you later. Hopefully the United Nations will get their act together and settle this. To be honest with you… I shouldn't say this."

"What?" Jayne said.

"I know you well enough, Isabella," Michael said. "You were going to say that the UN should settle this with the guy because while you don't approve of his ways, you think what he is asking for is reasonable."

"You know me too well, Michael," Isabella said. "I know you shouldn't speak like this out loud. Especially when you are on the police force and investigating this guy's murders."

"We appreciate your candidness, Isabella," Jayne said. "You always tell it like it is. No bullshit. It is a refreshing trait that I wish more people exhibited. No worries from my end for your honest opinions."

John and Michael nodded in agreement.

As Isabella was about to walk out, she turned to Jayne and John.

"There was one difference that I should point out. She had two pictures in her pant pocket. One is Jesus. The other guy, I have no idea."

Isabella handed the crumpled pictures over to Jayne.

"I didn't go to Sunday school regularly," Jayne said, "but there is no doubt that is Jesus."

John nodded.

"Do you recognize this guy, John?"

John thought for a while. He opened his phone and punched some letters in a search engine. Then a big smile came on his face, like a kid who has just figured out where his parents are hiding the Halloween chocolates. "I most certainly do."

"Who is it then?" Jayne said.

"Ginny was quite a philosopher. The first time we met her, she went on about how imagination was a dangerous thing. Remember, Jayne?"

Jayne nodded. Isabella and Michael looked puzzled. John picked up on their bewilderment.

"It's a fascinating thought. I will have to describe to you in detail over a beer some time. The second meeting I had alone with her, she went on about our jobs, how they were similar, citing another philosopher. This time it was Plato."

"This guy is Plato?" Jayne said.

"No. I am getting to who this guy is."

"Today would be nice, John," Jayne said.

"After she got me thinking about Philosophy, I started reading a book that was a fantastic summary of all the great philosophers of all time. You should read it some time."

John could tell his partner was getting impatient.

"At any rate, the picture is of this guy." John showed Jayne the same picture on his phone. "It's the great Chinese philosopher Kong Qiu, otherwise known as Confucius."

"I have heard of him," Jayne said. Isabella and Michael nodded in recognition of the name. "But what do Jesus and Confucius have in common? And what do they have to do with any of this?"

"I don't know yet," John said. He was now sitting at Ginny's desk, frantically searching his phone, alternating with his interview notes.

"While Sherlock thinks," Isabella said, "we will go have the difficult conversation with Jonas Clavette."

"Jesus and Confucius," John whispered to himself. "Jesus and Confucius."

"It doesn't matter right now, John," Jayne said. "Let's have one more look around then get Ginny's body to Doctor Vista."

"I would like to look around again," John said. "I just feel there is something we are missing here."

"No problem, John," Jayne said. "Let's start by interviewing Louise Agat."

As they closed the ultrasound room door behind them, Jayne turned to the other three.

"I guess the CC mystery is solved. We know what that stands for."

"Carrying Capacity," John said. "There goes the Club de ockey Canadien theory, right Jayne?"

"Yes," Jayne said, managing a smile. "Yves Lavallée seems a long time ago now, doesn't he?"

"I miss that guy," John said. "E was ha nice man, ey?"

Inspector Lake, Captain Lahr and Detective Chandler all managed a little smile. But nobody's heart was in the mood to laugh. All deaths are difficult, but when you have seen this captivating, vibrant woman alive only a few weeks ago, seeing her inert, bloodied body was all that much more gut-wrenching.

10

"He is back on the line, madame Beaudry," Marie Meadows said.

"Should we bother trying to trace him?" Marie-Hélène said.

"I doubt he will screw up. But we can try," Marie said.

"Hello again, madame Beaudry."

"Hello. I presume you have had enough time to mull over options, mister Angel?"

"I have. I will agree to an arrangement that meets our objectives regarding the Paris agreement and sets up prospective policies regarding a two-child personal limit, followed by mandatory adoption."

"That's great news, Angel."

Marie-Hélène Beaudry was relieved. She did not enjoy the spotlight that had been placed on her in the past few weeks. She was also secretly a huge fan of the policy. "I will have my team draft something up today. We can sign the agreement tomorrow."

Assuming Marie Meadows is as good of a lobbyer as she claims to be, thought Marie-Hélène.

"However," Soul continued. Marie-Hélène raised her eyes at the prospects of a clause that would defeat their deal. "I feel that since I am being conciliatory, you can concede two additional items. After all, your new policy will force me to change the tattoo I have on my right arm."

"Tattoo? You are seriously talking to me about a tattoo right now?" The remark brought laughter to the very tense Security Council room.

"Yes, madame Beaudry. My tattoo is of a beautiful Oasis, with the numbers one and four, then the letter u, then numbers one and four, then the letters u and s.

Marie-Hélène Beaudry thought for a few seconds.

"I get it. One for you and one for us. Sorry, mister Angel. You will need to have someone scratch out that first number one and replace it with a two. Please don't make the UN finding you a reliable tattoo artist part of this arrangement."

"I won't. But for my willingness to cooperate, I would like the following two clauses added to the agreement."

"What are those?"

"For one, all investigations into the martyrs' deaths will cease, and my entire team will be given amnesty by all the involved countries. No exception."

The Security Council room buzzed with discussion. Fortunately, Marie-Hélène Beaudry had anticipated this request, and had previously received approval to go ahead with a pardon clause if this became a critical component of achieving a deal.

"Go on. What is your second one?"

"One member of my team not only agreed to be a soldier in the first phase, but when her personal situation changed, she bravely agreed to be a martyr for the second phase. I would like this agreement named after her, in light of her immense personal sacrifice for the safety of our planet."

Marie-Hélène Beaudry was both moved and impressed by this story, but given the delicate events involved in this matter, she restrained her natural instincts to express her emotions and gratitude.

"I think both of those requests can be honored, Angel. I will sign the agreement in front of the cameras tomorrow at nine AM. I will then email you the documents for your signature, and we can conclude our deal. And conclude the killings."

"You have my word, madame Beaudry. Until tomorrow, then."

11

John's mind was once again spinning. He leaned over the body, had a prolonged look at the incision with his cell phone light, then turned to Jayne.

"How fast can Doctor Vista have a look at the body?"

"We can get it over to him within the hour, John. I can call him to do a stat autopsy early this afternoon. Why?"

"I still feel that there is something we are not piecing together, here. Jesus. Confucius. And maybe my imagination is running wild, which Ginny taught us is a dangerous thing, but this incision looks different to me. Plus, I would like him to tell us if Ginny had Xenon on board."

"Then let's get this autopsy done, Detective," Jayne said. "I will call over to the Pathology lab right now."

CHAPTER 17

TWO BIRTHS

1

Although the February days were getting longer, the sun had already set by the time Dr. Vista had called Jayne to let her know that he was ready. Jayne met John at her office and they both made their way down the Pathology area together. They waited outside of the entrance panel to catch their breath after racing down the stairs. Dr. Vista sounded quite excited over the phone.

"Do you remember the code?" John said.

"Yes, 7-2-8-4. PATH. I have to say you surprised me with that moment of brilliance, John."

"Didn't think I was up for that level of thinking, did you?"

"Can you blame me? It's not like you displayed Mensa-like intelligence on that first day, Hunter!"

"True, but you have to admit, Jayne, you weren't exactly the most welcoming partner that day either!"

Jayne nodded, smiling.

The panel light turned green at the same time as the door buzzed.

"OK, here we go again," Jayne said.

"What is the worst part you think," John said, "the sight of the bodies or the Vista view."

"Vista for sure."

"The smell of formaldehyde or the Vista fragrance?" John asked.

"Vista again. This is when I would kill to have another bout of acute sinusitis."

"You're mean, Detective Chandler," John said, with a wide grin. "Do you know why he smells this bad?"

"Why?"

"So that blind people can find him disgusting also!"

"Stop!" Jayne said, laughing out loud. "Totally inappropriate. Especially when his wife...."

"Good evening, both," Vista said. "You two seem rather chipper tonight."

"Well, Doctor Vista," Jayne said. "You sounded pretty excited on the phone. You have a captive audience arriving."

"Excellent," Vista said. "Come on in then, and we will get started."

2

Seeing someone you have met on their death bed is a difficult sight. Seeing that person on the autopsy table, under the bright operating room lights of the laboratory, was not a site John was prepared for.

"I am sorry, Doctor Vista," John said. "I am just going to have to excuse myself for a minute."

John raced out of the laboratory, dry heaving, until he could have a seat and feel some of the cool basement air. He was dripping with sweat. After a few seconds, he managed to regain his legs and his composure and headed back into the laboratory.

Jayne managed to limit the reaction by staring at anything but the body.

"You OK, John?" Jayne said, as he walked back into the autopsy suite. "Your color is certainly better."

"Yes, thanks," John said. "Sorry about that. That is embarrassing."

"Don't worry about that, Detective," Vista said, with a rare empathetic tone in his voice. "Totally common and normal reaction. Particularly as I understand that you knew the young lady."

"I did," John said, feeling bad now for his derision of the sympathetic Pathologist. "Please, carry on, Doctor. I will sit on this stool, if that is alright with you."

"No problem at all, Detective. Now let's begin. I know you two are very busy and thus I will get to the main points and specifically Detective Hunter's two questions. There are many more similarities than differences when comparing this case and the two others. Once again, the victim was carrying twins. Twin boys."

John bowed his head to acknowledge the passing of Jonas and Ginny's two sons. Doctor Vista continued.

"To get right to your first question, missus Fremlin did have evidence of Xenon in her blood. No doubt, she was anesthetized like the others."

"You already sent the blood away for testing?" Jayne said.

"No. Due to the interest in this chemical, and the risk of future need to measure it, the Police Chief allowed me purchase the measurement device. Your father is a man of vision, Detective."

John nodded unconvincingly. Only Jayne picked up on the nuance.

"Did she have the same amount of Xenon on board, Doctor?" John said.

"That is a difficult question to answer, Detective. You see our tool is a qualitative measurement, rather than a quantitative one."

"It detects the presence of Xenon, yes or no, but not the actual amount?" John said.

"That is correct," Vista said. Looking back at the body, he took a deep breath and continued. "Now, what else can I tell you? The incision was in the same location, there was still no evidence of trauma. Still no other major organ changes."

"No rash like Lynne Nanton?" Jayne said.

"Right, no rash," Vista said. "The only skin finding other than the incision was the same 'CC' engraving around the belly button. Have you figured out what that stands for?"

"Carrying capacity. At least that is what we think," Jayne said. "That is the term the Angel used in his message to the United Nations."

"Yes of course," Vista said. "I didn't watch any of that, but my colleagues from around the world mentioned it to me when we spoke."

"What about my second question, Doctor?" John said.

"Now that is fascinating." Dr. Vista's eyes lit up. His face was beaming. Jayne and John had not previously seen this side of his appearance, which dramatically changed their superficial, negative impression of his looks.

"I think you are on to something, Detective Hunter," Vista said.

John smiled, partly due to pride, but mostly at seeing the perplexed look on Jayne's face.

"After receiving your phone call, Detective, I looked back at my notes on the Nanton and Augustine cases. In both instances, the carotid incision was twelve millimeters deep on the right side, and ten millimeters deep on the left."

"What does that mean?" Jayne asked.

"Roughly speaking, it takes two millimeters to go through the skin layers, then another two millimeters to get through the subcutaneous tissue. That will take the incision to the carotid. The carotid is about five to six millimeters in width."

"It would take ten millimeters to completely transect the artery, Doctor?" John said.

"That is correct. And that is how deep the killer went."

"But you said twelve millimeters on the right side of the incision?' Jayne said.

"Correct, I did. That very likely means that the killer plunged the scalpel initially on the right side of the incision. It is only natural to go deeper with our initial plunge, then cut a little more superficially as we go across with the incision. This is very suggestive…"

"That the killer in the first two cases was right-handed, correct?" Jayne said.

"You got it. A right-handed person, who is facing their victim, would likely supinate their wrist. Meaning keep their right thumb to the outside of their body rather than turn it to the center. They would then start their incision on the right and proceed in a right to left fashion."

"The cut gets shallower as you move to the left," Jayne said.

"Exactly, Detective. The findings lead me to believe that a right-handed person killed missus Nanton and Doctor Augustine. However…"

"Let me guess, "John said. "It's the opposite with Ginny?"

"Precisely." Dr. Vista approached the body and pointed with his index finger. "In missus Fremlin's case, the incision is deeper on the left-hand side of the incision, and gets more superficial as we proceed to the right."

"A lefty killed Ginny, then?" Jayne said.

"I am almost certain," Vista said. "Of course, I am presuming that the hand position would be supinated with thumb in the lateral position. It is possible that a killer could turn their hand and move their thumb to the medial side…"

"A more backhanded approach," John said, mimicking the hand position.

"Right," Vista said, "but I don't think they would do that. At a minimum, what I am certain I can say, is that the killer in the first two cases is different than the third one. You were right, Detective Hunter," Dr. Vista said. "Congratulations. Pretty astute for such a young Detective. The apple doesn't fall far from the tree, I guess."

Again, unconvincing nod from John, and again only Jayne noticed.

"He is a bright guy," Jayne said. "A real keeper. Thank you, Doctor Vista, I appreciate you putting a rush on this one and keeping you late again. You should get home to your wife."

"Thank you. No trouble at all. Detective Hunter, you told me, the first time we met, that there was still hope that Betty could recover. Well you were right again. She is now speaking in full sentences, has almost full use of her right arm, and is starting to walk with a walker. I think YOU are the Angel, Detective Hunter!"

Dr. Vista's eyes filled with tears, as he gave John and Jayne a big hug.

"That's fantastic news," John said. "Thanks for the uplifting update, Doctor Vista. All our best to Betty."

As the autopsy room door closed behind them, Jayne turned to John.

"Let's go, Angel. It's been a long day. We now have potentially two different murderers to sort out."

"Angel my ass. If only he knew what I have said about him. This Angel is going right to hell!"

3

"Hunter, are you up?" Jayne said, after calling him early at home on his cell phone.

"I am," John said. "Did you see that? The United Nations has called a press conference in fifteen minutes."

"It will be on all the stations. I will call you again when it is on," Jayne said.

Fifteen minutes later, as had previously happened, all the normally scheduled shows were interrupted for yet another announcement from Marie-Hélène Beaudry.

This time, Marie-Hélène was back in front of a large desk, holding a document that appeared several pages long.

"Good evening once again, ladies and gentlemen. As you are all likely aware, a second wave of 111 murders hit the world two days ago. That brings the total number of victims, from the group led by a man we know only by the name of Angel, to 222. After prolonged, careful deliberation with the United Nations Security Council and General Assembly we have decided to take measures to put an end to the murders. It was our priority to seek peace in the world, and provide comfort and safety to all, but in particular, pregnant women everywhere. Preserving international peace and security is the main role of the United Nations. The document I hold in my left hand, which I will now sign, assures that the murders will stop."

Marie-Hélène Beaudry paused her speech to sign the agreement.

"I will now send the document to the Angel, who will sign it."

Marie-Hélène's staff took the document away. She continued to address the cameras.

"The details of the agreement will follow. Suffice it to say, that in return for the immediate cessation of the violence, the United Nations has agreed to forge ahead with concrete plans to implement the Paris Agreement in all 193 member countries of the UN. In addition, all 193 member countries have agreed to prospectively impose a population growth cap, by way of limiting each family to two children of their own. Beyond that number, families will have to adopt using a new, international adoption agency that will promote cooperation and collaboration within and across countries. The two-child limit is more lenient than what the Angel had asked. Therefore, given the priority to end this violence, the United Nations has agreed to two additional clauses requested by the Angel."

Marie-Hélène Beaudry rearranged her papers, before reading the additional clauses.

"The first of these is to cease investigations into the previous murders and provide full amnesty to the Angel's team. The second is to name the agreement after a young woman who believed in this cause so staunchly that she agreed to be a part of the team during the first phase of this process, while volunteering to be a victim in the second phase two days ago."

There was significant movement of staff behind Marie-Hélène Beaudry.

"I have just received the signed document from the angel. He has included a video that my team is uploading now, of him signing the agreement."

The TV screen showed a cloaked man, sitting at a table in a dark room, who proceeded to sign the papers with his left hand.

"That is now final, ladies and gentlemen. I am happy and relieved to present to you the official version of: the Primera Agreement.

4

"Did you hear that?" John said, carrying on his cell phone conversation with Jayne. "It all makes sense now."

"What?" Jayne said.

"Jayne, what would be the first rule that you would associate with Jesus Christ and his teachings?"

Jayne pondered the question for a moment, then answered.

"Again, not a lot of Sunday school sessions for this girl, but I would say the basic rule is treating others like you want to be treated."

"Very well done, Jayne. The golden rule of Christianity: "Do as you would be done by". Jesus then goes on about respecting others like you want to be respected, and love your neighbor like yourself."

"No argument, but what does have to do with this case?"

"I am getting there. You and I both had suspicions about Ginny, from the first time we met her. You had picked up on her lack of patience with pregnant women."

"I remember."

"The second time I met her, she went on about how the planet was doomed due to climate change. She said we needed to fix it and she had thoughts on how to do it. Is that starting to sound relevant to these cases?"

"Yes, but Ginny Fremlin is now lying dead in Doctor Vista's lab. This hardly seems like her idea on how to solve the world's problems."

"But that is where Confucius comes in. Jesus said: "Do as you would be done by." Five hundred years before, Confucius had said basically made the same statement, only he used negative wording. Confucius said: "What you do not desire for yourself, do not do to others." Think about that for a second, Jayne. What if Ginny Fremlin was the Calgary arm of this international organization. What if this organization, for some reason, made her the test case for whether any of this could work: the Xenon, the CC, the incision with the fancy German name?"

"Pfannenstiel is what Doctor Vista called it."

"Right. They set out with this mission to make a point that couples should have one kid of their own, then adopt. Who becomes your first target?"

"Women carrying twins."

"Yes. Only what if the person seeking out these targets acquires the very condition that she was targeting?"

"Then you would have a tough decision to make."

"Yes, you would. I would suggest it would be a deep, philosophical debate. From a deeply philosophical person. Duty and loyalty versus self-preservation and survival. That brings us back to Confucius..."

"What you do not desire for yourself, do not do to others," Jayne said.

"Bingo, Jayne. Ginny Fremlin chose duty and loyalty over her own life. She did to herself what she did to others. Ginny Fremlin is Primera."

"And though maybe a warped cause for some," Jayne said, "she did it with the altruistic goal of saving our planet."

Jayne went silent as she reflected on John's conclusions.

"Your theory is brilliant, John," Jayne said. "There is only one flaw that I can see."

"What's that?" John said.

"Actually, it is a flaw that I can't see."

"What do you mean?"

"First of all, I am not sure how technically she could administer the anesthetic, then make the incision."

"Would be tricky, I admit. But possible. Probably she would not have been fully anesthetized, or not anesthetized at all, which makes her actions even more heroic."

"OK. But in that case, where was the scalpel? It wasn't at the murder scene. She might be very skilled, but surely she couldn't raise herself from the dead and make a scalpel, and possibly a rag full of Xenon, disappear from the room!"

John reflected. His theory of a solo effort was certainly contradicted by these points.

"The only explanation," John said, "is that she had someone involved in her cause clear those materials after her death. But who?"

"Jonas?" Jayne said.

"Shit! I told Isabella I would go see him yesterday and it completely slipped my mind. I will go first thing this morning. I doubt Jonas would help Ginny. He loved her too much to agree to any of this."

"The Angel?" Jayne said.

Both Jayne and John went silent.

"It's the Angel," Jayne said. "You saw the video of the signing. He signed it with his left hand. That would corroborate Doctor Vista's incision findings."

"It would, I guess," John said. "But he is not the only lefty in the world."

"Is Jonas left-handed?" Jayne said.

"No," John said. "Jonas mentioned that he and Ginny were both superstar right-handed pitchers at the Christmas party. I think our left-handed Angel must have made a trip to Cowtown in the past few days!"

"It all makes sense," Jayne said. "Speaking of trips, I guess I won't be visiting the BMW headquarters this weekend. The United Nations gave them all amnesty! That's not going to go over well."

"Agree. The world will be full of some pretty pissed off police forces!"

"Let's get ready now, John, we have a lot to discuss with your father."

5

As he promised to Isabella, though a day late, John left to visit Jonas at his home. He was not looking forward to this conversation, though felt encouraged by the words of Marie-Hélène Beaudry and his findings about Ginny.

"Hello, Detective Hunter," Jonas said. "Please come in."

John walked in and warmly hugged Jonas. He expected a much more morose and disheveled-looking person.

"Please call me John, Jonas. How are you doing?"

"About as well as can be expected, I guess. Yesterday I was shocked and angry. I didn't even know Ginny was pregnant! But a lot has happened since Inspector Lake gave me the news. Happenings that give me a sense of comfort and hope."

John thought he knew what Jonas meant, but asked anyways.

"What do you mean?"

"I am sure you heard the words of the United Nations President. This Primera person. I think it was Ginny."

"Why do you say that, Jonas?"

"Ginny was crazy about this climate change stuff. She would do anything to save the planet. I even think she would do this. Every year, she would go off to these climate change conferences, all over the world. Morocco, Germany, Poland, Spain. She would come back electrified about the contacts she made and the plans they had."

"Did she mention any names?" John said. He realized right away that he was taking the discussion to an interrogation, which was not appropriate for Jonas at this time. The amnesty would also preclude any further investigation.

"No, she didn't. But I have to wonder if it was this magic Angel."

John collected his thoughts as to how he would present his theory to Jonas.

"Jonas, I think you are correct. Detective Chandler and I came to the same conclusion.

"How?"

"We found pictures of Jesus and Confucius in Ginny's pants. You know better than I that she was big into Philosophy. I think she linked those two people, basically by their shared motto…."

"That you shouldn't do to others what you are not prepared to do to yourself," Jonas said.

"That is what we think. We think Ginny joined this organization with great intentions to save the planet. Then she got pregnant. She probably agonized over this decision but then arrived at a conclusion guided by Jesus and Confucius."

John let Jonas assimilate this information then continued.

"Jonas, I can't go into details, but I can tell you that some of the evidence we collected is very convincing that Lynne and Gemma were killed by the same person. But a different person murdered Ginny."

"Murdered. Wow, when you hear that word, it's just so shocking."

"It is. I'm sorry to have to use that term. But the Angel said that the victims did not suffer, and I believe that. Confidentially, I can tell you that they were all put to sleep before anything violent was done to them."

"Thanks for telling me all that. I realize that you can't share all the details."

"When Marie-Hélène Beaudry confirmed the two roles this Primera played," John said, "it all made sense."

"Primera," Jonas said. "I looked it up. It means first in Spanish."

"Which makes total sense. They probably would have named it the Ginny Fremlin agreement, but decided not to for your safety and protection. We don't know how the Nanton and Augustine family would react."

"They would certainly be like I was yesterday: angry. Angry not only at the person who did this to my Ginny, but angry at the entire world. Angry at everyone who has a partner, a child. Angry at everyone who gets to live the life that I should have lived with Ginny!"

Jonas stared blankly out the window, obviously trying to process all of this.

"John, I have to say, I have let religion slip out of my life in recent years. You would think something like my wife being murdered would have killed my faith even more. But so much has happened, so many signs, that if anything I think my faith has been revived."

"That is good, Jonas. That will help you heal."

"Starting with this whole pregnancy," Jonas said.

"What do you mean?"

"We never thought we would have kids. I had a surgery as a child in THAT area."

"You don't have to share this with me, Jonas."

"No that's OK, John. They had to remove a testicle, and apparently my second one wasn't working very well either. Ginny getting pregnant, with twins no less, it feels like…"

"You got help?"

"Yes. And I know Ginny wouldn't cheat on me. Divine help has happened before, John."

"It sure has, Jonas."

"But there is more. Little things. Probably stupid things. After Inspector Lake left yesterday, I went upstairs, lay on my bed, and cried until there was nothing left inside me. When I got up, I started looking at Ginny's pictures on her desk. There was one picture of her she hated. It was an old high school picture of her playing volleyball. Ginny always turned that picture to the wall. But yesterday, she was facing me. It was like she was trying to make me laugh. And it worked."

"That's amazing," John said.

"Then I came back downstairs. As I sat at the kitchen, I heard a tapping sound on the window. There were birds that were tapping. But not just any birds. Ginny's favorite birds: robins. Robins, in February? And guess how many."

"Three."

"Exactly. A mother and her two babies. In February? How is that possible?"

"I can't explain it, Jonas."

"The last sign happened around nine PM. I was feeling awful again. I went outside on the patio and looked at the sky. It was a completely cloudy night except for one clear spot. In that small opening was a full moon. The moon had a small cloud above it and below it that looked like eyelashes. It looked like Ginny was staring down at me. But that's not the end of it. Right beside the moon was a celestial body, the only one visible in the entire sky. It was Jupiter."

"The Roman God of all Gods."

"Yes. Ginny and Jupiter sat there for ten minutes looking at me. When I stopped crying, I started feeling a peace that I have never felt. Then the clouds moved in and covered them completely. It was like Ginny was wrapping things up and moving on to her new life. But first, she wanted to look down on me and tell me "Hey, everything is OK with me. Everything will be OK with you"."

"That is powerful, Jonas. It is hard to explain all of that without a powerful force in action."

"That is why I feel better than I would have thought today. I'm sure I will flip back and forth between all of these emotions."

"You will," John said. "You will, Jonas. For weeks. Months. Years."

"But those experiences make me think that when someone dies, they are given a certain amount of time to signal their loved ones that everything is OK and will be OK."

"Jesus spent forty days doing that, but he had a whole bunch of people to reassure."

"Right. Ginny basically had me, and a mother with whom she had a love-hate relationship. She signaled me, and now she is off to another life. I am not sure what that is. Maybe it's in this place we call heaven. Maybe it's a whole new life on one of these billion planets that God created. And when I think of her, it sends her warmth and pleasure, and when she thinks of me, I get those same feelings. It's like a text to another world, only the text is sent by emotions rather than words."

"That makes a lot of sense to me, Jonas. Since my mother died, I of course get waves of sadness, but sometimes I also get an overwhelming sense of calm and reassurance. I never could explain it, until now. Thank you for this conversation."

"Thanks for coming over, John," Jonas said. "It has been really helpful. I hope we can stay in touch."

John hugged Jonas and left him, with a profound sense of invigoration from this life-altering exchange.

6

"Soul, Ruprecht, my dear friends, welcome to beautiful, sunny Puerto Rico," Mikhaël Leddy said. "I should say welcome home to you, Doctor Fernandez."

"Thank you, my friend," Soul said. "I have been away such a long time that it doesn't quite feel like home. La Perla is certainly sunny, but I would say far from beautiful."

"On that point, you will get no argument from me, Soul," Mikhaël said. "But La Perla and its people were perfect for what we needed to accomplish. As you said, a little bit of money in La Perla gets you ample access to volunteers and secrecy."

"Thank you for coming personally to the airport, Mikhaël," Ruprecht said. "You could have sent someone for us."

"No. I left my assistant Hans Vonn Boechorstein with our new addition. I was looking forward to seeing you gentlemen. Though it is with a sense of sadness that I meet you without Ginny."

"We all miss her, Mikhaël," Soul said. "But Primera is with us every step of the way."

"I truly feel that," Ruprecht said.

The three men had climbed into Mikhaël's car and started their drive that would take them through some of the toughest neighborhoods in the world.

"We took eggs from two local women, named Sofia and Maria," Mikhaël said. "We then manipulated the embryos in a manner very similar to what I described to you before, and reinserted two embryos into each of the two women. One of the women was briefly pregnant but lost the child early. The second carried a boy to near full term, and delivered him without complications last week. The woman is doing fine post delivery."

"That is amazing work," Ruprecht said. "You are a cool customer, Mikhaël, dealing in such high stakes science."

"It's not that stressful," Mikhaël said. "A wise man once told me, "It's just life and death after all". Isn't that right, Ruprecht?"

Ruprecht laughed at hearing his expression said back to him.

"She understands that her involvement with the child will end soon?" Soul said.

"Yes," Mikhaël said. "That was the arrangement. The woman was chosen to mimic the health of a delivering mother post environmental holocaust. She is very poor, and very malnourished, making her breast milk of poor quality. She feeds the boy three times per day, and will be at his side for eight weeks."

"She will then relinquish all contact with the child?" Ruprecht asked.

"Yes," Mikhaël said. "Money buys you detachment around these parts of the world."

"Did you make all the modifications that you described to us in Phase two last year?" Ruprecht said.

"I did," Mikhaël said. "You will see that the boy's physical appearance is like what we saw in the mice. Very little hair and quite bumpy skin, if anything bumpier than the mice. Not a very attractive baby."

"I don't care what people say," Ruprecht said. "But no baby is all that attractive. They all look like my homely, pudgy friend Bobby from Leipzig."

"I think this boy is probably a little uglier than even your friend, Ruprecht," Mikhaël said. "Normally I would say he has a face that only a mother can love, but I don't even think his mother can bear looking at him."

"But he lives, and that is the key point in all of this," Soul said. "And living independently, I gather?"

"Almost. Other than the little bit of breast milk, the lactulose, and the protein supplements. Difficult to know where he is at as far as his nutrition. He has not gained weight in the past week, which is not uncommon, but has not lost weight either. I am quite encouraged about that."

"And his interactions?" Ruprecht said.

"All babies are pretty useless that way in the first few weeks, so that will take some time to judge as well."

They were now in the heart of La Perla. Soul quietly took in the surroundings. It brought back a great deal of memories of his childhood, his parents who sheltered him, his family. Memories that for the most part he had suppressed and wished to forget.

They drove by a billboard adverting the new Star Wars movie, 'The Rise of Skywalker'.

"Even in such a destitute place," Ruprecht said, "they still love their Star Wars."

"It's a sad comment on humanity," Soul said. "We live in a world obsessed with a mythical force in a Hollywood movie. This same world progressively ignores the ultimate force around them: God, and the immaculate nature He has created for them."

"And don't forget the intricate science God has created," Mikhaël said. "Humans are fascinated by a force that is able to choke someone or move rocks, but forget the amazement of what happens after two small cells come together to create the highly complex beings known as humans."

"Amen, Mikhaël, Amen," Soul said.

The three men approached the small, dilapidated home that had become Dr. Mikhaël Leddy's makeshift laboratory, and birthplace for the next wave of humans. The Angiospermae. Self-sufficient, resilient humans, who could survive pretty much any disaster, in any environment, on any planet, if they had adequate exposure to sunlight.

They walked through the door. After a brief hello and handshake to Hans, Soul Fernandez, Mikhaël Leddy, and Ruprecht Barren turned to the small bedroom in the corner of the diminutive home.

In this room was a woman holding a baby. The room was bright, with the day's sunlight beaming through the large skylight window. Sunlight that served to provide warmth, comfort and nourishment to this miraculous baby boy.

"Ruprecht, Soul, I would like you to meet Maria, the mother of the child."

Soul cupped Maria's loose right hand with both of his and kissed her forehead.

"Eres la madre más hermosa que he visto," Soul said, to the most beautiful mother he had ever seen. Maria stared into Soul's piercing look. The new mother felt overwhelmed with emotion, as tears began to stream down both sides of her face.

Soul's eyes turned to the newborn child.

"Say hello to the child, Soul," Mikhaël said. "Say hello to Christian. Named in honor of your faith, Christian Heinrich Heine of Düsseldorf University, and the father of Embryology, Heinz Christian Pander."

"What an appropriate name," Soul said. "Also recognizes the epic work of Robert Christian with the Georgia Guidestones."

"Are you…" Ruprecht started.

"For another time, my friend," Soul said. "Let's just say that the Guidestones align well with all of my principles: population control, uniting humanity, and considering nature first."

Soul turned to the child. It was his turn to be overwhelmed with emotion. Such an important birth to the world, born in the humblest of places.

"Soul," Ruprecht said, putting his hand on his shoulder. "You rose me from the dead, and now you have created life to preserve our life."

Soul looked around.

"This time there is no hay and no animals. But there is a beautiful mother, and there are definitely three wise men," Soul said, turning to Hans, Mikhaël and Ruprecht.

"I have no gift for the baby," Soul said, "except for the tears of an angel."

And with that, Dr. Soul Fernandez, the angel from the east, blessed the child with tears from heaven.

AFTERWARD

I would like to thank Mr. Stephen King. When I started this journey, I read his book called "On Writing". Mr. King, I apologize in advance for my book, and I certainly don't think anyone should hold you responsible for it in any way! Regarding writing, you said "Drink and be filled up": and so, I drank. I managed to keep the drink down, hopefully readers will also. In that book, you emphasize starting with a "What if…" idea. There is one of those in this book. In fact, I did listen to you, started with the "What if…" idea, and just went from there, letting the characters dictate the course of the book. I paid less attention to plot (as you suggested), and maybe it shows too much! The "what if" should be evident as you read this book. The "what if" is solved by one of the characters in the last chapter of the book.

Thank you to Dr. Tom Rosenal for giving me Mr. King's book, and, along with Mona Foss, my wife Heidi Coderre, and my son Paul Coderre, agreeing to be one of my first readers.

Thank you to my daughter Gabriela Coderre, who was the inspiration for the Angiospermae creation, and my son Marcus Coderre who read and critiqued the edited version of the book.

Thanks to all my immediate family, who heard of this book ad nauseum far before a single word was written.

Thanks to all those who contributed their middle name, and the first street (or town) they lived on, for the characters in the book.

Thank you to farmer Tim Calon who allowed me to combine canola with him, while giving me the inspiration for the climate change counterarguments found throughout the book.

Lastly, I would like to acknowledge and thank the authors of "The Philosophy Book: Big Ideas Simply Explained" (DK publishing). The book was an amazing resource for me.

CPSIA information can be obtained
at www.ICGtesting.com
Printed in the USA
LVHW091305230720
661366LV00002B/347

9 780228 833192